# CHERISH MY DESIRES
# MALCOLM & STARR PART III

## STEELE INTERNATIONAL, INC. A BILLIONAIRES ROMANCE SERIES BOOK 9

## CHARMAINE LOUISE SHELTON

*Cherish My Desires Malcolm & Starr Part III*
Copyright © 2021 by Charmaine Louise Shelton

All rights reserved. No part of this book may be reproduced or transmitted in any form or by any means, electronic or mechanical, including but not limited to photocopying, recording, or by any information storage and retrieval system without written permission from the author.

ISBN: 978-1-7369748-2-7 (Paperback)
ISBN: 978-1-7369748-1-0 (eBook)
Published by CharmaineLouise New York, Inc.
Sexy Fantasies Fulfill Your Desires Publications

*Cherish My Desires Malcolm & Starr Part III* is a work of fiction. Names, characters, businesses, places, events, and incidents are either the product of the author's imagination or used in a fictitious manner. Any resemblance to actual persons, living or dead, or actual events is purely coincidental.

# CONTENTS

*Free Book*   v
*Also By Charmaine Louise Shelton*   vii
*About STEELE International, Inc. A Billionaires Romance Series*   ix
*About Cherish My Desires Malcolm & Starr Part III*   xi

1. Starr   1
2. Starr   9
3. Starr   17
4. Starr   27
5. Malcolm   34
6. Malcolm   45
7. Starr   53
8. Malcolm   61
9. Starr   72
10. Malcolm   82
11. Malcolm   96
12. Starr   106
13. Malcolm   114
14. Malcolm   125
15. Starr   136
16. Malcolm   149
17. Starr   161
18. Malcolm   167
19. Starr   178
20. Malcolm   188
21. Starr   200
22. Malcolm   211
23. Malcolm   223
24. Starr   231

| | |
|---|---|
| 25. Starr | 242 |
| 26. Starr | 254 |
| 27. Malcolm | 263 |
| 28. Malcolm | 274 |
| The STEELE Family | 281 |
| Note From Charmaine Louise | 283 |
| Next Series in the STEELE World: STEELE International, Inc. - Jackson Corporation Series Crossover | 285 |
| Coming Next: Tempt My Desires Lachlan & Haley Part I STEELE International, Inc. - Jackson Corporation A Billionaires Romance Series Crossover Book 1 | 287 |
| *Welcome to CharmaineLouise — The Sensual Lifestyle* | 305 |

# FREE BOOK

**Get the start of the STEELE International, Inc. A Billionaires Romance Series with** *Discover My Desires Sebastian & Lola Prequel* **FREE!**

**Click Cover Below** or visit **bit.ly/CLBooksNewsletter** to subscribe to my newsletter for latest news and launches, books from my author friends, and sizzling reads in book promotions. Plus, start reading the steamy billionaire romance *Series Prequel* of Sebastian Steele and Lola Lewis.

Their stories. Their discovery of unknown desires…

# FREE BOOK

# FREE BOOK!

EXCLUSIVE FOR SUBSCRIBERS!

## ALSO BY CHARMAINE LOUISE SHELTON

**STEELE INTERNATIONAL, INC.**
**A BILLIONAIRES ROMANCE SERIES**

Discover My Desires Sebastian & Lola Prequel
(Available Exclusively to Subscribers)

Fulfill My Desires Sebastian & Lola Part I

Heighten My Desires Sebastian & Lola Part II

Ignite My Desires Roger & Leonie Part I

Stoke My Desires Roger & Leonie Part II

Justify My Desires Roger & Leonie Part III

Deepen My Desires Sebastian & Lola Part III

Capture My Desires Malcolm & Starr Part I

Embrace My Desires Malcolm & Starr Part II

Cherish My Desires Malcolm & Starr Part III

A Trilogy of Desires Sebastian & Lola Parts I-III

A Trilogy of Desires Roger & Leonie Parts I-III

A Trilogy of Desires Malcolm & Starr Parts I-III

Series Extras

Series Playlist

## STEELE INTERNATIONAL, INC. - JACKSON CORPORATION
## A BILLIONAIRES ROMANCE SERIES CROSSOVER

Tempt My Desires Lachlan & Haley Part I

Tease My Desires Lachlan & Haley Part II

Grant My Desires Lachlan & Haley Part III

Intrigue My Desires Harris & Kat Part I

Decode My Desires Harris & Kat Part II

Honor My Desires Harris & Kat Patt III

A Trilogy of Desires Lachlan & Haley Parts I-III

A Trilogy of Desires Harris & Kat Parts I-III

Series Extras

Series Playlist

# ABOUT STEELE INTERNATIONAL, INC. A BILLIONAIRES ROMANCE SERIES

**Welcome to the titillating world of the multibillion-dollar global company and the love affairs of the family that controls it.**

**STEELE International, Inc.** is a series of interconnecting Billionaire romance. Follow the Steele family as they fly around the world chasing the women they love and their happily ever afters. Get ready for glitz, glamour, and steamy romance books. What's better than that? The Jet-set Lifestyle has never been hotter...

The Desires Series is not for the tea set; it's for the top-shelf vodka straight up in a pretty crystal glass coterie!

**Don't miss any of the sizzling romance books in the STEELE International, Inc. A Billionaires Romance Series:**

Discover My Desires Sebastian & Lola Prequel (Available Exclusively to Subscribers)

Fulfill My Desires Sebastian & Lola Part I

Heighten My Desires Sebastian & Lola Part II

Ignite My Desires Roger & Leonie Part I

Stoke My Desires Roger & Leonie Part II

Justify My Desires Roger & Leonie Part III

Deepen My Desires Sebastian & Lola Part III

Capture My Desires Malcolm & Starr Part I

Embrace My Desires Malcolm & Starr Part II

Cherish My Desires Malcolm & Starr Part III

A Trilogy of Desires Sebastian & Lola Parts I-III

A Trilogy of Desires Roger & Leonie Parts I-III

A Trilogy of Desires Malcolm & Starr Parts I-III

Series Extras

Series Playlist

# ABOUT CHERISH MY DESIRES MALCOLM & STARR PART III

Malcolm

This is the conclusion of a rebel, bad boy billionaire and my laid-back LA girl, brown-eyed beauty's steamy love story. It's been one hell of a trip that almost saw the last of me—the last of us.

Will I make the most of my resurrection? Or will I screw up... Again?

Starr

That man has put me through all sorts of changes—Shibari; stalker ex; mountain lion... Now, he pulls this stunt on top of everything we've faced. With an unexpected pregnancy? Oh hell, no! Where's my mala?

Take the leap with Malcolm as he learns the true meaning of unconditional love with his Starr from Beverly Hills to Laucala Island to the Exumas in their too-hot-for-words second chance billionaire romance.

Their love story is a standalone romance trilogy in the series. Get a glimpse of their dynamism in other books.

**Anthem: "Leather and Lace" Stevie Nicks and Don Henley**
**https://www.youtube.com/watch?v=Ob4cgakHwsQ**

**Playlist:**
**https://www.youtube.com/playlist?list=PLXwYvn0e218AaAPcbS9RFC_N-z5VLXJjX**

**Visit CharmaineLouiseBooks.com**

## STARR

"I'm going to turn in early tonight. I have a private yoga session to teach at six tomorrow morning. So no hanky-panky, Mr. Steele!"

I shimmy out of my lover's embrace as we lie on the sofa in the media room of my Benedict Canyon Drive mansion. We just finished watching the rom-com movie my girls were raving about. It lived up to the hype, even if the male lead isn't as sexy as my man. Well, then again few men can compare to Malcolm Sexy AF Steele!

His gray eyes zing me, set my nether regions afire with carnal lust. The full lips and angular jaw coupled with his thick, tousled ebony hair I love to run my fingers through then pull the silky strands. All six feet, four inches of pure muscle developed from years of MMA fighting and extreme sports. Either clean shaven or a 5 o'clock shadow covers his firm jaw. The dominating sex god with wings tattooed across his powerful back and a Prince Albert's piercing on his ten-inch dick captured my heart despite our crazy love triangle start.

Vicky Reynolds Malcolm's ex-psycho-sub who happened to be my client unbeknownst to me. The same client who sought to ruin my company Starr Light Fitness & Wellness Beverly Hills in her zealous desire to reclaim her Dom—now my Dom—and get that ring. Vicky the Hollywood royalty actress who tends to name-drop her great-grandfather the founder of a movie studio, her father a major producer, and her mother a screen siren. Crazy woman!

"What if I say I can get you off in under five min—"

The ding of a text message from my lover's mobile disrupts his lascivious counteroffer and pulls me from my musings.

Not tonight, Vicky. You won't get in the middle of me and my man! I giggle to myself then sashay toward the door, wiggling my fingers to wave good night to Malcolm. But to be sure I escape his amorous demands, I rush through the house and up to my bedroom. The way we go at it, I'd never sleep and my client would not appreciate me yawning throughout her session.

"Babe! I have to go into the office. I'll be back later. Get your rest. For now!" Malcolm yells up from the foot of the stairs to me on the second floor.

Momentarily saved by the proverbial bell!

Minutes later I hear Malcolm's Ducati Desmosedici motorcycle rev its way out of the garage and down the driveway. Yeah, a two-hundred-plus-thousand-dollar motorcycle. My man is a badass rebel multibillionaire—and an Alpha Dom to boot!

Malcolm *The Enforcer* Steele.

The second son; the rebel; the bad boy multibillionaire playboy of the Steele family, as in STEELE International, Inc. His family's multigenerational, multibillion-dollar luxury real estate development and management company based out of The STEELE Tower in New York City. Malcolm is the President of STEELE's Entertainment Properties Division and the First VP of the Board. He oversees their casinos, hotels, and resorts and generates the most revenue of all divisions.

That's how we met, through our partnership negotiations for SLFW Beverly Hills to expand to a location in the Caribbean and in to international fitness retreats at luxury resorts.

I followed my hippies turned into super successful environmental law attorneys parents'—Peace and Sun Knight, aka Jordan and Belinda—footsteps to their alma mater, Stanford University. Undergrad I received a degree in economics, then continued on to the B-School. Not exactly the Law School, so I couldn't join their law firm Knight & Knight LLP with eight offices around the country. I wanted to forge my path.

Health and wellness became my focus after my first trip to Rishikesh as a teenager. It helped me to regroup from the taunts of the It Girls of Beverly Hills Junior High School. Then stayed with me through adulthood.

I wanted to combine my love of wellness with helping others. So I opened my center nine years ago at 25 as my initial goal with Adrienne Anthony my CMO and General Manager of my SLFW Beverly Hills.

We met at Stanford Graduate School of Business. Everyone referred to us as Night & Day since we contrasted in our appearances and attitudes. From our long, curly hair with Adrienne's light brown and mine dark brown to her green feline eyes and my sorrel brown angelic eyes to her buttery pecan-colored skin and mine the color of warm chestnuts. I have dimples to her sharp cheekbones. But we're both five feet, six inches with curvy fit bodies from our years of yoga, Pilates, and strength training as certified teachers and students.

Again alike with our hippie vibes, independent nature, and outgoing bubbly personalities. We're loyal and open to a fault. Resourceful and trustworthy round out our traits. Where Adrienne has a tattoo of a peacock wrapped around her foot up her ankle to symbolize success, I have shooting stars on the back of my neck for wishes.

My close friend Lola Lewis when we met then Steele, paid it forward when she made the connection for me to STEELE through Malcolm since my center falls under his Entertainment Division's purview. Lola attended my first international retreat on the private Laucala Island in Fiji and loved it. Especially since the yoga and meditation recalibrated the petite spitfire and owner of Lola's Coterie —the luxury lingerie and evening wear brand—after she broke up with her then boyfriend, Alpha Dom Sebastian Steele, the eldest of the five siblings. Malcolm is Baz's doppelgänger. At thirty-six and only two years younger than Sebastian, people often confuse the brothers or think they're twins.

Each sibling shares the same Steele genetic traits and works at STEELE International and has a board position: Sebastian took over the helm from their father Morgan as CEO and Chairman of the Board while Sebastian remains president of the Retail Properties Division; Roger, president of the Residential Properties Division and Second VP; Harris and Haley, fraternal twins, co-founders of the subsidiary STEELE Technology and Cyber Security and Members. Each of them head divisions best suited to their knowledge and interests. While their mother Shelley runs their STEELE Foundation, their family's philanthropic foundation that builds and manages attractive, affordable housing for urban, lower-income families. The name is a play on the house foundation, being strong and supportive like steel.

Malcolm and I have known each other for over three years and been together for twenty-one months after we broke up because of a misunderstanding with Vicky. Seeing your boyfriend fucking another woman after he invites you over to his penthouse would end any relationship. But of course it was a ploy by Vicky. The man she was fucking on Malcolm's Sunset Strip penthouse roof deck was the concierge and not my man... It cost us time together, but we're back together. Thank God and every deity in every religion's pantheon!

For whatever reason Vicky moved to Johannesburg and has disappeared from our lives since Haley found out Vicky was behind the mysterious occurrences at SLFW that disrupted my business. Again, thank God and every deity in every religion's pantheon! Although I believe in my heart of hearts, her abrupt relocation is Malcolm's doing—not that I care, since Vicky is outta here!

I laugh out loud as I take a shower.

Since Malcolm had to go into the office unexpectedly, I settle in bed and read my book to wait up for him. Undoubtedly he'll be back soon. Nothing could be that time-consuming at this late hour.

"Hey, My Angel. Wake up, babe. I'm back. Did you get your rest? I have plans for you…"

Malcolm murmurs as he strokes my soft cheek with his calloused pad of his thumb.

My open book slides from where it slipped to my chest to land on the bed as I roll towards Malcolm's warm embrace. I sigh and stretch languorously, certain his mouth will land on my peaked brown nipples. A throaty moan slips from my parted lips. Back bows and arms reach overhead. I spread my thighs wantonly.

Fingertips skim along the insides of my bare arms from my crossed wrists to the outer curve of my D-cup breasts. A thumb flicks over my silk-covered nipple, then with an index finger pinches the bud hard like a clamp.

I tremble in erotic delight.

Malcolm's tousled ebony hair tickles the sensitive skin of my inner arm as he leans over to take my other nipple into his warm, wet mouth. A hand and a mouth tease me.

A mewl escapes from my lips.

"Wake up, babe," Malcolm murmurs against my skin as his mouth slides down my belly to cover my mons.

My hips raise from the mattress when his lips close on my swollen clit.

He slips his arms beneath and around my legs, then places his palms against my inner thighs to spread me wider. His broad shoulders keep my legs separated as he settles in to feast upon my sweet nectar. Lips, tongue, and teeth partake ravenously.

Unable to move my legs and trained to keep my arms above my head in a submissive position, I toss my head side to side as the carnal pleasure and pain rolls through me.

"Wake up, babe," Malcolm murmurs as he slides his cold body over my heated one.

His ten-inch dick rests limp at the entrance to my welcoming core.

Caught up in the echoing sensations of his mouth on my breasts and pussy, I writhe beneath him, lips parted in a silent plea for more.

An icy chill blasts through my bedroom.

My writhing changes to a shiver.

"Wake up, babe," Malcolm murmurs, his cool breath hangs between our faces. "I need you."

I open my eyes, a seductive purr at the back of my throat.

Malcolm's once handsome face floats above me.

His skin no longer olive toned, but gray, like his soulless eyes sunken in their sockets; his mouth agape in agony. Blood drips from the back of his head to land in droplets on my cheek.

His face contorts in pain.

On a stuttering breath he murmurs, "I love you, My Angel…"

"MALCOLM!!!" I gasp.

# STARR

"MALCOLM!!!"

Sweat drenches my skin as I jolt awake screaming his name, terrified by the nightmarish vision. Disoriented, I shudder as I wrap my arms around myself, gasping for air. My tear-filled eyes sweep around my bedroom frantically. Then settle on the bed beside me.

Empty!

With a cry I jump from the bed, snatching the tangled, damp sheets off of my body.

"Malcolm?!?!?!" I cry, racing to my en suite bathroom.

Empty!

"Malcolm?!?!?!" I yell as I rush through my bedroom doors into the hallway.

From the top of the stairs, I scream his name again.

Silence.

Panicking, I pivot and run back to my bedroom. My hands shake as I unlock my iPhone to call Malcolm's mobile.

It rings to voicemail.

I call his office number.

It rings to voicemail.

The clock shows thirty minutes passed since he left. I must have been more tired than I thought and fallen asleep instead of reading my book.

Where is he?!?!?!

Then it hits me. Malcolm's microchip!

With the back of my hand, I swipe tears from my cheeks. Then I open the app Harris created to track all the Steeles and me—thanks to Delia Shaw's madness with kidnapping The Twins.

I click Malcolm's profile.

His vitals pop up on the screen.

Yellow, not green.

"NOOOOOOOOOOO!!!" I scream.

Should the person's vitals change from green to yellow or to red, Harris programmed the app to dial the local police and medics and provide the GPS coordinates automatically. Thankfully, help should arrive shortly.

The GPS view shows Malcolm somewhere along Benedict Canyon Drive, close to my home.

I pray to God and to every deity in every religion's pantheon for Malcolm to hold on.

"I'm coming, baby. Don't you dare leave me!!!" I say, praying my words reach him as his message reached me in that horrific vision.

As I run to the mudroom, my iPhone rings. A glance at the screen shows Harris' name. I answer as I slip my bare feet into my Hunter rubber Wellington boots. I disregard the fact I'm only clothed in silk sleep shorts that cover my ass barely and a camisole.

"Oh, Harris!" I wail as I fling the mud room door open to the garage. "I'm going to him—"

"Starr!!! Where are you?!?!?" Harris shouts.

"Home! Malcolm got a text from Anton to meet him at the office! Malcolm left thirty minutes ago on his motorcycle! I'm driving to the location now!" I respond, speeding down my driveway.

My mobile connects to the Tesla Model X Long Range as Harris' voice booms through the speakers.

"Hurry, Starr!!! Hurry. FUCK!!!!" He yells. "Don't hang up! Stay with me, and I'll guide you to the location. I see your blip and his on my screen. The live feed is loading now."

I floor the pedal as I hit Benedict Canyon Drive. Only moments pass before Harris tells me to stop and to get out. My headlights reveal debris from some electronic thing, gravel strewn across the side of the road, and tire marks.

"Go down the incline!" Harris directs now on speaker. "WHAT THE FUCK?!?!?!"

With the flashlight from my iPhone, I rush headlong down the steep ravine, following the path created by Malcolm's Ducati. Just as I reach the canyon floor, the sound of scuffling reaches me. I scan the area, but don't see Malcolm.

The flashlight picks up a trail of blood leading to movement in the grass.

I blink and look again.

No fucking way...

A mountain lion has Malcolm by the leg, dragging him deeper into the underbrush.

My stomach drops.

"STARR!!!! A LION!!! DON'T GO—"

I trip over a large branch in my haste to rush forward and drop my iPhone. Harris' voice still yells over the speaker.

The movement stops.

Adrenaline races through my body as I leap up, grab the branch, and charge the mountain lion. An almighty roar rips from my mouth, louder than the lion's hair-raising growl.

"LEAVE HIM ALONE!!!" I scream, swinging the branch like a giant club before me. "GET AWAY FROM HIM!!!"

The mountain lion crouches, ready to pounce on me. It has no desire to share its meal.

I brace myself in a warrior's stance, ready to defend my man and myself.

"BRING IT YOU FUC—"

A shot rings out just as the mountain lion springs in the air.

With a surprised screech, it crumples to the ground.

Shouts from behind me filter through my mind. So preoccupied with protecting what's mine, I didn't notice the police and the medics yelling at me.

I ignore their commands to wait and run to Malcolm. As I drop to my knees beside him, the branch falls to the ground.

"MALCOLM!!!" I scream.

Tears pour from my eyes once again.

He's still and his hand cold to the touch.

From my years of anatomy studies, I know better than to move him. He may have a spinal injury from the crash. God forbid.

"NOOOOOOOOOOO!!!" I wail, as a police officer lifts me to my feet.

A flurry of activity precedes the air ambulance's arrival. They place Malcolm—strapped to a board with a neck brace and an oxygen mask on his face—inside. The door shuts. Police officers tell me they'll take me to Cedars-Sinai Spine Center.

Wrapped in a blanket, I huddle in the back of the cruiser. The adrenaline rush leaves me shivering and dazed. The police officers' words of comfort wasted. All I know is Malcolm doesn't look good. At all.

"Ms. Knight?"

I startle at the sound of my name. I fell asleep again. A glance up shows a woman—dressed in a business suit and not scrubs—stands before me in the waiting room.

"Malcolm?!" I cry. "Is he okay?!?!?!"

Her mouth twitches, not quite a smile or a grimace.

"The doctors are still with him. I do not have an update for you," she responds. "I'm the CEO of Cedars-Sinai Spine Center. Morgan Steele wanted me to touch base with you and to give you a staff mobile. Mr. Steele will call momentarily. Should you need anything, do not hesitate to call me."

I nod mutely and thank her as I take the mobile and her business card. Then watch her leave.

My stomach roils.

When I arrived, a nurse insisted I shower in the staff locker-room and change into a set of clean scrubs. She explained I can't help Malcolm if I'm not at my best. Afterwards she gave me a cup of chamomile tea and a blanket, then led me to a private waiting room. Before she left, she told me the Steele family is in route to the hospital.

I feel a bit better, but still achy from my fall. Only Malcolm concerns me. It's been hours, and no word. A tear spills down my cheek as I hug the mobile to my chest like a lifeline. With my parents on an eco retreat in Belize, I can't reach them. Awake again, I feel so alone.

The ring of the mobile brings me back to the room.

"Morgan!" I cry.

"Starr, honey, thank you for saving our son!" he exclaims as his voice cracks with raw emotion. "We landed at LAX and will be there soon."

In the background, I hear Shelley.

"What do you need, Starr?" He asks for her.

"Only Malcolm," I cry pitifully.

There's a pause as Morgan girds himself.

"I know… I know," he murmurs as Shelley wails.

"Mr. and Mrs. Steele?"

A chorus of yeses fills the waiting room as the doctor enters with two others.

Morgan and Shelley, Sebastian and Lola, Roger and Leonie respond in unison as they rise from their chairs.

Haley, Harris, and I stand with them, eager to hear any news after hours of silence.

Morgan steps forward—the patriarch and Alpha Dom of all his sons.

"Morgan Steele. How is my son?" He asks.

The doctor gestures for everyone to sit.

Shelley screams.

Or is that me?

Arms catch me as my world fades to black.

"—FINE. Make sure she stays hydrated. Her temperature is a bit higher than normal, so monitor it. Ah, there you are, Ms. Knight."

One of the other doctors smiles at me as I open my eyes.

Heat floods my face when I notice everyone around me with concerned expressions. I make to sit up, but Lola's hand on my arm stops me. I glance at her, and she shakes her head.

"I... I'm so sorry to interrupt—"

"Nonsense! You have been through a lot of stress, Starr," Morgan chides. "How do you feel?"

"Fine, thank you. But, Malcolm? Please?" I answer.

Our gazes shift back to the doctor.

"I apologize for scaring you. Mr. Steele is being monitored in the ICU. The surgery went as expected," the doctor pauses. "He's had extensive damage to his spine and the back of his skull, not to mention the mauling of his calf. He came in unresponsive and remains in a coma—"

Shelley's heart-wrenching wail sends a chill through me.

Lola sobs and pulls me close.

I'm too numb to react.

The doctor continues, but his words blend incoherently for me.

Malcolm. Unresponsive. In a coma.

"How long until he wakes?"

Sebastian's question breaks through my haze.

I sit forward, praying for good news.

The doctor shakes his head as he replies, "We cannot predict when someone in Mr. Steele's condition will awake or if he will—"

This time I howl in anguish for my mate.

My stomach roils again. I jump from my seat and rush to the corner where a trash can stands. The tea and remnants of our dinner erupt from my mouth.

"*Chérie, oh chérie!*" Leonie croons as she kneels beside me and rubs my back.

Lola joins her and whispers, "Breathe, Starr. Remember your deep cleansing breaths, honey."

No yogic pranayama or sutras can ease the pain of my broken heart.

Malcolm, oh, my Malcolm!

# STARR

"I still can't believe what you did. Charging a full-grown mountain lion with a measly stick? Total badass Starr!"

Harris as always uses his jokester ways to make light of the situation—even a situation as dire as my love being in a coma.

In response, the corners of my mouth turn up slightly. If any other time, I would laugh at the absurdity of me facing off with a hungry, wild beast over its next meal. Now, not so much.

A month has passed since Malcolm's life-altering accident. And no change.

Even with the Steele billions of dollars, we can only do but so much to help my love. As the doctor said that fateful night, only time will tell the outcome of Malcolm's condition.

The Steeles will have none of it.

Not a clan to sit back and allow life to lead the way, Morgan held a strategy session only hours later. He invoked his substantial influence to take over a section of the hospital and to gather the best doctors, researchers, and physical therapists from around the world for a video conference. Within a relatively short period, they devised a plan and designed a custom facility dedicated to Malcolm and his recovery. The following day, they descended upon Cedars-Sinai Spine Center, ready to heal my love.

Malcolm's medical team wasn't the only ones to make a major move unexpectedly.

Morgan and Shelley took up permanent residence in the President's Suite at STEELE Beverly Hills. Roger, Leonie, The Twins, Daphne, and Nanny Grace moved in to a long-term mansion rental next to my home—*"to be near you, chérie"* as Leonie said. Harris moved into Malcolm's Sunset Strip penthouse.

After two weeks of staying at the hotel, Sebastian, Lola, and Haley returned to New York City. Since Lola is pregnant with their twins and needs to see her OB-GYN on a regular basis, they didn't move permanently.

The siblings divided STEELE International responsibilities too.

Sebastian claimed the East Coast since he needs to be in New York City as CEO and head of his Retail Division. Roger took over Malcolm's Entertainment Division and the West Coast operations in addition to his Residential Division. Haley chose the East for her and Harris' Technology and Cyber Security.

The other half of the Dynamic Duo remained in LA.

Besides his STEELE duties, Harris is working with the police on the case since they recovered a drone from the scene of Malcolm's accident. Harris has shared little information with us, but I know he and Haley are wizzes and will solve any problem.

And like his family, I devote myself to my man. After my initial hysteria, I drew upon my inner strength, inner warrior, and absolute love for Malcolm to gain the power to never leave his side. While I may not have a medical degree, I intend to nurse him back to optimal health. The powers of prayer and intention are strong.

Adrienne—BFF that she is—stepped in to handle SLFW Beverly Hills and Resorts along with the retreats until further notice. She keeps me up to date with weekly meetings here at the hospital, but I trust her to run my company in my absence. Márcia Souza—the Brazilian petite spitfire also known as my administrative assistant and a yoga substitute teacher—helps Adrienne and updates me regularly. My team amazes me, and I am grateful for them.

With a sigh, I think of my one regret: I told Malcolm no when he asked me to marry him over a year ago. Often as I sit at his bedside reading to him, my mind wanders to thoughts of *what if?*

What if I said yes?

We may have been in our penthouse at The STEELE Tower, and he would have taken the private elevator to his offices.

We may have been in our beachfront mansion at Steele Southampton Village, and he would have taken our Sikorsky S-92 Executive Helicopter from the Island to Manhattan.

We may have been paragliding above the magnificent cliffs of Miraflores overlooking the Costa Verde, and he would have been unavailable.

A tear trickles down my cheek, and I try to blink more away as I turn my head from Harris.

"Ah, Sis, I'm so sorry. You know me, just trying to make you smile. Instead like a dummy, I made you cry—" Harris' words cut off as his voice cracks on a sob of his own.

Yet he manages to hug me close in his powerful embrace. His hard body and build so like his brother's give me a moment of respite.

Then I recall Harris' use of "Sis" as a term of endearment, and it makes me cry harder since that's what he calls his sisters-in-law, Lola and Leonie. He views me—like they all do—as Malcolm's.

And I could have been if I weren't so *as the Universe takes me.*

Fool!

"Come on, honey, have some chicken noodle soup. You'll feel better."

My mother's suggestion as she smooths her hand along my back brings me out of my pity party.

I nod and loosen my grip on Harris.

Then I smile at my mother. We look exactly alike. Sorrel brown eyes full of love as she peers at me. Smooth chestnut-colored skin glows from healthy eating and regular exercise. Long, curly, dark brown hair pulled up in a topknot. Dimples highlight her sculpted cheekbones when she returns my smile. She's a beautiful woman in her late fifties.

"Yes, eat. You look a bit wan," Shelley adds in concern. "Remember your health is important, Starr sweetheart."

Again I nod. If Malcolm's mother can show strength and grace, I can too.

The Moms settle me at the dining table in the waiting room turned living room with comfy chairs, sofas big enough to sleep on if not in one bedroom, and desks for work.

When I lift the cloche covering the soup, the smell makes my mouth water. And not in a good way...

I rush to the trash can and empty my stomach contents. In the back of my mind, I wonder why I can't seem to hold food down. But I chalk it up to the stress.

"Starr, I will not hear another excuse. You will see your doctor today," my mother states in her no-nonsense-attorney voice.

With a feeble nod, I agree.

A call to my PCP's office, and I'm scheduled for later in the afternoon. Fortunately, it's during Malcolm's second physical therapy session of the day. Those are the only times I leave his side for an extended period.

"Good morning, Mr. Steele has finished his PT. You're free to join him in his suite," one of his private nurses tells us from the doorway.

"Oh, no, you won't!" My mother says, placing her hand on my shoulder as I rise from the table. "Eat the crackers and drink the tea before you return to Malcolm."

Shelley agrees, then goes with Morgan to their son.

Harris steps out to get some fresh air.

Alone, Sun turns to me.

"Starr, honey, Shelley is correct. You don't seem well"—my mother raises her hand to stop me from speaking—"You worry your father and me. Tell me, how are you doing really?"

Through more tears, I confess to Sun my fears, regrets, and my wishes. My parents and I are extremely close, so I share everything with them.

They didn't judge me when I told them I'm in the BDSM lifestyle and share a D/s relationship with Malcolm. Being hippies who keep fluid minds, they understand my desire to give up my control to a powerful and experienced Dom in a power exchange. Through their interactions with Malcolm, they respect my choice of him. Even my father admits he likes Malcolm.

My mother understands my heartache at not being his wife and my guilt at not giving him the one thing he ever asked of me after wearing his collar. Now I may never marry the love of my life.

"Starr, sweetheart, always remember my favorite yogic piece of advice," Sun starts. "Be equally thankful for what you perceive to be good and for what you perceive as bad. It all happens for a reason. Either way, you don't let it disturb your inner peace. Strive for tranquility no matter the outer circumstances."

Fresh tears fill my eyes as I clutch at my mother. Deep inhalations of the calming floral notes of her signature perfume relax me as they have since I was a child. The peace her scent instills in me dries the tears from my eyes and the pain from my heart.

I vow to be strong for Malcolm and for me. We may not know now why the accident happened, but we will get on the other side of this situation. Our love will thrive forever.

"THE DOCTOR WILL SEE you in a moment, Ms. Knight. Kindly have a seat in the waiting room."

I smile at the receptionist for my PCP, then sit. Another waiting room…

Fortunately, the wait isn't long. The nurse calls me shortly after I arrive and ushers me into the examination room. She checks my vitals and notes my temperature is slightly higher than normal. She takes my urine sample and leaves the room, saying the doctor will be in.

I answer some emails from Márcia while I wait. Then I glance up when the door opens, and the doctor walks in with the nurse.

"Ms. Knight, you mentioned nausea, super tender breasts and nipples, food aversions, and fatigue during the last few weeks. Do you have any idea why?" My doctor asks.

I have to hold back an eye roll. Isn't that why I'm here? To find out what's bothering me???

"Yes, doctor," I respond instead.

She smiles and says, "Well, I think your gynecologist is better suited to your needs. Or I can refer you to an OB-GYN."

I stare blankly at her. Maybe I'm more tired than I thought. What is she getting at?

"Ms. Knight, congratulations! You're pregnant!" She says, now grinning broadly.

I sit back on the exam table in shock.

When the doctor suggests I make an appointment with my OB-GYN, the puzzle pieces started to fall into place. After her bombshell announcement, the pieces fit snuggly. After she assures me there's no mistake, I call my gynecologist who happens to be an OB-GYN. Dr. Leticia Sánchez has an appointment in half an hour.

My mind still works to process the information even after Dr. Sánchez confirms my PCP's diagnosis. Diagnosis?! Ha! Life-changing pronouncement.

How the heck did I—a doula who's helped women with their pregnancies—miss my own symptoms?!?!

I was so focused on Malcolm; I lost sight of myself.

Malcolm!

My heart pounds as I think how fucked up this whole situation is for us. He's made hints and overt comments about having babies with me. I've felt the tug of my ovaries being around The Twins, Daphne, and Slade. Now Lola's expectant twins.

Lola!

She's 14 weeks, and I'm 16. We'll be pregnant together! Give birth days apart! Who will be our doulas?!?!

By the time I return to Cedars-Sinai Spine Center, I'm a jumble of emotions. Damn hormones!

There's only one person I want to see, need to see. My love, my Malcolm.

Quickly, I slip past the door to the living room. A peek through the window of Malcolm's bedroom of his suite reveals a nurse taking his temperature. I nod at her as I enter and close the curtain.

With a smile, she leaves us.

I have to swallow around the lump in my throat as I stare at my love.

Malcolm lies in bed motionless save for the rise and fall of his chest powered by a machine. He's still unresponsive to his surroundings. Regular massages and grooming keep his skin with a touch of color and his hair and facial hair well kempt. One would assume he was asleep. But unlike a deep sleep, any stimulation cannot awaken Malcolm, including pain. Nor hear my stifled sob.

I take a deep cleansing breath to clear my mind of what I perceive to be negative, to give way to the flow of positivity. I'm pregnant with his babies. Twins.

As I stand beside his bed, I take my love's hand in mine. I bring it to my lips for a soft kiss, then place his palm on my lower belly. The belly I thought was growing because of the cortisol running rampant in my system. No, it's our babies trying to tell their Mommy they need me too. And their father.

"Malcolm, my love. Guess what? Your wish came true. You put your baby in my belly. Two babies, in fact! Here, my love, see for yourself! Two little blips. Two Mini Malcolms! You marked me from the inside with your seed and out with your collars. Now you have to put your rings on my finger, my love I. Am. Yours. We need you, Malcolm Steele. Come back to your little family. I won't tell anyone because I want us to tell everyone together. Okay, my love? I love you so much."

Determined to be strong for all of us, I blink the tears away as I place his limp hand back on the bed.

Then I settle into my chair for my constant vigil.

# STARR

"Ms. Knight, today we'll do the twenty-week anatomy scan to gauge the development of your twins. We can also determine your babies' sex, if you like. The ultrasound takes about thirty to forty-five minutes. If you watch the monitor, I'll point out some details. Would you like that?"

The sonographer smiles at me encouragingly as she applies the gel to my melon-sized belly.

With their watchful eyes, my mother and Shelley noticed the roundness of my usually flat stomach and added my symptoms to deduce I was pregnant a week ago.

*"Starr, sweetheart, what do you have to tell me?" My mother asks as I walk past her to sit at a desk in the hospital living room.*

*Shelley and Morgan read to Malcolm in his suite. Roger and Harris have meetings at STEELE Los Angeles. While Leonie visits a project site for her STEELE Children and Young Adults Division. Sebastian formed it almost two years ago for her to incorporate for residential nurseries, bedrooms, playrooms, and playhouses and for hospitality kids clubs and play areas. As the head of the division. She reports to Roger and to Malcolm, respectively.*

*I gaze over my shoulder at my mother as my hand unconsciously lands on my belly. When I notice the natural reflex, my hand drops to my side.*

*Damn! Did she notice?*

*"What do you mean, Mom?" I ask, busying my hands with my booting up laptop.*

*When my question silence meets my question, I risk a glance in her direction.*

*Sun sits with her head tilted to the side, a perfectly arched eyebrow raised, and her full lips pursed. Her expression of doubt confirms my suspicions.*

*Flowy shirts and baggy joggers do not fool my sharp-eyed mother in the least. Damn!*

*My hand resettles on my babies bump as tears threaten to fall.*

*Damn hormones!*

*In fact, damn this whole fucked up situation!*

*My shoulders shake as my mother wraps her arms around me.*

*"Oh, Mom!" I sob. "Only Malcolm knows, but does he hear me???"*

*She rocks me and whispers words of love and support. Her soothing presence draws the confession out of me in a rush of blubbered words. She holds her comments until I finish on a hiccup.*

*"I'm trying to be strong for Malcolm, our babies, and for me.*

But it's so hard. I miss him so much! I'm scared out of my mind he won't wake up. Oh, Mom!" I end.

Sun dips the linen napkin from my half-eaten lunch into the glass of ice water, then dabs it on my flushed face.

"Hush, child of mine. You and my grandchildren will be fine. We come from a long line of courageous women capable of thriving despite the circumstances," my mother says as she cups my face.

Then she continues, "As for Malcolm, he has the absolute best care. Our prayers and thoughts surround him in the light of healing and love. He is young and strong. Continue your vigil. I believe he hears you and senses your presence. The babies will give him even more to fight for. You'll see. He loves you beyond any doubt."

I nod and take a deep cleansing breath.

"Now, show me my grandchildren," my mother says with a grin. "Your father will be overjoyed! He's at court, so we can tell him when he comes by later."

I grab my portfolio, and she takes my hand to lead me to a sofa. At last, I can caress my babies bump outside of Malcolm's suite. Surprised, I rub my hand over a spot one of Mini Malcolms kicked, and I laugh.

"Oh, Mom! Feel this!" I exclaim.

"Starr?"

So engrossed in the scans from today and the first of weeks ago, we don't hear Shelley and Morgan enter the living room.

A clearly distraught Shelley stands a few feet away. Normally a striking woman in her late fifties, her expressive brown eyes swollen and red from tears, stare at me. Her shoulder-length, wavy black hair pulled back in a messy bun appears greasy.

*Worry lines form between her elegant eyebrows. Shelley's feisty New Yorker personality takes a backseat to weariness. She's a shell of the shopgirl who captured Morgan Steele's heart when he visited one of his family's retail properties years ago.*

*Understandable since it's been weeks her second son lies unresponsive in a coma. She and Morgan just returned from visiting Malcolm, and she sags against her husband for support.*

*Their gazes shift between my belly and the ultrasound images in my mother's hands.*

*A glimmer of hope fills Morgan's platinum gray eyes as they widen in wonder. His sons get their handsomeness from their father. My heart constricts seeing Malcolm in his features.*

*Unsure of how they'll react to the news, I offer a smile to the Steele Matriarch and Patriarch.*

*"I'm nineteen weeks pregnant with Malcolm's twins," I say confidently.*

*Shelley faints.*

*When Morgan rouses her, she grabs me and cries. My tears join hers along with my mother, and even Morgan sobs.*

*When our eyes no longer fill with tears, Shelley sits back and clutches my hands.*

*"If anything happens to my son, you carry his babies... all that would be left of him on this Earth... Please... Please let us be a part of your and their lives, Starr... I know Malcolm would want us to care for you and for them," Shelley says as her voice cracks with pain.*

*Too overcome by the thought of anything happening to Malcolm, I can nod and squeeze her hands only.*

Now, as I lie on the exam table, Shelley squeezes my hand. I turn my head from the monitor to her.

"Oh, Starr, will you find out their sex? I'm sure Malcolm would love to hear. What a wonderful present," she says softly.

In the week since I told her out about my pregnancy, Shelley transformed. She and Morgan went to their President's Suite after my announcement. The next afternoon, they returned refreshed. Shelley told me she had a spa overhaul from head to toe and booked one for me in an hour. *"No more moping around being sad! We have to be strong for Malcolm's babies—and you of course, Starr, honey!"*

Morgan assured me even though I am a brilliant, Independent young woman with mighty, wealthy parents, he and Shelley guarantee Malcolm's babies and I will want for nothing. Morgan then presented me with a document outlining the trust funds he created for Mini Malcolms and a document for palimony retroactive by nineteen weeks for me.

Despite my protests, Morgan and Shelley insisted and had my parents as backup. Outnumbered, I gave in, and my heart swelled with love for them.

As it does now.

"Yes, Shelley, let's find out," I respond, as I return her squeeze.

My mother smiles and kisses my other hand.

Flanked by The Moms, we watch the monitor as the sonographer points out different parts of Mini Malcolms. When she pronounces both twins are healthy with one a female and the other a male, The Moms and I burst into tears.

This time tears of joy!

. . .

"WELL???"

"Don't keep us in suspense, Starr!!!"

"Come on, Hot Mama! Fess up already!"

I can't help but to giggle as my father, Morgan, Roger, Leonie, and Harris gathered in the hospital living room and Sebastian, Lola, and Haley via video conference demand to know Mini Malcolms' sex.

"Okay, okay!" I laugh with my hands up, palms out in surrender.

I glance at my mother and at Shelley on either side of me, then face the group.

"Malcolm and I are pregnant with... a girl and... a boy!!!" I announce, holding my babies bump and grinning like a Cheshire Cat.

Whoops and hollers fill the air. Harris wolf whistles while Leonie throws her arms around me.

"I'm so happy for Malcolm and you, *chérie*!" *The Lion* says as her amber eyes glow with happiness. "Lola and I sent a trousseau from my Lola's Coterie maternity lingerie and loungewear collection to your home. I have a few pieces here for you, too! It never hurts to feel sexy, *non?*"

"Yes! Welcome to the Sexy Mama Club, Starr!" Lola says, blowing kisses from the flat screen TV. "Now Baz's and my twin girls will have another girl their age! The grandkids will be even, four girls—Daphne, yours, my two—and four boys—Rodolphe, Gaspard, Slade, yours!"

Roger pulls me in for a hug and says, "Congratulations, Starr! Malcolm will be so happy to have one of each!"

My father and Morgan embrace me while The Moms pass out crystal flutes of Champagne.

"None for you, preggies!" Haley teases as she lifts her flute with Sebastian. "We'll have enough for the two of you!"

We spend more time chatting about nurseries—Leonie to the rescue!—expectations, and most effective practices. Everyone tries their best to keep the mood festive since it's Christmas Eve. As the French tradition Leonie—the half Tunisian, half Parisian megamodel turned interior designer—reminds us it's time to open presents.

After a while, I excuse myself and go to Malcolm's suite. Time to celebrate the news with my man and to give him his presents—two framed scans of each twin.

"Merry Christmas Eve, my love," I whisper as I kiss his soft lips. "Our Mini Malcolms are a healthy girl and a healthy boy! And guess what? Lola and Sebastian are having girls! Can you believe it? Wake up soon, my love. I can't wait for you to see your presents. We love you, Malcolm."

# MALCOLM

"—Change in his lips mean? Where—"

My mind dredges through mud worse than the quicksand I stumbled in near the Amazon River. None of my limbs move despite my brain's demands. Not even my eyelids open.

What the fuck is wrong with me?!?!?!

The voice fades in and out as I try to make sense of this world I'm trapped in.

Pain shoots through my heavy head; a dull pounding beats in my ears; blackness alternates with a spark of light beyond my sealed eyes.

"Mr. Steele? Can you hear—"

*Yes!* I scream, but the word rattles in the back of my throat. My thick, dry tongue sticks to the roof of my mouth. I try to cough, swallow, but nothing happens.

"—Malcolm! Can you hear me?"

My Angel?

What is she doing here? In fact, where the hell am I?

Her anguished cry cuts through the mud, pushing the viscous goo to the edges of my mind as I try to make sense of my surroundings. If only briefly.

Another flash of pain wipes my response from my mouth. Bile fills it. The acid burns.

Fuck. Me.

"—Ms. Knight, please—"

"I'm not imagining things! I caught the corner of his mouth move!"

My Angel's distress triggers my protective instinct. With a Herculean effort, I part my lips. Even to my ears, the hiss sounds nothing like the word *stop*. But it's enough to get someone's attention.

"Mr. Steele? We heard you. Just a moment. Let me get the doctors."

The unfamiliar voice says more to My Angel, but I can't decipher their words.

Another attempt to open my eyes or to speak makes my head hurt. Instead, a groan slips past my lips.

"Malcolm, baby. It's me, Starr. Don't try to move anything, baby, please. Just wait for the doctors."

My Angel's plea gives me pause.

*Doctors?*

My brain scrambles with the additional information. Like a short circuit, the word triggers a rush of disjointed memories.

Watching a movie with My Angel.

The crunch of leaves.

Stars.

The revving of a motorcycle.

Vicky Reynolds.

A mountain lion!

My eyes fly open at the horror.

Pain slices through my skull. Light blinds me. More voices.

My eyes close.

"Fuuuck!!!" I groan.

Immediately darkness descends. Urgent whispering. A door opens.

"Malcolm!"

*Mom?*

"Oh, Shelley! He's awake!" My Angel exclaims.

"Mrs. Steele, Ms. Knight, please stay back."

I lift my head, but it's still too heavy. Again the words don't form properly, only an incoherent jumble of sounds falls from my parched lips.

"Mr. Steele, this is Dr. Stevens. We closed the shade to block the sunlight from your room. You can open your eyes now."

I focus all of my effort on my eyelids. Open dammit!

Still darkness.

"Excellent, Mr. Steele. I'm going to use my penlight to check your responsiveness. Don't attempt to speak yet," Dr. Stevens says.

My eyebrows pinch together.

What the hell is he getting at? I can't see a damn thing.

A spot of light appears before me, then gets closer. My sluggish eyelids blink to block the unwanted brightness. The light alternates between my eyes a few times.

"You're doing very well, Mr. Steele. Blink once for yes and twice for no. Do you understand?" Dr. Stevens asks.

My eyelids close and open for an affirmative response.

A gasp nearby draws my attention. I turn my head, but pain shoots from the back of my skull to between my eyes like a scalpel sliced my head in two. A garbled cry escapes my mouth, and I close my eyes to shut out the excruciating pain.

"Keep your head still for now, Mr. Steele. We'll give you medication to ease the discomfort," Dr. Stevens says as I pick up movement from my left.

I blink once, then my world fades to black once again.

WHISPERING VOICES AWAKEN ME. It takes a moment to reorient myself as my eyes open to a dimly lit room. I shift my gaze left and right, but I can't distinguish shapes, only a brightness. What the fuck?!

"Malcolm, my love, you're awake."

*My Angel.*

My lips move, but my tongue still sticks to the roof of my mouth. A straw touches my lips.

"Drink some water, sweetheart."

*Mom.*

I take a few sips and swallow past the cotton stuck in my throat.

"Excellent son, very good."

*Dad?*

Another memory flash puts the pieces of the puzzle together.

I didn't die in the canyon. I'm in a hospital.

Thank fuck!!!

MY ELATION at being alive lasts as long as it takes for the doctors to tell me I was in a coma for two months and paralyzed from the waist down. They say it's an improvement since the paralysis was from the neck down when I arrived. The doctors gave me a bit of encouragement when they told me being awake is the next step in my recovery and to give my body time to heal.

But on top of that fucked up shit, I'm blind as a bat. Well, at least they think it may be a temporary affliction because of the impact of my fall.

Yeah, my fall somehow caused by Vicky Fucking Reynolds. That vindictive broad. I should have hired a real hitman to off her ass and not an actor to scare the shit out of her. Obviously my plan didn't work.

Harris and the police plan to meet with me tomorrow morning. The doctors don't want me to deal with but so much in one day. The less stress the better.

I agree wholeheartedly.

The only bright spot is Starr, My Angel who grounds me always. From what I could tell, she was in the room while the doctors delivered the bad news. But now she sits beside me. Alone at last.

However, my mind races faster than my heart, as I wonder whether she thinks less of me now. My Angel risked her life to save mine. She fought a damn mountain lion. Talk about love...

But does she still want me? Half a man? She's stayed by my side for two months knowing my situation, so that's a positive. But I can't determine her state of mind since I can't see her face...

Fuck!!!

A squeeze to my hand stops my brooding.

"Hi, my love," My Angel whispers as her soft lips brush my knuckles.

"Hi, Angel," I respond, disheartened.

"I missed you so much," she says as her voice catches.

I may not be able to peer at her, but I can perceive her distress. It makes my heart ache even more. How the hell can I comfort her when I want to cry like a baby?

This shit is so fucked up.

* * *

"It's time to finish that bitch once and for all!!!"

I can sense my little sister's vehemence without being able to put eyes on her. A vision of Haley leaning forward with silver sparks flashing from her dove gray eyes as she slams her palms on the conference table appears in my mind's eye. Along with Baz and Lola, Haley is on his Gulfstream G650 en route to LAX.

The police and my attorney, Engelbert Douglass, left moments ago after I gave my statement of the night's events.

As it turns out, Harris used the drone I knocked to the

ground with my glove to track the owner through the drone's serial number. Some tech nerd who stalked Vicky in the past exchanged jail time when he agreed to follow me for her. The conniving broad dropped her charges against him to use his cyber skills and drones. He sang like a canary when the police arrested him for his involvement in my accident.

Now with my statement confirming her voice and words over the drone's audio feed, they'll extradite Vicky from South Africa and begin her legal case. She won't get out of this so easily with a first-degree attempted murder charge.

But Haley has other plans.

"Don't look at me like that! I mean it, Baz! These females are going crazy for my brothers. First Roger, now Malcolm. Uh uh, no!" She interjects.

"Haley, we will handle this situation through the proper channels. Do you understand?" Our father's commanding tone stops any further discussion as Haley mumbles her concession despite the fire still burning in her molten platinum eyes.

Besides Morgan, my mother, Starr, Roger, Leonie, and Harris sit in my room. The direction of their voices clues me in to their locations. As though I still have my vision, my head turns towards them whenever they speak.

The brightness of the light increased. So the doctors have me wearing some shields to protect my "sensitive eyes" from the glare. Last night My Angel told me she refused to let them keep me in the dark with the shades drawn: "You need sun in your life, no different from before."

My concern for her no longer wanting me lessened as we spent the night talking. She held my hand and chatted on until we fell asleep, exhausted after the long day—a barrage of tests for me. It hurt like hell when I couldn't wrap my body around hers and hold her tight to me. Instead, My Angel kissed my lips and slept in another bed. Out of my reach.

I fucking hated my life right then.

Now it's not much better.

I'm with Haley. Finish that bitch!

But what the hell can I do about it?

I'm a bedridden, former enforcer who can't even see to dial a phone number to make the call.

Fuck. My. Life.

And *fuck* you Vicky Fucking Reynolds!

\* \* \*

"Angel? Angel, is that you?"

I whisper the words, afraid the vision before me is a mirage—a trick of my weary mind.

A couple of weeks passed—or so they tell me since I can't see worth a damn—and instead of just light, I glimpse a shape beyond the shields. A figure in the form of My Angel with her back to me. I recognize her long, curly hair atop her head as she does a yoga pose. That is, if my eyes don't deceive me. I remove the shields for a better look.

The figure gasps and whips around, then grabs what appears to be a high chair to steady herself.

"Malcolm?! You see me?" My Angel asks, shocked.

No denying the soft lilt of her voice. It's My Angel, and I can see her!

YES! YES! YES!

I don't realize I shouted out loud until a nurse rushes into my room.

"Mr. Steele, are you all right?" She asks as she hurries to my bedside.

The concern on her face is clear, just as clear as the tears shining in My Angel's sorrel brown eyes wide with surprise.

"I can see you! Angel! I can see you, baby!" I shout and sit forward with my arms open.

She covers her mouth and comes into my embrace. As soon as she settles on the bed, I bury my face in her neck. My tears mingle with the dampness of her warm skin from her yoga session. I inhale her coconut and frangipani perfume.

Heaven on Earth! My Angel!

"Oh, Malcolm!" She sobs as she pulls back to look into my eyes. "Oh, Malcolm, my love! Thank you, thank you!"

The door bursts open before I can say more. My mother and father rush in, followed by the doctors. After a moment for my parents to see me for themselves, the doctors ask everyone to take a seat. I watch my father usher my mother with her arms around My Angel to a sofa.

The doctors perform more tests and pronounce my

vision returned in full. Another improvement in my healing process.

Thank fuck!

Unfortunately, no change in my lower half. Still unresponsive to their pokes or whatever they do since I can't *feel* anything...

The medical team leaves with assurances to step-up my treatments since I have my vision back. They can add alternative methods to the routine.

Good. I'm sick of this shit already.

"Malcolm, sweetheart! You're doing so well!" Shelley says, as she approaches my bed.

My father adds, "We are so proud of you, son!"

But I only have eyes for My Angel.

My gaze travels from her curly bun to her gorgeous heart-shaped face down to her tits. Wow, they're bigger than before. Or am I seeing things? No matter, I'm a T&A man, anyway. When my gaze lands on her belly, I cock my head to the side in wonder. Maybe my vision isn't fully restored. Her normally flat stomach appears distended. I shake my head and close my eyes, then reopen them to double-check.

"Did you gain weight?" I blurt out.

In my periphery, my mother and father glance at each other, then leave the room without a word.

My Angel bites her lower lip and averts her eyes as she puts her hands on her swollen belly.

What an asshole thing to say!

"Babe, I'm sorry—"

"I'm pregnant—"

We speak at the same time, and I think my hearing may have gone just as my vision returned. I cock my head again and lower my gaze to her stomach.

She moves forward and takes my hand to place it on her belly.

"Malcolm, I'm pregnant with twins"—she reaches to the nightstand and holds picture frames in her hands—"Your baby girl and baby boy. They're twenty-four weeks now."

As she speaks, my hand jumps. My wide eyes lift to hers, and she giggles.

"One of them says hello to their daddy. That was a kick or a punch," she says. "Here, another one."

My jaw drops as my brain re-circuits to comprehend her words.

My Angel is pregnant with my babies?!?!?!

Fuck. Me.

# MALCOLM

"Trust funds and monthly palimony guarantee Mini Malcolms and Starr well taken care of. Even though Starr insisted our actions were unnecessary. Your mother and I implemented them while you were in a coma. We want to ensure you do not need to concern yourself with your family's well-being. We want you to just focus on your health, son."

My father's words register barely as I sit stewing in a wheelchair. A wheelchair.

Another month and shit in progress.

Fuck. My. Life.

What started as optimism has swiftly plummeted to doubt.

Doubt I'll ever walk again.

Doubt I'll ever make love to My Angel again.

Doubt I'll ever take care of my babies or make children again.

Doubt I'll ever be a real man again.

Instead, a sense of self-loathing suffocates me. Each failure in my physical therapy sessions results in another layer of disgust wrapping around me like gauze on a mummy. I might as well join the dead with the lack of worth I now represent.

Everyone from the doctors to my family tries to encourage me. Hell, they even arranged for a shrink to meet with me twice a week. As fucking if. I kicked his ass out of my room the minute he started with his gobbledygook. Not impressed.

What I need is to get the fuck out of here. I can't think straight with all the constant, unwanted attention. In the back of my mind, I know my family means well. But I haven't had a moment alone to process my predicament.

Despite her best efforts to comfort me, My Angel even grates on my nerves.

I'm tired of her New Age hippie words of enlightenment. There's but so much deep breathing, meditation, and dharma talks I can take. I'm not that man anymore.

With an inward sigh, I recall our first argument—one of many in the past couple of weeks.

*"Time for your morning meditation, my love!"*

*Starr's melodic teacher's voice fills my room.*

*I squeeze my eyes shut and slow my breathing, hoping she won't notice I was awake. I just do not have the energy to deal with this right now.*

*It was a hell of a night with the usual horrible dreams plaguing my mind. Each night they're different but with the same theme—I can't walk. Helpless.*

*Last night was the trapped in an unending corridor of a hospital with a snarling creature just beyond my vision stalking me. I fall out of my wheelchair and use my forearms to crawl along on my stomach, legs trailing limp behind. Sweat drenches my skin, causing the pajama top to stick to my back. The salty fluid burns my eyes as it drips from my forehead. Not one of the doors I heave myself up to reach the doorknob opens. I fall back down to the floor and continue my quest. Escape.*

*Just thinking about the nightmare makes my torso shudder.*

"Are you all right, Malcolm?" Starr asks as she places her small palm on my not-so-muscular-anymore chest.

"No!" I yell as my eyes snap open to glare at her. "No, I am not all right, Starr! I am a fucking mess. Okay?!"

Her soft gasp and stricken face do little to assuage my anger. An anger that I keep simmering beneath a placid surface, hidden from my family and the medical team. Only the psychiatrist caught the full force of my fury. Now Starr is at the receiving end.

Tears fill her eyes. She averts her gaze to my bed. Her attention goes to straightening the covers on my legs.

The legs I cannot feel.

"Stop!" I snarl.

Starr brings one hand to her heart and the other to her swollen belly. A sob escapes her parted lips as she backs away from my bed.

"I—I'm so sorry, Malcolm," she says softly without gazing at me. "I don't mean to upset you—"

"Enough. Just go. I need to rest," I interject as I turn my head towards the window, not wanting her to see my tears.

*A moment passes before Starr leaves me alone. Alone, to drown in a pool of self-pity.*

*Good.*

*I slam my fists into the mattress with my eyes squeezed shut, tears spilling out, and my mouth open in a silent, anguish-filled scream.*

*More tears creep from the corners of my eyes to puddle in my ears. A roar fills them, making my head pulse. The weight of it all is unbearable.*

*I cannot take much more.*

Now as I half listen to my father, I wonder if Starr will even stay since she and our babies are more than financially stable thanks to my parents' foresight. Or their belief I would have succumbed to my injuries and never awoken from the coma…

After each fight—all one-sided—I tell her to go. But Starr always returns, undeterred by my histrionics. Dark circles rim her eyes and a bit of her free spirit drains. Yet she the glow of impending motherhood surrounds her like a protective shield. Nothing can take away from her innate beauty. Not even the pain I cause her.

Damn, I'm a miserable asshole.

"Malcolm."

My father's commanding tone drags me from my thoughts.

I shake my head to clear it from the jumble and lift my gaze to his stoic face.

He scrutinizes me for a moment. Sharp gray eyes bore into my very soul. One could hear his brain analyzing the situation, trying to make sense of his wayward second son.

I tumble back in time to my rebel teen years. Many a day did I stand before Morgan Steele to face his disappointment at my misbehavior. Never one to follow the rules, it was an everyday occurrence.

Sebastian took the role of eldest sibling seriously and made it his mission to watch over the rest of us as the leader. Roger *The Responsible* middle child served as the mediator with his intense stare and need for order. The unexpected twins Harris and Haley—the youngest jokester son and the baby girl—had everyone fawning all over them.

Me? I was the second son; the rebel; the bad boy billionaire playboy of the family. Even before I had my own billions. The one with the back tattoo from shoulder to shoulder around to my pecs of wings to symbolize freedom from family constraints and the flying as I sped along on my motocross bikes. Later, the Prince Albert piercing to give optimal pleasure to the many women I bedded.

My parents could have recorded the scoldings they gave to me and set them to auto play. Not that it mattered.

Now I'm a grown ass man, not here for chiding.

"Yes, Dad?" I ask with a stubborn lift to my chin as I meet the Alpha Dom's gaze.

Only the slight narrowing of his eyes provides any sign of his annoyance with me.

Too damn bad.

I'm the one who's suffering. Sitting immobile in a fucking wheelchair. No end in sight based on the dismal progress I've made since I awoke.

My father schools his features then responds, "Malcolm, we cannot fathom what you must go through. Nor will we make light of your feelings. However, keep in mind you have a responsibility to yourself and to Starr and to your babies. Get your head in the game, son. Do all you can to improve your situation. It may not be ideal in your mind, but it is the situation you must deal with. We are Steeles, and we let nothing stop us. Do you understand, Malcolm?"

I take a deep inhalation and a slow exhalation to calm myself—damn if Starr's New Age technique comes to the forefront.

"Listen, Dad. I'm trying here. A stalker ex almost killed me; a mountain lion almost ate me. In a coma; temporarily blinded; paralyzed from the waist down; my girlfriend is pregnant with twins. It's a whole lot to 'deal with' and not that easy, you know," I respond truculently. "Give me a break already."

He opens his mouth to speak, but I hold my hand up. I'm not that teenager anymore.

"I appreciate what you and Mom did for Starr and for the babies. For me with this custom facility and best-in-the-world medical team. Thank you. But I need some space. Some time to myself," I say. "Please."

Without hesitation, my father nods and responds, "I understand, son. Know that we love you and want the best for you. I'll speak with our family and the doctors. However, you must continue with your healing plan. Nonnegotiable, Malcolm. Do I have your word?"

I nod; he raises his eyebrow.

"Yes, Dad," I respond, knowing how Starr must feel when I demand a verbal response during our playtime.

"Very well, son," he says.

He embraces me, then strides out of the door.

A relieved sigh slips from my mouth as I navigate the wheelchair to the window. If I can't walk outside, I might as well stare at the bustling streets of Beverly Grove. The six lanes of traffic forming South San Vicente Boulevard stretches before me. Fortunately, the treated windows block the noise. Although I would welcome the distraction of honking horns and sirens.

How much time passes, I'm not sure. But the soft cough behind me makes me glance up. Reflected at me is the vision of My Angel.

Her sorrel brown eyes meet my stormy gray ones questioningly.

"Excuse me, Malcolm. I don't mean to disturb you. I will respect your request for time apart from us. But before I go, I want to let you know I love you with all of my heart, body, and soul, and I will be here when you are ready," Starr says in a voice tinged with sadness.

Her passionate words knock the wind from my lungs. I jerk with the force of it, and my head snaps to my chin and back. An incoherent grunt pops out of my mouth.

My Angel takes my visceral reaction as her dismissal and hurries from the room as best as she can at twenty-eight weeks pregnant with twins.

Just as the door clicks shut, I find my voice.

But it's too late. Starr left. Only the aroma of her coconut and frangipani perfume wafts around me.

Once again, I take a deep inhalation to imprint her tantalizing scent on my brain. Then a slow exhalation, saddened by the loss of the last vestiges of my love.

I am alone.

# STARR

"*How* are you doing, *chérie?*"

The concern in Leonie's feline amber gaze causes tears to fill my eyes. I shift to face the antique dresser she added to Mini Malcolms' nursery in my home —one of the five she designed—to avoid her noticing my pain.

More like gut-wrenching pain from being abandoned while pregnant by the one man I love and trust more than any other before him. The man with whom I want to spend the rest of my life. The man who captured my heart.

How could Malcolm do this to me? His Angel.

If anyone told me he and I would end up separated by not only miles but blocks put up by his mind, I would have laughed and told them not my Malcolm. Not my love.

Yet here I stand two weeks after he requested space from his family, thirty-weeks pregnant preparing for the arrival of our babies without their father.

Sure, I understand and respect Malcolm's need for

some time to acclimate to a life vastly different from the one he had before being paralyzed. Cave diving; paragliding; kitesurfing; hell just walking down the damn street. At this time, not possible. And it must cause him a lot more pain than my sense of abandonment.

But my heart aches still.

So many nights I spent in his hospital room wishing he could hold me in his arms and ease some of the pangs of pregnancy. Rub my back; massage my calves; soothe the pulsing ache at the apex of my thighs. I know women I've helped as a doula spoke often of their increased sexual desires, but I never expected to be this needy. And BOB while watching the sex and dungeon videos Malcolm and I made do not cut it in the least. No Battery Operated Boyfriend can make up for the girth and length of Malcolm's ten inches of velvet covered steel wielded with such skill. Nor the two-dimensional image of him, even in all its glory on the giant screen in my media room. My greedy pussy clenches at the reminder.

Damn that man for being so self-involved!

What about me and my needs—including the horny ones, huh?

How does he expect me to go through pregnancy, birth, and raise twins by myself?!

Every day we're apart it's a constant struggle for me to continue being empathetic. And the raging hormones don't help my emotional rollercoaster. Not even my daily—now twice a day—meditation sessions help me refocus.

I'm nearing my wits' end.

If it weren't for my parents, my girls—Adrienne, Lola,

Leonie, Anita, Billie, Blair—and of course the Steeles, I don't know what I'd do. But as my mother told me, *we come from a long line of courageous women capable of thriving despite the circumstances.* This too shall pass, and I will come out stronger for it.

And my babies will only know love and joy. They will never know their father didn't spend time with me while I carried them. I just pray he'll be at their birth.

Each day I record our pregnancy progress so Malcolm won't miss one moment of Mini Malcolms' development—or the beauty of my body he's missing! After I shower and rub nourishing oil on my damp skin, I stand naked before the full-length mirror in my dressing room to record front, profile, and back views. Then I take still shots and place printouts along with the official ultrasound scans in the journal I write my musings in throughout the day.

What started as a way to document our babies since Malcolm was in a coma now is a means to provide him with the experience secondhand. His being absent is his choice.

So how am I doing? Not so great, to say the least…

"Oh, honey, don't worry. We're here for you," Billie says in her Southern Belle drawl when a sob slips from my trembling lips. "And for your little broccoli bunches!"

I can't help but to giggle through the sadness at her reference to the size of Mini Malcolms. Each time I see my OB-GYN, Billie wants an update so she can tease me. It's become our running joke.

As she wraps her arms around my shoulders, her Granny Smith apple green eyes twinkle with mirth. With her wavy, medium-blonde balayage hair and pecan-colored skin, Billie reminds me of Tyra Banks' doppelgänger. Billie is curvy like the megamodel, but a petite version at five feet, four inches.

Her joking is just what I need to drag me from the funky mood. I say a silent prayer of thanks she's spending more time at Lola's Coterie Beverly Hills than in her base at the boutique in STEELE Las Vegas' luxury mall. Since meeting her as Lola's West Coast assistant, Billie and I have become fast friends. When Lola promoted Billie to COO, we celebrated with a weekend getaway to Napa Valley.

I wish I had a glass... no, make that a bottle of wine now. I rub my broccoli-filled belly and giggle. Well, maybe not *right* now.

"I know, and we thank you," I respond as I hug Billie in return. "You do not know how mind-blowing this whole situation has been. I wish that woman never messed with Malcolm and caused the accident. But I am grateful for your support. All of you. It means so much to me and helps make it a bit better."

"That's what friends are for, Starr!" Anita chimes in with a smile on her honey brown face beaming at me from where she sits cross-legged on the floor folding onesies. "We'll always have your back."

Indeed.

Last week she moved into my guest house. As my doula, Anita wanted to be close to me during the last weeks of my pregnancy—not all the way in Paris. She's a yoga instructor with a flourishing practice I know from our fitness world and my partner for the cafés in my SLFW Beverly Hills and

Resorts. She's also the wife of Roger's luxury gym business partner, the former world heavyweight champion Norman Green. He relocated with her and will train out of his Beverly Hills facility. It's also nice to have their young daughters here for Mommy practice.

Along with Daphne at nine months and The Twins Rodolphe and Gaspard at two years old, I'm getting lessons in newborns, toddlers, and pre-schoolers. Whew!

On the babies' front, I'm covered. However, a man, not so much.

Roger and Harris try to make up for Malcolm's absence. They bring foods I crave, surprise me with goodies for Mini Malcolms, and put together their mobiles and custom baby monitors. Harris—the self-proclaimed *Bad Boy Bachelor For Life*—even offers to go with me to my doctor appointments. I pass on the visits, but love him for the thought.

Instead, The Moms go with me. They helped me to select a nanny with a nursing background who can assist me with twins. Patience Beck came highly recommended from the agency Leonie, then Lola used. One the überwealthy and celebrities use to hire their nannies, nurses, and governesses. Their training is top-notch in everything from changing a diaper to language lessons to disarming a would-be kidnapper. Although Morgan arranged a security detail at the ready since The Twins' kidnapping put everyone on high alert.

Nanny Patience presented as the best candidate—even aside from her name. Besides being appropriately trained and smart. She fits in with my personality, has the stamina to handle twins, and is a widowed, early fifties, mature woman. Zero interest in my man adds to her pros column. She'll be on call twenty-four, seven and live in the two bedroom, two bath apartment above the garage.

"However, I don't appreciate you leaving me to handle Anton Alexeyev," Adrienne huffs as she rolls her feline green eyes. "That man takes advantage of Malcolm and you being out of the loop to pester me all day!"

We laugh at her melodrama.

I know without a doubt the striking Russian giant weakens her resolve to fall hard for a man. Who can blame her with him resembling sexy AF Dolph Lundgren as the Russian boxer in *Rocky IV* with shoulder-length hair and glacial blue eyes?

As Malcolm's friend from Harvard University undergrad and B-School turned Vice President, Development for Entertainment Properties Division, Anton oversaw the partnership between STEELE International and SLFW. Adrienne unknowingly charmed him with her beauty, brains, and fluency in his native language. Not to mention disinterest in him makes her the perfect conquest for the Alpha Dom. She's been mum about their relationship so far...

"Girl, like you don't love it!" I tease Adrienne with my own exaggerated eye roll. "We see you!"

She snorts and returns her attention to organizing the walk-in closet.

"Well, I'm just glad Starr likes Mini Malcolms' nurseries. My favorite is the one at Steele Southampton Village. There's something about the tranquility of a beach to soothe babies," Leonie says as she fluffs the pillow in one glider.

"I don't just like them, I love them!" I exclaim. "You did an awesome job with each nursery matching it to the mansion's decor yet giving them a unique feel. My parents love theirs too, as do Shelley and Morgan. I can't thank you enough, Leonie."

A twinge of sadness pokes at the tenuous edges of my happiness. The thought of Malcolm not being pleased with me changing rooms in his penthouse at The STEELE Tower in New York City and at his Hampton's beachfront mansion makes my stomach flip. Leonie started work on them as soon as I found out I was pregnant, while Malcolm was still in a coma. Now he's awake.

Shelley and Morgan assure me Malcolm won't mind despite his current standoffish behavior.

It pains me to think he would demand their removal considering they're for his babies. But with the way he's acting, who knows?

I give my head a firm shake to dislodge the gut-wrenching thought. No time for negativity, Starr Knight! I admonish myself.

Now there's a positive thought... Starr Steele.

Perhaps if I ask Malcolm to marry me, he'll see I love him unconditionally.

Whether or not he can walk, our love supersedes any setback. Together we can overcome the blocks he's set in his mind. I won't let him lock himself away from me, his babies, or his loved ones. No more than I left the blinds drawn in his hospital room.

Malcolm needs the light and the love of those closest to him, despite his pushback.

I refuse to give up on us, on our little family. I'll give him another two weeks. After, I'll propose to the man I love—then, now, and forevermore.

My heart lifts, and a smile of pure joy spreads across my face.

"Honey, you are the epitome of a glowing Mommy-to-be!" Billie says.

Leonie claps her hands and adds, "Oh, *chérie*! You are simply stunning!"

Adrienne and Anita express their agreement with grins of their own.

I smile and rub my babies bump.

It's not my glow alone; it's Malcolm and our love that shines so brightly.

Soon we'll be together again.

# MALCOLM

"Thanks, bro. I appreciate you helping me out with my office. I need to do some work or I'll go crazy sitting around here all day long. It's time I focus on my work for STEELE."

Harris pauses at my words as he connects the monitor to the new computer he set up in the living room area of my suite at Cedars-Sinai. He turns a steely stare in my direction. The chill radiating from his gray eyes sends a shudder down my spine.

What's eating his ass?!

When I ask, Harris narrows his eyes into points as he glares at me. The space between his eyebrows furrow and his nostrils flare. He takes a deep breath.

"Really? It's time for you to focus on your work for STEELE?! What the fuck, *bro*?! How about you focus on your pregnant girlfriend?! Who do you think needs you more? Starr or STEELE? I'll help you out... It damn sure ain't STEELE!" Harris rails at me.

No sign of the jokester younger brother in sight. He's spitting mad with eyes blazing shards of platinum into me.

Well, damn.

"Listen, Harris. I do not need—"

"You do not need? You do not need?! Fuck you, Malcolm! You see those scars from fangs on your calf? Starr risked her life to save your sorry ass when a damn mountain lion was dragging you away to devour you. I saw the crazy sight with my own eyes, and it nearly gave me a heart attack! She stayed by your side every damn day and night. And this is how you treat her?! Damn, even if Starr wasn't pregnant—with your twins by the way—she doesn't deserve the cold shoulder you're giving her. How the hell can you justify icing her out of your life like this? You dumb fuck!" Harris continues, not slowing for air in his tirade.

Each time I open my mouth, it sets him off. All I can do is sit here and take his shit.

Like I want to be away from Starr?!

No, I don't! But what the fuck am I going to be able to do for her? And for our babies?! Riddle me that, little brother?! Little brother who's never been in a serious relationship a day in his thirty-two-year life!

"Fuck off, Harris!!!" I roar.

He shuts his mouth, but glares at me before he shakes his head with a look of pure disgust.

"No! *You* fuck off, Malcolm and get your shit together," Harris bites out. "I'm only helping you because Dad said so. Otherwise, I'd leave your sorry ass to wallow in your pool of self-pity. So. Shut. The. Fuck Up. and let me finish so I can go see how your pregnant girlfriend is doing. Without you, loser."

Well, damn.

I sit stunned silent in the wake of Harris' fury. I can only watch as he finishes hooking up the computer. My mind reels. No one has spoken to me as he has since Baz and I had our arguments as teens. And even then, Baz didn't admonish me to the level Harris has.

Maybe I am being a total dick to Starr.

But she doesn't need a paralyzed man in her life. What the fuck can I do for her or for our babies other than give them money? And my parents took care of that issue with the trust funds and palimony.

Starr needs to just move on without me. Live her best life. Not to be saddled down with a gimp like me.

My mind drifts back to the disappointing conversation I had with my lead doctor this morning.

*"It's been five months since the accident; the last three with me awake from the coma. I follow all of your team's directions; complete my physical therapy and strength training; hell, I even meet with the psychiatrist twice a week. Yet no new progress. Tell me your honest, medical opinion: will I ever walk again, doctor?" I ask.*

*Dr. Stevens stares at me for what seems an eternity before he responds.*

*"Mr. Steele, as I said when you woke, we cannot give you a definitive answer or a timeline. We can only adjust your treatment plan according to the progress you make using the best research and therapies available. It is a process you must trust," he says.*

*Now it's my turn to stare at him.*

"So you're saying I may never walk again?" *I press for a more concrete answer.*

*He shakes his head.*

"Equal odds for you to experience a full recovery or for you to remain at your current state. I assure you we do our best for you, Mr. Steele."

*The last fragile thread of hope snaps. I free fall. This time the thrill of the extreme sport disappears.*

"Stay positive, Mr. Steele. That can be the most effective course to maintain," *Dr. Stevens says before he leaves me sitting in my wheelchair despondent.*

"—And if you think Mom and Dad or any of the others are happy with your stupid behavior, think again, fucker."

Harris' declaration jars me from the disappointing memory. Then the door slams with enough force, the artwork on the walls shake as he storms out of my suite.

So lost in my thoughts, I hadn't realized he finished installing the computer. The login screen blinks silently with the STEELE International, Inc. logo awaiting my credentials.

Starr or STEELE?

Right now, it's still STEELE.

With a sigh, I type in the required information and set to work.

This is what I need right now. No one understands what I've been through or the hell I face every. Single. Damn. Day.

***

"It's good to have you back, Mr. Steele. We'll be sure to add you to all status updates and communications going forward. Should you need anything, just let us know. Good day!"

I smile at the screen before ending the video conference call with my Entertainment Properties Division. I gave myself a week to get up to speed on the various projects and this week marks my full return as the head.

Roger didn't argue with me about resuming my role from him. He only gave me shit about Starr. Again.

I wish they would back the fuck off already. If Starr's not complaining, why do my siblings need to berate me constantly? Hell, even Lola read me for filth a few days ago.

Fuck!

I shrug it off and lift my gaze to Anton.

The giant Russian pins me with his glacial stare.

"I am glad to see you back at work. But doing shit for your woman? Not glad, *zhopa*," he tsks with an aggrieved shake of his head.

I raise my arms in the air and glare at the ceiling in a silent plea for strength to deal with more bullshit. My blood heats in my veins. I'm sick of being treated poorly.

With a roar I respond, "Not you too, Anton. ENOUGH!"

I wheel around the desk and make quick work of the distance between us to face him head on. Our eyes on level since he's remains seated at a table allows me to square off with him.

Sure I may be in my wheelchair and legless, but my

upper-body strength returns with each personal training session. I point my index finger in his face and snarl.

"Get the fuck off my back, *zhopa*! You do not know what the fuck you are talking about. And I damn sure do not need your judgement of my personal life! Either you are here to work or get the fuck out!" I say in a menacingly low growl.

Anton raises his eyebrow and slowly shifts his gaze between my finger in his face and my blazing eyes.

"You better get off the painkillers, Steele. Do not tempt me to beat your *zhopa* right here, right now. You damn sure need someone to knock some sense into you," he responds with his Russian accent thickening in his anger. "We have work to finish. Then I will take my leave of you. I am a man who handles his responsibilities."

My head explodes.

"Fuck. You—"

A polite cough from the doorway interrupts my rebuttal. I swing around to see who stands at the door.

Forget Anton… Fuck. Me.

It's Starr.

*Starr*

Today is the day. I will ask Malcolm Steele to step into the light of our love forever. I will ask him to marry me.

My heart flutters as I walk off of the elevator at the hospital. I nod to the nursing staff at their station, not wanting to stop and chat as I would normally. There's no need to check in the living room since Shelley told me she and Morgan were taking a spa day.

It'll be just Malcolm and me—no disruptions. Or witnesses if he tells me no, like I told him so many months ago…

With a deep cleansing breath, I shake my head and roll my shoulders back to rid myself of such negative thoughts. Get thee behind me!

As I near Malcolm's suite door, I hear shouts from within.

For a moment I consider leaving. I don't need him in a foul mood when I'm about to risk a proposal. Then I decide the risk of losing him proves greater than a hit to my ego. I take one more breath and knock on the door.

Malcolm's raised voice prevents him from hearing me.

He really shouldn't get himself so worked up. Nothing is worth elevated blood pressure in his medical condition.

I open the door and survey the room.

An enraged Malcolm points at Anton, who has a deceptively calm appearance. Knowing the Russian, I can tell he's pissed too.

I cough to bring their attention from ripping each other's head off to focus on my presence.

Their heads whip in my direction.

The fire in Malcolm's eyes resembles molten platinum.

A shudder trips down my spine. I clutch my babies bump protectively. I'm not at all concerned Malcolm would harm me. But he looks ferocious.

Our eyes lock—mine wide, his wild.

"Malcolm?" I judder.

"*Dorogoy*, come in. I was just about to take my leave," Anton says with a bright smile as he rises from his chair and gathers his things.

Malcolm's nostrils flare and he bites out, "Starr is not your *sweetheart!*"

Oh, dear. Perhaps I should rethink my proposal now, after all...

Anton ignores Malcolm and double kisses me before he exits the suite without a backwards glance at his best friend.

My eyes shoot up at the growl from Malcolm. I take in his flushed face and heaving chest. I don't know what they argued about, but it has Malcolm out of sorts.

"Would you like some cool water?" I ask as I move further into the suite. "I'm a bit parched myself."

I add the last part to not isolate him. So I proceed to the mini refrigerator and remove two bottles of Fiji Water. I smile to myself. The brand has become our favorite since our trips to the island chain. Then I go to his side.

Malcolm sits silent as I pass a bottle to him. His eyes study my face.

His intense gaze makes me blush.

"Well, I missed you too, Mr. Steele," I joke to lighten the mood. "I'll bring a framed photo the next time I come, and you can stare at it all day!"

After I sit in the chair Anton vacated, I take a much-needed sip from the frosty bottle. Then clear my throat and set our bottles on the table.

"Malcolm, I know you said you needed some space. But

I want to ask you a very important question," I say as I take his hands in mine.

Once again his eyes search my face, and I keep my expression open, hoping to share my unconditional love for him through it.

I take one final cleansing breath before I begin:

"Malcolm Steele, you mean more than the world to me. In fact, you are my sun and my moon—my everything. I love you beyond mere words. Over three years ago, you captivated me as I sat on the beach in St. Barth's while watching you kitesurf. Throughout that time, you taught me to embrace my desires by trusting you with my heart, body, and soul. Our love is unconditional. Nothing can tear us apart—no psycho sub or hungry mountain lion. I am yours and you are mine. Together we have our Mini Malcolms as proof of our love. I ask you to bind me to you forever, not just with your Shibari ropes, but with your commitment to me, to us, to our babies. Malcolm Steele, will you marry me, your Angel?"

Silence descends on the suite. Not even Malcolm's breath sounds from his parted lips as his mouth hangs open. Whether his reaction is a good shock or a horrible one, I cannot decipher as I continue to hold on to his now sweat-dampened hands.

Malcolm stares at me as his eyes darken. Then he drops his gaze to our hands clutched on his thighs. A strangled noise comes from the back of his throat. He pulls his hands from mine and wheels his chair backwards—away from me.

"I cannot even feel our hands on my lap," Malcolm whispers, again wild-eyed.

I sit frozen as he pivots the wheelchair to turn his back to me.

His shoulders droop, then shake.

His chin drops to his chest, and he brings a fist to his mouth.

A gut-wrenching sob tears from his lips as his body convulses with each anguished cry.

I jump to my feet and go to Malcolm as fast as my body allows at thirty-two-weeks pregnant. My heart breaks and tears fill my eyes when I see my powerful Alpha Dom boyfriend so broken. Not once since he woke up did Malcolm display this level of pain and sadness. I knew he was hurting, but not to this extent.

"Malcolm, oh, Malcolm, my love," I start as I frame his face in my hands. "It's okay, baby. Just let it out. I'm here for you. Always."

I cradle his head to my babies bump and rock him as I hum while praying to soothe him and to give him strength. He wraps his arms around my back and clings to me while his sobs reach a peak.

We stay as one for a long while until Malcolm gathers himself and pulls back.

I wipe my tearstained face and lean over to kiss his full lips.

He turns away from me. Again.

"No," Malcolm whispers.

I stare at his profile blankly. *No?*

"I am a broken, angry, and bitter man, Starr, and I

vowed to protect you. Even if that means protecting you from me," Malcolm says in a more firm voice as he stares at the wall. "Go, Starr. I can do nothing for you like I am. The babies will bear the Steele name. I will make certain they and you are financially secure for life. But I can do no more."

Without sparing me a single glance, Malcolm wheels himself away from me one final time. The bedroom door of his suite shuts with a resounding click in the silent room.

The pieces of my broken heart turn to dust, and my tears wither away.

# STARR

"I do not give a damn what you say, Starr Knight! By the time I finish with Malcolm Steele, he will not need to worry about being 'a broken, angry, and bitter man!' He will not have to worry about a damn thing!"

I imagine steam pouring from my father's nose, mouth, and ears as his pecan complexion reddens with his rage. His obsidian eyes flash with each step he takes as he storms around the living room in my parents' Bel Air mansion.

After Malcolm's harsh dismal, I was so upset I needed the comfort only my mother and my father could provide for me. I love my girls and their support, but I needed more. Much more.

I still don't know how I made it from Malcolm's suite, then outside to my new SUV.

Morgan and Shelley gifted the chauffeur-driven Black Badge Rolls-Royce Cullinan to me when my babies bump made it difficult to drive my Tesla. The future grandparents explained the SUV would prove a more convenient method of transportation to get around with the babies. They insisted Ernest Rowland—a member of STEELE International's security team based in Los Angeles—join my detail and serve as my driver.

Even though I protested initially, I was thankful to have him waiting outside of the hospital. I was in no condition to drive. One look at my facial expression, and Ernest ushered me into the backseat. The comfort of its sumptuous interior with the scent of lavender wafting from the built-in diffuser wasn't enough to soothe me.

I asked Ernest to take me to my parents.

As we drove the thirty minutes along Sunset Boulevard, my mind replayed the scene on repeat, analyzing every detail and nuance. The expression of concern around Anton's eyes; the tic of Malcolm's cheek as he ground his molars; his eyes shifted from stormy gray to closed off while I opened my heart during the proposal.

By the time Ernest helped me from the Cullinan, nausea made me weak and my stomach roil. My parents weren't home yet, so he helped me to a sitting room and put my legs up on a sofa. He disappeared and returned with a cool glass of water. Then he offered to stay until my parents returned. I assured him I would be fine and told him to take the rest of the day and tomorrow off. With a sympathetic look, he left.

Tears welled in my eyes at his simple actions.

Ernest, my parents, Morgan, Shelley, my girls... Hell, even the man who held the elevator as I waddled towards it exhibits more care for me than my boyfriend and the father of our babies!

After I pulled the cashmere throw over me, I cried myself to sleep curled in a fetal position on the sofa. Rest evaded me as nightmares of being abandoned in the hospital room or alone giving birth plagued me.

I gave up on peaceful sleep.

Instead, I made my way to the kitchen for a cup of lemon ginger tea. Leonie hooked Lola and now me on to the tasty beverage. Perfect for upset tummies.

As the water heated in the kettle, I rubbed my babies bump and murmured words of love to the only bright lights in my life. I vowed to give them my all and to stop pining over Malcolm. They need me more than he does, apparently. And they deserve a home full of warmth and love.

So as I learned from one of my favorite movies—*Like Water for Chocolate*—the power of emotions and cooking, I put a stop to my tears. I refused to have my sadness transferred to my babies. Their happiness supersedes my despair.

By the time my parents arrived from their law firm, I made up my mind. I will care for my babies to my fullest without Malcolm Steele. They will bear his name and receive his monthly child support in addition to the trust funds, as they deserve. However, I will no longer accept the monthly palimony. I only agreed to it since I believed Malcolm and I would marry.

Silly Starr no more!

So as my father steams—not at all peaceful like his

adopted name—I await an opening to tell him again I can handle my life. I only ask for their support. And not the reckoning of Malcolm Steele...

"Starr, honey, let your father talk to Malcolm. And I mean *talk*, Jordan. I cannot believe he would behave in such a callous manner. He's been such a pleasure," my mother says, shifting her gaze from my father to me.

Whenever she reverts to his given name, Sun means business.

From my father's chastened expression, he understands. With a growl, he spins on his heel to stalk towards the liquor cabinet where he pours himself a double straight up of Michter's Bourbon. The ultra-premium Kentucky Bourbon is his liquor of choice. He tosses it back without a flinch and pours another. His piercing eyes go to my mother.

"Sun, would you care for a drink?" He asks gruffly.

"No, darling. One of us needs to maintain a clear head," she replies with an eye roll.

She returns her attention to me and pats my leg.

"Honey, men are funny creatures. When they hurt, they either withdraw or lash out. In Malcolm's case, he's done both"—she pauses to cup my cheek as a stray tear leaks from my eye—"Honestly, I'm surprised he hasn't broken before now. You have four weeks until Mini Malcolms' births. Time heals all, Starr."

Across the sitting room, my father snorts as he finishes his second Christofle rocks glass.

Our gazes lift to him.

He shakes his head and mutters to himself.

"You'll just talk to Malcolm. Right, Dad?" I ask.

With a sigh, he strides back over to where my mother and I sit on the sofa. He perches his six-foot-five-inch frame on the edge of the armrest and kisses my forehead, then my mother's lips.

"Starr, sweetheart, I cannot imagine what you are going through—or Steele for that matter. But I will repeat for you what I told him over a year ago and then the afternoon before his accident."

My father goes on to tell me—verbatim as the attorney he is—his conversation with Malcolm about our relationship.

*"Understand Starr is my only child and means everything to her mother and to me. Our family unit is inseparable. Starr shares every aspect of her life with my wife and with me. She made us aware of the situation with Vicky Reynolds and her declination of your proposal, along with the lifestyle she's chosen with you. My daughter is an intelligent, grown woman who thinks for herself. However, Starr is still mine to protect by any means necessary. I am no Quinn Peters. You were together for eight months; broke up for two; back together for ten. Now what are your intentions with my daughter, Steele?"*

*"Peace, I respect Starr, Sun, and you—your family dynamic. I love your daughter with every fiber of my being. I value her and the life I want to build with her. Starr may have said no once. But I am a patient man determined to prove my worthiness. I ask for your permission for her hand in marriage now. So when Starr is ready, we will have your blessing."*

*"I appreciate your candidness and your respect. Starr loves*

*you and in time will say yes. You have my blessing. But... Do. Not. Fuck. Up. Steele."*

Then Malcolm's conversation with my father about a second proposal.

*"Labor Day went well with our families meeting for the first time officially. So I'm glad you and Sun will join us in the Exumas on Bougainvillea Cay for Thanksgiving. Especially since I plan to propose to Starr."*

*"Excellent, Malcolm! Exactly what I expected to hear from you. I believe you'll get your yes this time. Sun and I look forward to spending Thanksgiving with family."*

My mouth falls open.

I did not know Malcolm planned on proposing to me again. I was just excited both of our families would join for the holiday. Spend time getting to know one another while enjoying the tranquility of Lola and Sebastian's private island in the Bahamas.

Damn that Vicky Reynolds for finally destroying our love!

Despite my recent pledge to not suffer sorrow, tears slip from my eyes as I sob uncontrollably. The heart I thought couldn't hurt anymore shatters.

What if the accident didn't happen?

Where would Malcolm and I be right now, five months later?

How happy would we be together instead of miserable apart?

I squeeze my eyes shut and swipe at the tears.

No more, Starr!

As my mother suggests, I will give Malcolm more time and take a coping mechanism from him.

Between now and our babies' expected birth date, I'll focus on my Starr Light Fitness & Wellness business. Ernest can drive me so I can spend at least four days at the center. It will keep me busy just as Malcolm returning to STEELE International must do for him by the looks of the office he set up and Anton being present with his laptop. With the nurseries finished and my home ready for the twins' arrival, I can turn my nesting to my original baby—SLFW Beverly Hills and my jewelry making. It's time for a new collection for the center's boutique and those at the SLFW Resorts.

Refocused, I smile at my loving parents to reassure them.

My mother stops fussing with the throw around me as my father returns with a fresh pot of lemon ginger tea. They gaze at me expectantly when I clear my throat.

"Mom, Dad, I love you so much and am grateful for your love and support," I start as I clasp their hands in mine. "Now that I know Malcolm planned to propose again, it gives me the strength to believe in our love again and to not let anything break us. I'll give him the time, as Mom said. Meanwhile, I'll get back to work on SLFW. Adrienne can use my help as a buffer for Anton!"

They laugh, knowing Anton's potent attraction to my bestie.

Just as then the chef enters to announce dinner is ready.

My stomach growls louder than my father from earlier since I haven't eaten in a while, too nervous about my proposal. Once again we laugh as I link my arms through theirs and head to the dining room.

* * *

"WHAT DO you think of this set, *chérie*? I love the sheer panels on the legs!"

I glance up from the rack of clothes to see *The Lion* modeling a new tank top and matching leggings. Never one to notice her impact on others, Leonie sashays on her legs for days around the boutique at SLFW Beverly Hills while clients gawk at her flawless beauty.

No makeup, wavy mahogany mane in a high ponytail, and barefoot one can't help but to admire Leonie. She stuns the crowd, whether on a Parisian catwalk, on a billboard in Times Square, or in workout gear. With her flat toned abs peeking out, no one would guess she's the mother of three children under the age of two years old.

I grin at my close friend.

"Fantastic! The gold highlights your caramel skin perfectly. Here, try this on next," I respond.

She flashes her billion-dollar smile and takes the hot pink leopard print catsuit, then ducks into the changing room.

"You know, I could play *Dress Up Leonie The Lion* all day, you know!" I tease. "No wonder they pay you the big bucks, girl."

Leonie's tinkling laughter fills the shop and carries to the lobby where clients waiting to check in or who sit at the café tables turn to the sound. She reemerges moments later, crawling on the floor like a big cat. Her feline features play to her nickname. She roars then leaps to her feet, clapping her hands while giggling.

"I couldn't help myself, *chérie!*" She exclaims. "I knew you'd laugh, and it's good to see you in high spirits at last!"

I nod and think how it's been a week since I declared only happiness in my life. During that time, I've enjoyed getting back to work full time after being by Malcolm's side for months. And as I thought, Adrienne was more than enthusiastic about my return!

"Absolutely! I flew in just to check on you for myself. I needed to see your face in person to make sure I didn't have to beat my dumb brother up," Haley adds.

I grin as she throws imaginary punches and bounces on the balls of her feet.

"Okay, Ms. Muhammad Ali!" Anita trills. "Malcolm better watch out, or he'll get stung by the Champ! He said he'll come out of retirement if Malcolm doesn't get himself together."

We laugh at her reference to Norman making Malcolm his ninth TKO.

"Well, get in line because my Dad is on deck raring to go at him!" I giggle.

"His brothers too!" Leonie says as she comes back out in her yellow terrycloth romper and Nikes. "Roger is beyond pissed. But, he insists Malcolm will come to his senses by the time the twins are born. So no worries, *chérie, non?*"

I nod and with a sweep of my arm along my body I respond, "*Oui!* I agree. Besides, he cannot deny all of this!"

Haley lets loose with a series of wolf whistles.

"Yeah, Starr! That's it, girl!" Anita claps. "A man will throw away a bone, but he'll keep the meat!"

That old adage has us cracking up so loudly everyone within hearing distance turns in our direction.

Red faced with tears of mirth spilling from our eyes, we make our way to the café for lunch. As I pass the shop girl, I ask her to wrap the girls' purchases up and to put the bags to my office.

Adrienne meets us halfway with a smirk on her face.

"Okay, what's the joke, ladies?" She asks, cocking her head to the side. "I could hear your cackles and snorts as I walked past the front desk."

Haley jumps into a fighting stance, and Anita faces off with her as they pretend to box. Anita mimics an exaggerated upper cut, and Haley crumples to the ground. Mrs. World Heavyweight Champ raises her fists in the air triumphantly as she prances around in a circle around her ninth TKO.

"I see!" Adrienne laughs. "Well, let's get you a steak to replenish your protein, Anita."

Steak has up cracking up all over again while Adrienne stares at us in wonder.

Leonie loops her arm through Adrienne and says, "We'll explain over our lunch of champions, *chérie*."

As I follow them past the surprised clients, I say a silent prayer of gratitude for my girls.

Yes, Starr, this too shall pass, and you will come out stronger for it. I smile to myself, rubbing my and Malcolm's babies bump.

# MALCOLM

"Don't fuss, sweetheart. You're perfectly fine. Are you certain you want to wheel yourself? No need to overexert yourself before we get to the courthouse."

My mother smooths the Full Windsor Knot of my platinum silk tie and adjusts my navy blue striped suit vest. She winks at me and smiles.

"No one is as handsome as my sons. Well, other than your father, and you look exactly like him!" She adds, fluttering her eyelashes.

My return smile resembles more of a grimace. I appreciate her attempt to lighten the mood. But I can't help wondering if my being in a wheelchair will make me appear weak in Vicky's eyes. I'd rather not witness a triumphant gleam in her eyes.

Once her Alpha Dom; now her victim.

How far I've fallen.

This will be the first time I see Vicky since three months before the accident.

When I had her naked, bound, and gagged in a dank, underground bunker with a menacing Russian who encouraged her not to fuck with my or Starr's lives. After I entered the room with its dirt floors, rough-hewn stone walls, timbered ceiling, I presented her with two options: sign an agreement and leave or stay there with him.

The Russian actor I hired scared the piss—literally—out of Vicky.

She chose the agreement.

Vicky moved to Johannesburg, South Africa—far from any STEELE or SLFW property—immediately; ended her acting career—already in shambles from Operation Nightingale—officially; never contact Starr, myself, or any of our connections directly or indirectly.

It wasn't a raw deal. Especially since she violated the five-year civil harassment orders. I could have pressed further charges.

In hindsight, I wish I had...

For this major infraction, the court ordered Vicky extradited from South Africa to stand trial for the accident that nearly killed me. The process was lengthy. But when she arrived two months ago, I wasn't ready to have her see me.

Fortunately, my medical team didn't approve of the added stress of a trial at that time. So Dr. Stevens informed my attorney. Judge Susan Dixon—who handled my other cases against Vicky—accepted their decision and moved the trial date.

Another stroke of luck was the tech nerd Vicky used to follow me and to direct the drones.

When confronted with the enormity of his involvement, he ratted Vicky out. Being a techie, he kept detailed accounts of every single one of their communications—written and visual. His court-appointed attorney—bogged down with other cases—offered no type of defense for him. The attorney recommended he plead guilty with a chance for a lesser charge and sentence based on his testimony against Vicky—the mastermind behind the accident.

Engelbert conferred with me and my family. He thought it best to go after Vicky the hardest. The techie would still serve plenty of time. But his limited resources wouldn't allow for any financial recompense.

Roger—who had a similar situation with his stalker and her sidekick—agreed with Engelbert. After further discussion, during which everyone voiced their opinions, we agreed as a whole. As Haley said, *"Deep-six, that bitch!"*

Now Haley's voice draws me from my musings.

"Malcolm, I'm with Mom. At least let me push you to the Sprinter. The press is out front, and our security team roped off the rear entrance to prevent a crazy paparazzo from sneaking in," Haley adds.

Again, I appreciate the help, but I'd rather not have my little sister push me, a man. It's bad enough a male nurse has to come with me to help me in and out of this damn wheelchair—carry me like some overgrown baby. At least he's dressed in a suit and not in his regular white uniform.

I open my mouth to decline her offer when Sebastian speaks.

"Thanks, Haley. But I'll take care of Malcolm. He's too big for you to handle, even in a chair," he says with a smirk.

And like that, our older brother naturally steps into his role of caring for his younger siblings. He nods at my grateful expression and steps behind my wheelchair.

I also appreciate him coming to the trial instead of staying in New York. Lola—at thirty-two-weeks pregnant with twin girls—can't fly so close to her due date. She has their nanny and her doula to help her, not to mention the rest of their staff.

Lola didn't want to hear my suggestion: Baz not come. She reminded me I was already on very thin ice with her over Starr and to not push her buttons further.

Starr.

Despite me being a total jerk and her being thirty-four-weeks pregnant, she's meeting us at the courthouse with her parents. She's set to testify and refused to do it via video conference. Judge Dixon granted Starr the option to appear in person or via video since she's two weeks out from her due date.

When I found out about Starr testifying, I called to tell her to put the babies' and her health first. I need nothing happening to them on my account. I couldn't bear it. No more losses.

She kept the conversation brief and only on confirming her decision. Then she hung up.

And I thought I would have to end the call. Not that I can blame her.

It'll be awkward seeing Starr, too. We haven't seen each other since her proposal.

Just remembering hearing her gasp when I told her no proves painful. I knew then I couldn't look her in her sorrel brown eyes and took the coward's way out. Wuss that I am.

Again, how far I've fallen.

Baz steers me out of my suite and to the back entrance of Cedars-Sinai Spine Center. True to what Haley told me, Mercedes-Benz Sprinters sit right outside the door and STEELE security man the perimeter.

Thank fuck since the media went into a frenzy with news of a first-degree attempted murder of a member of the STEELE Quaternity by a Hollywood Royalty starlet in a jealous rage. Add on the love triangle involving BDSM and international tabloids had their newest fodder.

Yeah, the STEELE Quaternity... The media dub Sebastian, Roger, Harris, and me the moniker for being the most sought-after of the world's eligible billionaires. Well, that was prior to Lola and Leonie snagging Baz and Roger off the market. And boy, did the world go wild when that happened.

So for one of the two remaining to almost die at the hands of a famous actress, they clamored for details, exclusives, insider information, the works. The hospital had to dismiss an orderly and a nurse for sneaking a photographer onto my private floor and for recording me during my physical therapy session, respectively.

After tips from other staff members, my security detail intercepted the cameras and the iPhone before they could share the images and the video. What people will do for a buck...

Engelbert enlisted the power of STEELE's public relations department to counteract any negative press. They also implemented campaigns to present me most favorably. Highlights of my philanthropic work with STEELE Foundation. Multiple interviews with prominent individuals and businesses to support me as an upstanding business executive. The PR machine fills the networks and publications on a global scale daily.

It's easy going to the courthouse.

Until I spy the crowd of onlookers, international television crews, and photographers out front.

I have a flashback to Roger's court appearances. Not a pretty sight. Except this time no one is chanting, "Off with his cock!" This time I'm perceived as the victim, not the woman involved.

The drivers take us to the rear of the courthouse where once again the secured area hides no cameras. We pull up behind a Cullinan and disembark. When the nurse sets me in my wheelchair, the Cullinan's doors open and Peace steps out.

He shots me a scathing glare before he walks around the back and leans in to the other open door. Legs swing out and dainty hands reach for his more sizable ones. Followed by a head of curly dark brown hair appears.

Starr.

She scoots forward and into her father's arms. He steadies her before he wraps his arm around her lower back. She graces him with a beatific smile. He says something to her, and she laughs, cupping her much larger belly.

Damn!

A sensation I haven't felt in a long time burns within me. I recognize it barely—possessiveness.

That should be me Starr smiles at so lovingly, my caveman snarls.

Starr must sense my heated stare as she flicks her gaze in my direction.

Her father follows her gaze, then says something to her.

She nods and the light that only moments before filled her sorrel brown eyes dims.

Damn.

Suddenly my view of Starr gets obstructed by Haley and Leonie rushing to her side making a fuss. Anita and Norman exit a Mercedes-Benz G-Wagen and make their way to her, too.

The forward movement of my wheelchair jolts me. Baz pushes me to Starr.

Her gaze returns to mine, and we stare at one another.

"Thank you for—"

"You look good—"

We speak at the same time. Then shake our heads and start again.

"No, you look beautiful—"

"You're welcome—"

Again we talk at once.

This time Peace interjects.

"Judge Dixon hates when people are late to her courtroom. Let us get going. Starr needs to sit," he says in a clipped tone of voice.

My father agrees, and we proceed to the courtroom.

Surreptitiously, I glance at Starr. She is more than beautiful. She's stunning. A glow makes her normally gorgeous face even more angelic. The way she cradles her babies bump so protectively makes me want to wrap her in my arms and hold her close where no one can hurt her or the babies.

I snort to myself.

*I* fucking hurt her…

Damn!

We continue on inside the courthouse en masse. Anton along with my boys—his cousin and my MMA trainer Borya *The War Defende*r Alexeyev and my cousin and business partner with LEVELS our BDSM Dance clubs Lucien *The Sexy Chef* Jackson—wait inside the entrance. Their presence for support and as character witnesses, especially since they've seen me with Vicky and know the type of person she is. They too greet Starr first before they turn to me.

Again a growl threatens to rip from between my curled lips at the sight of them putting their arms around her, even if they're only hugs. I. Do. Not. Like. It. At. All.

Baz gives me no time to process these unexpected emotions wreaking havoc with my mind. He presses on and doesn't stop until we're outside of the courtroom. Then he pauses and leans down to speak so only I can hear him.

"Malcolm, are you ready for this?" He asks.

Again, I have to give it up to him. Baz's protective behavior for his family shines through. He knew what I was feeling as we neared the double doors.

I nod and respond affirmatively.

He beckons for our security members to open the doors.

We enter, and all heads swivel in our direction. Countless eyes gawk at me, surprised I'm in a wheelchair.

I draw on my Alpha Dom to raise my chin higher and met their stares with a cool indifference. Yeah, I'm in a wheelchair, but don't think for one minute I'm some chump.

I am Malcolm *The Enforcer* Steele.

* * *

DAYS LATER, Judge Dixon had enough.

Vicky exploded at the sight of Starr pregnant. The actress could no longer adhere to the pretense of being an ingenue corrupted by a lascivious male who drove her to one moment of madness. She also went berserk when the techie took the stand against her and delivered damning testimony unrefuted by her lead attorney.

I never had a chance to recount the night since Harris pulled video footage from security cameras of the mansions along Benedict Canyon Drive into a complication. The entire scene unfolded in one agonizing clip from the moment I left Starr's garage to me being harassed by the drones to my Ducati Desmosedici motorcycle flying over the embankment.

The body-cam footage revealed Starr charging the mountain lion with a stick while the police officers shouted for her to stop. The moment the lion leaped in the air to attack her, my stomach dropped.

A chill snaked down my spine as I watched, transfixed by the replay. I think of a thousand different ways I could have handled the situation.

Stop and call the police.

Stop and smash the drone before the other one showed up.

Stay at home and make love to My Angel.

The last had me wishing I could still feel my cock...

Each day Starr arrived with her parents and waited to enter the courthouse until I arrived. Wanting to show a united front, she never wavered from supporting me.

Until I caught her grimacing, and I told her to go home and rest.

Starr put up a protest, but gave in when her mother, Anita, and Shelley told her it was best. She gave in grudgingly. But her parting shot to Vicky was a kiss to my lips that made my heart stutter and the ex-psycho-sub scream.

Since that day I wonder if it was all for show. But I don't allow the seed to plant itself too deeply in my mind. I still can't do anything for Starr or for the babies.

Still, I can't stop thinking about her, about us. And how differently things would stand had I handled the situation any other way.

The only good thing is Vicky Fucking Reynolds is out of our lives permanently.

Engelbert proved beyond a shadow of doubt Vicky demonstrated an intent to murder me, but failed. Judge Dixon—who made it clear she was none too pleased Vicky disregarded the civil harassment orders the judge issued—handed down the most severe punishment. Life in prison!

Take that. Take that. Take that!

The expression on Vicky's face was priceless. I wished I had a photo of it! Until then she held no regard for the legal system and obviously assumed she would get off scot-free.

Nope.

The bailiffs had to drag her from the courtroom, kicking and screaming obscenities at me, her attorney, then at Judge Dixon, when she dared to order Vicky to leave in silence. She was so out of line the judge issued fines and mandatory anger management sessions.

Vicky's parents and friends hurried from the courtroom, avoiding all eyes and questions from the press. Their security team had to shield her entourage from microphones shoved in their faces for statements and cameras.

I sat back in my chair, relieved it was all over. A weight lifted off of my chest. Then my mind jumped to Starr.

The urge to swoop her into my arms and make love to her in celebration was intense. But not possible. One, I can't feel my cock. Two, her OB-GYN due to stress put her on bed rest and couldn't be at the courthouse.

What should have been elation for us being rid of the ex-psycho-sub was a bust. So completely fucked up.

Still, I called Starr and gave her the news. Then I asked if I could see her. She agreed.

*"Thank you for being so supportive of me, Starr," I say sincerely.*

*Now it's my turn to sit beside her bed.*

*She rests in a chair by the window of her bedroom with her back against pillows and a cashmere throw on her lap. A delicate lace and satin peignoir in a soft pink sets off her luscious curves.*

*My mouth salivates at her now double-D size tits. I've always been a T&A man. But the fetish of adult lactation jumps to the forefront...*

*I have to shake my head to clear it. Not now, Steele.*

*"You're welcome, Malcolm," Starr responds quietly.*

*"I have to ask you something," I start, then continue when she nods her consent. "When you kissed me in the courtroom, was it for effect or because you meant it?"*

*Starr studies my face for a moment, then turns her head as tears shine in her eyes.*

*I give her some time to collect herself. When she doesn't answer, I place my hand over hers and squeeze.*

*"Starr?" I press.*

*She gasps at my touch and swings her head back to stare at our joined hands, then at my face.*

*I'm reminded of the day I first laid eyes on her at Baz and Lola's wedding. The face of an angel stares up at me. Her sorrel brown eyes widen in surprise as her lush mouth forms a perfect O. My cock may not twitch as it did then, but my heart and soul ache for her.*

*"I—I," My Angel closes her eyes and takes a deep breath as though clearing the stutter then begins again. "I kissed you because... because you seemed so alone, despite being surrounded by friends and family. I didn't want to leave you, but I needed to rest. So I kissed you to fill you with my strength as you've done for me in the past."*

*Her response hits me in the chest with enough force to shatter the block of ice surrounding my heart. The light of her love for me melts the remaining shards and cleanses my mind, body, and soul. The negativity I carried for months falls away, replaced by hope.*

*Now tears fill my eyes.*

*Without a word, My Angel slips her free hand behind my head and draws me to her breasts. The rhythm of her heart beating fast confirms her emotions are as high as mine. As she massages my scalp like she used to, I rub my thumb over her knuckles to deepen our connection.*

*Her babies bump sits so close to my face.*

*I realize I haven't touched it since she placed my hand on her belly months ago. My free hand slides over the round surface until my palm rests over her belly button.*

*A kick greets me.*

*I jolt and gape at My Angel.*

*A smile plays at the corners of her mouth, and her eyes sparkle with glee. She puts my hand back on the spot, then moves it around until another kick connects with my palm. We sit with both of our hands connected in a comfortable silence for a while.*

*"Can I come to their birth?" I ask in awe.*

*When My Angel doesn't answer, I lift my gaze from her belly to her face.*

*Tears of joy fill her eyes.*

*My heart clenches.*

*Through vision blurred by my tears, I cup the back of My Angel's head and draw her to me. My mouth crashes onto hers. Our teeth click and tongues twist as I engulf her with a kiss so full of emotion it's hard to breathe.*

*She matches my intensity.*

*When she moans into my mouth, all the barriers I erected to keep her away crumble into dust. I will let no one tear us apart again—not even myself.*

*This woman is mine all mine.*

# MALCOLM

"Oh, how adorable! I love the little pink bows on this onesie and the blue ties on this onesie. Oh and these, too! I can't wait to see Mini Malcolms in their new outfits! Thank you, Billie and Patrick!"

My heart soars as My Angel holds up the gifts from Billie and her lover Patrick Rockett—the CEO of Rockett Construction Company and STEELE International Inc.'s competitor. But that's another story.

Then my heart soars even higher when I think back to the last two weeks. Every day I visit with My Angel for hours. It's the total reverse as I sit by her side while she remains on bedrest as she did for me.

My Angel even made a joke about it, and it was easy for me to join in.

The best gift she gave to me was the journal along with videos she's taken since she found out about her pregnancy —our pregnancy. The daily snapshots and her thoughts help me make up for the time apart. When she gave it to me, I was so overwhelmed, emotions robbed me of the ability to speak. She cupped my face and kissed me softly in understanding.

Leonie gave me a tour of the nursery and presented the ones in my New York penthouse and my Southampton Village beachfront mansion. She arched an elegant eyebrow at me when I asked how they gained access and told me with a superior look to fuck off in French.

Roger pinned me with his intense stare and cussed me out, too.

But I held up my hands, palms out in surrender, and told them I was only curious, not at all angry. They're my babies, after all!

Once we passed that minor blip and we shared our feelings and concerns along with effusive apologies on my end, our transition back to a couple was smooth. I told My Angel I love her and she told me the same.

However, Peace, not so much.

He ripped me a new one, and I allowed it since he was absolutely correct. When he finished, I explained myself—something I do rarely. Peace's parting shot was for me to prove him wrong.

And I intend to wholeheartedly.

"You do not know how many baby boutiques Billie dragged me to until she found 'the cutest outfits.' So, I am beyond thrilled you love them!"

Patrick's Scottish rumble brings me back to the present.

We're in the garden of My Angel's mansion for virtual baby showers. Her girls surprised My Angel and Lola with the parties. The location of my sister-in-law's being on a terrace of her and Baz's penthouse in The STEELE Tower.

Instead of the baby showers being limited to women, they included the guys. Anita and Norman's daughters and Roger and Leonie's twins—Rodolphe and Gaspard—helped to hand presents to My Angel. While their baby sister, Daphne cooed on Roger's lap.

I'm sure Baz and Roger are no more pleased than I am to see Lachlan helping Haley hand Lola her gifts. Lucien's older brother, Baz's best friend, and the President of Liquor at Jackson Corporation is in New York instead of his home base in Aberdeen, Scotland. We love Lach to death, but our baby sister with an Alpha Dom? *Grrr.*

My mother, Sun, Leonie, Billie, Anita, and Adrienne decorated My Angel's garden while Haley and Blair did Lola's terrace. They decorated the garden in shades of pink and blue and the terrace in pink and cream.

Lucien provided My Angel and Lola's favorite dishes from his restaurants in both cities for their lunches. One of his pastry chefs crafted an incredible and delicious cake in the shape of a cradle. It was an edible piece of art.

Blair led us through silly games before the presents, all while we interacted on the giant screens Harris and Haley installed. So far the whole affair turned into a fun fete we've enjoyed for hours.

Luc Montaigne—Lola's mentor and the Parisian multi-billionaire head of his family's multigenerational Banque Montaigne empire—laughs.

"Well, Patrick, I know what you mean! Blair did the very same with me," Luc adds.

Both women laugh, as does My Angel.

Then she cries out.

Every head swivels in her direction.

She grimaces and drops the onesies in her lap as she grabs her babies bump with a second cry. She doubles over.

What. The Fuck?!?!?!

"Babe, what's wrong?!" I ask, panicked, as I reach for her hand.

She shakes her head and moans.

Everyone shouts and jumps up to rush to her side. Anita makes her way past Sun and my mother to crouch in front of My Angel.

"Starr, where do you feel the pain? And how strongly?" Anita asks, going into doula mode.

My Angel catches her breath and raises her head.

"My lower back has been bothering me all morning. A sharp pain in my lower belly and lower back just now. The pain radiates down my legs," she whimpers and clutches her belly with the hand not holding mine. "Ooooh..."

"Patrick, get the Sprinter. Leonie, get Starr's bag by the front door and put it in the van. Roger, Harris, lift Starr between you in a sitting position and put her in the van," Anita gives the orders calmly. Then adds, "Now!"

They rush to do her bidding.

"Norman, stay with the children and their nannies. Everyone else, get to Starr's suite at Cedars-Sinai. Her OB-GYN is Dr. Leticia Sánchez," Anita finishes as she follows my brothers and my woman into the mansion.

I roll my wheelchair after them, then watch as my

family and friends scatter for their vehicles. The front door closes, and I'm forgotten completely.

"FUCK!!!" I roar as I bang my fists on the armrests.

Just as I said: I cannot do shit for Starr or the babies! Hell, I can't even get myself in a fucking car to drive to the hospital. She has to depend on any and everybody else! My heart plummets.

"DAMMIT!!!" I yell.

"What's going on?!" Norman barks as he rushes from the garden, holding hands with his daughter and Rodolphe.

He stops when he sees me. Sympathy floods his face.

Great.

"Oh, man," Norman mutters. "Hold on, let me call Anita."

"No! I'll—"

"Malcolm! Bro, let's go! Starr's calling for you," Roger shouts as he and Harris storm back through the front door.

I sigh with relief as Harris pushes me to the Sprinter.

"*Sois sage et surveille tes frère et sœur, Rodolphe!*" Roger calls over his shoulder to his eldest son to behave and watch his siblings.

My Angel lifts her distressed eyes up when we reach the van, then smiles wanly.

"Malcolm, thank God! I need you," she cries, holding her hand out to me.

And with those words and action, my heart soars anew.

"MAAALCOLM!!!!!!"

The breathing exercises Anita had Starr do early on

during pre-labor go out the window twelve hours later. My Angel huffs and puffs like the wolf in *The Three Little Pigs*—although I would never tell her that now. She already snapped my head off for stroking her cheek.

We're in her private suite at the hospital.

Over the past couple of weeks, I had rooms next door to my suite converted into one for her and a delivery operation room. With twin births we don't want to risk not having access to all medical equipment and not having support available.

Plus, she can recover near me, and I can keep her and our babies close.

"Oh, my God!! How much more?!?!?!" My Angel bites out as she squeezes my hand so hard I fear my bones will break.

When I try to wiggle my fingers, she glares at me. Her sorrel brown eyes flash.

"You think that hurts, Malcolm Steele??? Well, let me—"

Her face contorts, and her body stiffens.

"Take a breath, Starr," Dr. Sánchez says, stifling a smile.

She peers between My Angel's legs to check the progress.

Fortunately, Dr. Sánchez is a woman. Otherwise, the caveman in me would gouge out the eyeballs of a male doctor.

"Okay, Starr, one more push. You can do it. The first baby is almost here," the doctor declares. "Push. Now!"

In what proves to be a Herculean effort, My Angel delivers Mini Malcolm I. Their piercing cries mingle in the tense air of the delivery room.

A new Steele enters our world.

My first child.

Tears fill my eyes as I gaze at mother and child—wait, daughter!

Our baby girl came first.

"Mr. Steele, you may cut her umbilical cord now."

Dr. Sánchez's words pull me from my ecstatic musings, and I glance at her. She holds out a pair of sterile scissors for me with a smile and a nod of encouragement.

Starr hums her approval.

Anita comes around to wheel me to the end of the table so I don't contaminate my hands on the wheelchair.

"Congratulations, Daddy Steele," she says with a grin.

My heart swells and my eyes well with tears. I blink them away as I take the scissors. Before I make the cut, my gaze goes to My Angel. So beautiful as she holds our baby girl to her breasts.

"Thank you, My Angel. I love you and our daughter," I say as she smiles.

"We love you, too, Daddy Steele," she replies.

The pediatrician lifts my baby girl from her mother. I wheel after the doctor as he carries my daughter off to the side in order to care for her. When he's done, he places her in my arms and announces she's a healthy 4.8 pounds.

I glance down at her red face. She's tiny, but my responsibility to her hits me like a breath-stealing blow from Borya. Her safekeeping ranks as my utmost priority, along with her soon-to-be-born brother and their mother. They are the fruit of my loins. I am their father.

. . .

"I HAVE HAD ENOUGH OF THIS SHIT! YOU DID THIS TO ME, MALCOLM STEELE! AAARGH!!!"

The seventeen minutes of familial bliss pass as the next stage of delivery has my son making his way into our world. Only our baby girl rests comfortably in a warm hospital crib nearby.

Anita dabs My Angel's face with a damp cloth and offers her more ice chips.

I sit like a lump praying the demon releases My Angel back to me before she slaps me like she did a moment ago.

I merely suggested she practice her deep cleansing breaths.

Her eyes rolled up in her head and her neck twisted to bring her face to face with me. I swear flames flew from her mouth as she cussed me out using language I didn't even know existed. And I speak four fluently.

Damn.

More contractions, more colorful words, more soul-stealing looks, more pushing, and our second twin makes his debut.

Mini Malcolm II—a healthy 5.2 pounds—joins his sister in a crib after I cut his umbilical cord, the pediatrician cared for him, and his mother breastfed him.

Mommy—My Angel once again—rests in her suite's bed as her gaze shifts between our babies and me. The nurse bathed her and rearranged the braid Anita had made. An expression of love and happiness makes My Angel glow like a celestial beauty.

I lift my mobile to take more photos of her. I already have a full album of Mini Malcolms throughout their birth and after. Their mother, not so many since she nearly broke my mobile when she swatted at it. She accused me of being too close and demanded to know who the hell wants photos of a sweaty woman in labor with two ginormous babies pushing through a quarter-size hole.

Now she smiles and beckons me to her side.

I wheel myself over and take her hand. I bring it to my lips for a kiss.

She cups my cheek.

"Thank you, Malcolm Steele. I love you; we love you," My Angel says softly.

A knock at the door interrupts us.

I roll my eyes, and she giggles.

"Come in," she calls out.

The door cracks, and Sun pops her head inside. Then my mother leans in. Both gaze at us questioningly.

"Come in, come in," I huff.

Then I chuckle when the whole gang bursts in the bedroom.

They gather around us, and Anita helps me to lift Mini Malcolms onto My Angel's breasts.

Sun coos softly as she strokes Mini Malcolm II's little leg. My mother rubs circles on the back of Mini Malcolm I.

"How are you, Starr, honey?" Sun asks. "You did it. But you need to rest. We promise not to stay too long."

My mother agrees, "No, we won't keep you, sweetheart. Only a quick peek. Then we'll leave you to rest."

"Congratulations, Little Sis, bro! Well done!" Roger says as he fist bumps with me and smiles at My Angel.

"Don't keep us in suspense any longer! What did you name Mini Malcolms, *chères?*" Leonie asks.

I peer at My Angel, place my hand over hers, and take a deep breath.

"Starr means the world to me. She completes me like no other. Now, with our daughter and our son, she gives me the moon and the sun to represent the other heavenly bodies in our universe. To keep with the Knight tradition of unique names, we'll name them after Greek gods: Selina for the moon and Elio for the sun. We present Selina Steele and Elio Steele," I respond.

My Angel cries out. This time not in pain of labor, but for joy.

"Oh, my love…" she says as tears slip down her flushed cheeks. "How perfect. Thank you."

My father grips my shoulder and smiles. "Well done, son, daughter! Powerful names for the next generation of Steeles. Today is a great day for our families!"

Peace holds his hand out to me.

I grip it firmly and look him square in the eye.

"Excellent, Malcolm. I'll be even more proud of you when you put your ring on my daughter's finger," he states.

"Absolutely," I respond confidently.

Then turn to My Angel and hold her hand again.

"Will you marry me, Starr Knight?" I ask.

"No."

Fuck me.

Not again.

# STARR

"I still cannot get over how you told Malcolm no. Again! *Mon Dieu, chérie!*"

Leonie fans herself dramatically as she widens her feline amber eyes at me.

Yeah, everyone's mouths dropped to the floor when I said no to his second proposal.

I even surprised myself. I was thinking about it but hadn't expected to say it out loud. My mind was still loopy from having given birth to Selina and Elio.

However, I always believe everything happens for a reason, no matter how I may perceive the outcome.

And in this case it is for the best.

After everyone left, I explained my reasoning to Malcolm.

*The sight of disbelief in Malcolm's eyes nearly changes my mind. His head snaps back, and his mouth gapes in shock. He blinks and shakes his head as if rousing himself from a dream—or a nightmare in this case.*

*"What?" He murmurs.*

*The Moms herd the group from the bedroom and out the main door of my suite. When the door clicks shut, I speak.*

*"Malcolm, I said no," I respond firmly.*

*He shudders and lets go of my hand.*

*I reach for his hand and hold it while I balance our babies on my breasts. A squeeze draws his stormy gray eyes back to mine.*

*"Why not?" He asks in the bedroom's silence.*

*"I, we—Selina, Elio, me, and you—need you to get yourself together, get back to the man I know. The powerful Alpha Dom who takes control and lets nothing or anyone stop him in his pursuits," I start, then grip his hand tighter when he tries to pull away.*

*"See. Just what you're doing now and have done since you awoke from the coma. You avoid instead of attack. Lash out in anger and cause pain instead of lash out in love and cause erotic pleasure," I say and press on when he opens his mouth.*

*"Yes, for the past couple of weeks, you've had a breakthrough. The trial ended not only favorably, but it ended Vicky Reynolds from your life giving you a new start, a reason to move forward. And I'm happy for you," I say and take a breath. "But you still have a way to go. And I don't mean with you walking or not. I love you as you are, period. You have to get back into your previous mindset of abundance and not lack."*

*I bring his hand to my lips and kiss his knuckles.*

*"The time apart from you taught me I had to put myself and our babies ahead of you if I were to be strong enough to care for them without you. And I intend to do just that. Our babies are my top priority, Malcolm. Your top priority right now needs to be you," I smile softly at him.*

*"I love you. So my no doesn't mean no forever. Just not right now. You have work to do, Malcolm Steele. And I expect you to get at it if you want to be a part of my life again,"* I end.

*He takes a moment to absorb my words and to scan my face that I keep open and full of love.*

*"I'm so sorry I hurt you, My Angel. Never will I push you away again. You continue to love me and to believe in me. Know that I love you and believe in us enough to vow I will be the man you, Selina, and Elio need me to be,"* Malcolm says passionately.

*"Thank you, my love,"* I say.

*"But I have one ask: stay here for a week, then allow me to visit you and our babies at your mansion,"* he adds.

*A Cheshire Cat smile spreads across my face as I nod.*

*"Words, Little One. I will have your words,"* Malcolm, my Alpha Dom, commands.

*I bite my lower lip and peek at him through my eyelashes.*

*"Yes, Sir,"* I purr.

*He smirks and kisses my hand.*

"What did Sting say about freeing someone you love? Well, I had to give Malcolm a chance to find himself again before we can be one," I tell Leonie as I sip my iced lemon ginger tea.

We're in my garden catching up after she returned from Paris.

She, Roger, and their babies flew home to take care of some business. Anita, Norman, and their girls left Beverly Hills with them. Norman has some boxers who need him in Paris. So I thanked them for helping me and promised to visit as soon as I could travel with Mini Malcolms.

Their nickname stuck since every day they take on

more of Malcolm's traits: ebony black hair, platinum gray eyes, and olives skin tone. Instead of waves like their father, their silky strands curl like mine. So even at only a month old, they resemble their Daddy.

And they couldn't satisfy him more.

Malcolm fusses over them whenever he's here. The gleam returns to his eyes each time he holds them against his chest. A permanent smile stretches across his face. It's as though they light him up from within.

My mother tells me it's the light from my star, Selina's moon, and Elio's sun that burns so brightly inside of Malcolm.

I just adore her views on life!

I made matching bracelets for Malcolm, our babies, and for me. Set in platinum to represent Malcolm with semi-precious stones for the rest of us. Moonstone promotes healing and balance and enhances one's intuition. Sunstone clears and cleanses all the chakras, restores joy, and nurtures the spirit. Starstone—the stone of ambition—resembles a starry night and promotes optimism and personal growth.

Malcolm was so impressed, he asked me to design a set of cuff links.

Since I'm on maternity leave from SLFW, I'm able to make them and other designs. My work with crystals always brings out *my* inner light.

"True. Roger says Malcolm asked his medical team to go back to review all of their research and his chart to come up with an alternative plan. He works hard at it every day. So, *your* plan is working!" Leonie exclaims.

I nod in agreement.

"Yes. Malcolm told me about his meeting with them. I'm so glad he's vested in himself truly now," I say. "He's not coming today because a new machine arrived he wants to exercise on. Already I see an increase in his muscle definition."

Leonie winks and says, "I'm sure you do, *chérie*!"

I throw my head back and laugh.

"Unfortunately, he's put the kibosh on any intimacy—Alpha Dom control, you know. But I'm sure you as a woman who's given birth to twins can appreciate me having no desire for a very well-endowed Steele man near me!" I laugh. "Although my hormones still rage…"

Leonie's laughter turns into snorts, and soon we're gasping for air.

"Okay, what's so funny?"

We turn around to find Haley strolling towards us.

She flew in with Leonie and Roger for some time with her West Coast niece and nephew. Since Lola had Sabrina and Stella two weeks ago, Morgan, Shelley, and Harris swapped cities with Haley.

I love how the Steele clan ensures all family members get time with each other.

Even to the point where Roger bought the mansion he and Leonie were renting, Morgan bought the one on the other side of mine, and Sebastian bought the one next to Morgan's. Not that any of the residences were for sale originally… They said they need a Steele West Coast compound.

Roger had his Residential Properties Division build a

secured perimeter fence enclosing all four mansions. Each will maintain its entry gates with the addition of guard houses. Harris' Technology team arranged all security, even updating the system he installed in mine after Vicky's mess started. The Steeles are sticklers for security.

The Residential team is also working under Leonie's direction to redesign the homes to Shelley's, Lola's, and to her specifications. As a surprise for Malcolm, I asked Leonie to reconfigure my primary bedroom suite, along with other key areas to accommodate his accessibility needs. Thankfully, an elevator already existed. The projects should complete in a couple more months.

"Oh, *chérie*, just about the virility of your—"

"Ah, no!" Haley shouts as she plugs her ears with her fingers and sings aloud.

Our laughter kicks up again.

\* \* \*

"Hi."

I glance up from breastfeeding Mini Malcolms in their nursery to see the man himself sitting in his wheelchair at the doorway.

He takes my breath away, and my hormones rage with need. A need only my Alpha Dom can satisfy. He hasn't shaved in a couple of days, so the five o'clock shadow skims along his sculpted cheekbones and chiseled jaw. Either the wind blew his hair, or he tousled it just the way it looks after my fingers tug at the strands while he eats me out.

Damn.

I shiver so hard my nipple pops from Elio's cherubic mouth and the milk dribbles from the turgid tip. My eyes jump back to Malcolm at the sound of a low growl.

My Alpha Dom licks his full lips and bites down on the lower one. His chest rises and falls beneath the black long-sleeved t-shirt, making his pecs stretch the fitted material. His biceps bulge and his bare forearms flex as he wheels himself further into the nursery.

Our eyes remain locked as he makes his way across the hardwood floor.

"Ms. Knight, the baths are ready for Selina and Elio—"

Nanny Patience must sense the sexual tension permeating the room. She stops mid-sentence and stares between Malcolm and me. She clears her throat.

"Since Mr. Steele has arrived, I'm sure he'd rather help you. Excuse me," she says hastily and leaves the nursery with a polite nod to Malcolm.

Without breaking our eye contact, Malcolm thanks her for her thoughtfulness.

When she's beyond earshot, his lips curl into a smirk and his eyes twinkle mischievously.

"Feeding without me, Naughty Girl? Well, it appears as though my son has had his fill. Shall I relieve him?" My Alpha Dom asks.

My lips part, and my eyes widen at his innuendo.

He's never referred to drinking my breastmilk before.

I swallow and blink.

My Alpha Dom cocks his head to the side as he stops in front of me. His eyebrow lifts in question.

"I... Uh... Yes, Sir," I respond breathlessly.

A full smirk spreads across his handsome face. He takes Elio from my arms and puts him over his shoulder with the cloth. He burps his son with ease.

"The little bugger was full," he quips.

My nostrils flare on a deep inhalation. Calm down, Starr. I exhale and nod.

"Yes, and Selina finished. Would you care to burp her, too?" I ask in a level voice.

"Of course. I *am* here for Daddy Duty," he smirks.

I want to growl at his teasing. Instead, I take Elio, and Malcolm lifts his daughter to his shoulder.

I rise from the glider, purposefully leaning my bare breasts in Malcolm's face.

Two can play this game.

Now he gulps and warm air fans across my sensitive buds.

Damn.

"I'll start on Elio's bath. You can join us," I say over my shoulder.

I catch Malcolm's eyes on my ass before he lifts his heated gaze to my face. Now I'm glad I wore the zipper-front terrycloth romper my butt cheeks peek out from underneath.

I adjust my Lola's Coterie nursing bra and sway my hips slightly as I walk to the en suite bathroom.

He groans.

I giggle to myself. Gotcha, Malcolm Steele!

Who's in control now, Alpha Dom?

The sub, that's who!

# MALCOLM

"Aaaahhhh... Mm mmm... Oh fuck!!!"
Wait, what the fuck?!?!?!

A red veil descends before my eyes as I envision another man fucking My Angel. Who does she have in her bed?! When did she start seeing someone else??? How can she do this to me, to us trying to rebuild our relationship?! And with my babies under the same roof!!!

Thankful for the new aerodynamic wheelchair that allows me to move quickly, I race down the hallway towards the partially open double doors to her primary bedroom suite. I make haste as I maneuver around the sitting room, spurred on by the sounds of her pleasure reaching a crescendo.

Fuck. Me.

When I reach her partially open bedroom door, I pause.

Maybe I should back off. Starr deserves a real man in her life. Sure I've proven I can care for our babies—change diapers; give baths; burp them. But I haven't taken care of

Starr. I haven't been able to give her the erotic pain she craves as my sub and the carnal bliss as my woman.

Obviously *he* can.

Crestfallen, I change direction.

"Oh, God... MALCOLM!!! Malcolm... Ahhh, Malcolm... Malcolm..."

My head snaps up.

Me?

Starr calls my name in ecstasy?

"Mmmmmm.... Malcolm..."

Her last moan confirms My Angel is still mine all mine!!!

I do a silent whoop as I fist pump the air with both hands.

Thank fuck!

I spin around and nudge the door open.

In the dimly lit room, my vision tunnels on My Angel lying sated atop rumpled linens alone in her bed. Eyes closed, her head thrown back against the pillows as her bare breasts heave from the exertion. One hand kneads a heavy breast while the other hand rests between her toned thighs pressed together, trapping her fingers in her pussy. A soft whimper escapes her slack mouth.

The musky scents of her sex and of her coconut and frangipani perfume waft through the air to tease my nostrils.

Tantalizing!

Quietly, I roll to the side of her bed. I lean forward and skim my fingertips from her inner calf to her knee.

My Angel gasps and jumps to a crouch.

"Tsk... Tsk... Tsk, Naughty Girl," I chide her.

"M—M—Malcolm?" She asks shocked.

I cock my head and ask, "Who else do you expect in your bedroom stroking your leg, Naughty Girl?"

She swallows and sits with her legs tucked beneath her ass.

"Uh, no one else, Sir," she responds with wide eyes.

"I thought not. But your naughty behavior needs addressing," I say.

She blinks, then opens and shuts her mouth.

I crook my finger at her.

Her heavy tits sway as she crawls towards me, ass high, head low. She bites her full lower lip when she stops before me. My well-trained sub sits on her haunches with her eyes downcast, back straight, and palms face up on her spread thighs.

Divine.

If possible, the intensity level of my gaze would scorch her soft skin already flushed with her arousal. I take in her beauty from her tousled curls—now reaching her middle back—to her heart-shaped face, down to her mouthwatering tits, and to her just-as-appetizing pussy; her engorged clit visible between the plump, soaked folds.

Fuck. Me.

I lick my lips and hold my hands out to her.

Without hesitation, she places her dainty ones into my sizable hands.

When I tug her towards me, she rises to her knees and makes her way closer to the edge.

"Lie down, knees bent with your feet on the bed," I command huskily.

Fully spread before me, I reacquaint myself with My Angel's most intimate places. Several minutes pass as I test her ability to remain in position despite her need for release. And release she needs based upon the puddle forming below her ass cheeks as her pussy weeps for my erotic touch.

Unable to resist, I lean forward and bury my nose between her folds. The tip brushes her sensitive bundle of nerves.

She whimpers but holds still.

I inhale deeply, then slowly blow my warm breath over her pussy and puckered hole. As both holes clench with want, My Angel mewls and her hips shift.

A predatory smile spreads across my face.

WHAP. WHAP. WHAP.

She yowls and jerks away as my thick, calloused fingers spank her swollen pussy, causing more fire to erupt across her sensitive flesh.

"Ah, ah, ah, Naughty Girl. Take your punishment for pleasuring yourself without my permission," I command in my stern Alpha Dom voice.

She whimpers but settles back in to position.

I soothe the ache with gentle laps of my tongue.

Her whimpers morph into moans. Then her hips lift. Again.

A sharp pinch to her clit, and my Naughty Girl squeals.

My tongue wraps around the tiny bud, engorged from her arousal and sucks. Hard.

"Oooooh, Sir... Please let me cum, Sir!" My Naughty Girl cries out.

I deny her with a grunt as I continue to feast on her succulent pussy. She's as sweet as ambrosia. How I've missed her essence on my taste buds.

Eager for more, I wrap my arms around the backs of her thighs and lift them over my shoulders, then sit up straight. Only her head, upper back, and arms remain on the bed in an erotic Half Wheel Pose.

My super flexible yogi. Perfect.

I alternate my ministrations between erotic pain and pleasure to heighten my sub's desire. A steady stream of moans and sighs sings in my ears. Our carnal energy flows around us.

So enthralled by her, I nearly miss the signs of My Angel on the brink of coming apart for me. Only when her inner thighs squeeze the sides of my head do I return to the bedroom. The quivering of her pussy walls; hands fisting the sheets; shallow pants from her parted lips.

My Angel needs to cum.

With a deep thrust of my tongue and with the tip of my finger stroking her G-spot, I give her permission.

"Cum for me, Little One. Cum in my mouth. Now!" I command, as my lips brush her wet skin.

Her hands rip the silk sheets as she presses her pussy further onto my face. The muscles of her taut belly tighten as a keen rises from deep within her to erupt in a high-pitched wail. It goes on unstoppable as I coax more of her sweet essence down my throat.

While her climax abates, I lap at her folds lazily and suckle her clit softly. I hum my approval.

"Good Girl," I purr.

"Mmmmmm…. Malcolm…" she mumbles from the bliss of subspace.

Yeah. You know that's right!

After I gloat for bringing My Angel over the edge, I don't want to break our connection. I grasp her ass and lower her onto my lap.

Again I'm thankful for the new wheelchair. Sans arms, My Angel settles her legs on both sides of my hips unhampered. One hand glides up her sweat-damp back to grip the back of her neck while the other holds her hip, pinning her against my chest. I bury my face in her neck as my breathing slows.

"Oh, Malcolm!" She exclaims and leans back to stare at me.

I frown.

"Malcolm, baby, you're erect," she says in wonder.

What???

She grins at me and adds, "Your dick, it's hard."

Stunned, I loosen my grip, and she slides to her knees in front of me. Her hands reach for the drawstring of my sweatpants.

"Oh, Malcolm! This is marvelous, baby!" She exclaims as she pulls the bow like a present she can't wait to unwrap on Christmas morning. Her eyes dance in delight at my ten inches tenting my sweats.

Just as she reaches inside, I come to my senses.

"No!" I snap as I yank her hands away and roll backwards.

My Angel's face drops, and her hands drop to her lap.

The fierce expression on my face makes her eyes lower.

I didn't even feel my cock grow. Not. One. Inch.

Fuck. Me.

I'm torn between horror and excitement as I stare at the massive bulge. My cock has a mind of its own and obviously its own nervous system. My legs remain numb…

"I'm so sorry, Malcolm. I didn't mean to—"

A cry over the high-tech baby monitor Harris designed for the Steele Grandchildren interrupts My Angel.

Thank fuck for the small things in life!

I give a noncommittal grunt and pivot for the door.

"I'll see to Selina and Elio. I'd like to spend Father's Day morning with them as I planned," I say as I roll away.

A gasp behind me makes me pause.

"Oh, Malcolm! Happy Father's Day, my love!!!" My Angel says.

Arms wrap around my neck from behind before she swings around to land in my lap, planting kisses on my face.

I still can't feel my dick poking her round ass. But I can't deny her and kiss her back with fervor.

"I'm sorry I snapped at you, My Angel. I just don't feel—"

She places her fingertips against my mouth and shakes her head. Glossy curls bounce around her gorgeous face as she smiles.

"No need to apologize. Especially for that monster! I'm

just glad he wants to play. When you're ready, that is, Sir," she says with a wink as she licks her lips.

Hot damn! That's my girl!

"Welcome to the Club of Fatherhood, Malcolm!"

"Yeah, bro! You are official!"

"Hear, hear!"

"Doubly, Malcolm!"

"*Félicitations!*"

I chuckle as my father, Baz, Roger, Peace, and Leonie's father Guy Beaulieu—the Parisian multibillionaire merchant—raise their Baccarat crystal snifters of Jackson Special Blend Scotch in a toast. I salute them with mine held high.

"Thank you, gentlemen! It pleases me beyond words to join your illustrious club!" I respond before I knock back a healthy swig.

My Angel and Leonie turned the garden into a men's club while Lola and Haley did the same on the deck of my parents' beachfront mansion at Steele Southampton Village.

Since Mini Malcolms can't fly yet—even on our private jet—we along with Roger and Leonie opted to stay in Beverly Hills at Steele West Coast. The rest of the clan escaped balmy New York City for the cooler Hamptons shore. They'll stay through Labor Day after The STEELE Foundation Annual Fundraiser. My Angel and I will join them for the event, since Selina and Elio will be four months old.

"Well, just don't get any bright ideas to add me to your club any time soon. No, thank you!" Harris quips, rolling his dove gray eyes.

"Ha! Your time is a coming, bro. Just you wait and see. That special someone will sneak up on you when you least expect her," Baz says from experience.

Roger and I nod in agreement.

My eyes drift to My Angel as she and Leonie sit on blankets surrounded by five of the eight Steele Grandchildren. The grandmothers—Sun and Leonie's mother Josy, the Tunisian beauty she resembles—sit beside them, playing with the little ones.

The sight infuses my soul with love.

I'm a lucky man.

A firm grip on my shoulder brings my attention back to the men around me and those on the giant screen. I glance up to meet Peace's gaze. Even without me sitting in the wheelchair, he has an inch on my six feet, four inches.

He smiles.

"I am proud of you, Malcolm. You've stepped up to your responsibilities admirably. I understand your new healing program shows improvement," he says.

For a minute, I think he's referring to my earlier erection since My Angel shares details of her life with her parents unashamedly. But then I know she wouldn't have told her father that not so little tidbit.

I return his smile and say, "Yes, the new regimen pleases me, and the results are impressive. As I said, I intend to take care of my family. They give me the strength to move forward."

"Excellent," Peace says with a nod.

After everyone eats and sits around relaxing, I go inside and make a call to Baz. He answers on the first ring.

"Hey, bro. What's up? Everything okay?" He asks, concern laces his voice.

"Yeah, thanks," I start. "But I have an ask of you."

"Whatever you need, you know I got your back, Malcolm," he responds without hesitation.

"Baz, if anything should ever happen to Starr or to me, promise you will take care of my children as your own," I ask my eldest sibling.

Silence descends on the call.

Then I hear Baz say something to Lola before shuffling comes over the line. A door slides open and closed.

"What's going on, Malcolm? Did the doctors tell you something you haven't shared with us?" He asks gravely.

I slap my forehead.

Damn! He must think I'm not much longer of this world. Hell, no! I'm here to stay with My Angel and my babies—with more to come if I get a say in the matter.

"No, bro! I'm perfectly fine. Trust me," I chuckle as I think about my first erection since before the accident. "Father's Day has me thinking. I want to be certain Selina and Elio are well taken care of. I know everyone would pitch in—including their maternal grandparents. But I know how you've always been our second dad. I may have given you shit as a teenager. But I've come to value you more than you could ever know, Sebastian."

My voice hitches, and I pause to collect myself.

Baz clears his throat, also caught up in our brotherly moment.

"Absolutely. And I ask the same of you for our little ones. We may have had our differences as kids, but you're my closest friend, Malcolm," he says. "I love you, bro."

And there you have it: Sebastian Steele, former Alpha Dom billionaire playboy turned husband, father, and softie!

"I love you, bro," I respond.

We're in the same boat. And neither of us would ever choose another. No matter how tricked out it may be. My Angel and Lola have us on lock.

# MALCOLM

"Just because you're in a *rolly chair,* you think I am going easy on you, Steele? *Net!* Don't be a *kiska!* Meow. Meow. Hands up. Now!"

As I combat a barrage of lethal punches and kicks from Borya, I second-guess my decision to switch from the doctor-appointed personal trainer to the former MMA world champion. He's merciless.

If I were in my full capacity, I could hold my own and sometimes overtake him. But now, not so much. However, I know it's the best move to get me back to peak performance.

After six months of being awake from my coma—nine in total since the accident—I'm more than ready for the next level. And I want it more than ever.

The ability to defend myself and my family—no matter my circumstances—runs high. Sure, we have a security detail, but I need to know I can step up. Well, *roll up…*

"Fuck you, Alexeyev! Is that the best you have or does retirement have you soft, *prisoska*?" I taunt the *sucker* as I block a vicious roundhouse kick to my head.

I follow the block with a punch to his inner thigh. Albeit I aimed for his balls, but he dodged the blow.

"Aha! So you want to play dirty, Steele? Bring it, *kiska*!" Borya growls.

I jerk my chin and smirk as I punch my fists together. Who's the *pussy* now?!

"Let's do this, *kiska*!" I sneer.

Thanks to my previous MMA training and my wonder chair, I successfully maneuver around the mat. Quick turns to one wheel allow me to pivot easily then use my other arm to fight. I even catch him with unexpected headbutts.

The first one causes the giant Russian to throw his head back and roar with laughter—or at least what he considers laughter, others barks.

"Well done, Steele! Sneaky fucker!" He guffaws.

Then comes at me like a freight train going downhill with no brakes.

Damn!

An hour later I'm sufficiently sore from the intense workout but amped. This is what I need to reach the next level. The strength training program designed by the medical PT helped me to regain my upper body muscles and to keep my lower half from atrophy. Borya makes me use my mind, needing to think fast to avoid being knocked the fuck out and the power of my muscles to thwart him. His sessions make for the perfect combination.

"What's your plan for the rest of the day? A catnap?" Borya smirks as we head to the steam room.

"Ha, ha, ha. Actually, no. I'm surprising My Angel with a Mother's Day brunch since Mini Malcolms arrived a few days after the traditional date. As hard as she worked to carry my babies, deliver them, then to care for them, she deserves Mother's Day every damn day," I respond.

"*My Angel* this. *My Angel* that. You are pussy whipped, Steele," he smirks. "But Starr is an excellent woman. Better than you deserve. *She* deserves it all. Just do not fuck up again…"

Borya narrows his eyes at me and smashes his massive fists together.

I shake my head and grin like the Cheshire Cat.

"Nah, bro. That wimpy shit is done," I say as I pull my t-shirt over my head.

"Hey, don't look at me!" Borya says, aghast.

I throw my t-shirt at him and roll my eyes.

"I'm not stripping for you, dumbass! My new tat," I tell him as I point to my chest.

Right above my heart I added a tattoo of a star with My Angel written inside and a moon with Selina and a sun with Elio orbiting around it. I had the best tattoo artist in LA come to the hospital a few days ago. He created the design based on my vision: My Angel and our babies as my universe. I left space for more baby names, at least two…

"*Velikolepnyy!* Now you'd have to scour your skin to remove Starr from your life. And it'll hurt *you* like fuck that time!" Borya guffaws.

I join in and agree not only is my tattoo *magnificent*, so is my little family.

"Oh, Malcolm! What a wonderful surprise! Thank you, my love!"

My Angel smothers me in kisses when she walks into the solarium of her mansion to find it decorated for Mother's Day and me sitting with Mini Malcolms in their slings across my chest.

I enlisted the help of my mother, our family's party planner and drill sergeant—as Lola and Leonie learned during the planning of their weddings. Sun proved her high-powered attorney skills when she negotiated the contracts with the vendors. She even had Lucien nervous when he offered to provide the food and the dessert.

Now I cup My Angel's cheek, smiling at her delight.

So worth it!

"No, thank you for giving me the greatest gifts—our babies, Selina and Elio. I love you, Hot Mama," I respond with a grin.

My Angel giggles at me teasing her with the nickname Lola coined for Leonie when she was pregnant with Rodolphe and Gaspard. Now all three women are a part of the club.

My brothers and I are lucky AF.

"Okay, Sexy Daddy!" My Angel purrs as she nips my earlobe and tugs on it.

Fuck. Me.

Now she's rocked me with the Daddy kink along with

adult lactation. If I could feel my cock, it would be hard as steel.

I shift Mini Malcolms to peek at my crotch. Yup, the anaconda wakes.

My Angel notices and licks her plump lips.

I smirk at her, then gesture to the table.

"Come, Naughty Girl. Let us eat," I command.

"Oh, yes, Sir. I'm famished, absolutely…" she purrs as her gaze darts to my lap.

Yeah. Fuck. Me.

I've created a sex-starved sub wrapped in a Hot Mama.

And I wouldn't have her any other way.

"Oooh! Are these dishes from Lucien's latest restaurant? I remember he mentioned a lobster frittata with golden Sevruga caviar. My mouth watered as he described it to me. Tell me this is it!" My Angel exclaims, clapping her hands.

Okay.

So when the hell did Lucien speak to my woman? And why did he make her mouth water?! My caveman demands an answer and a jab at *The Sexy Chef*.

My Angel giggles.

"What's so funny?" I snarl.

My question has her cackling and snorting as she fans her flushed face. Her dimples deepen as tears fill her eyes when I grunt incoherent words of irritation with my close friend. When I spear a slab of bacon with my fork and it shoots off the platter to the floor, My Angel loses her shit completely.

Try as I might to maintain a stoic expression, the frown

on my face flips as chuckles burst from between my pursed lips.

"You! You're so funny, Malcolm!" She titters with glee. "He's *your* friend, not *my* lover."

I growl.

Then reach across the table to grip the back of her neck, then pull her to me. My mouth captures hers in a display of dominant possession. Her gasp gives me full access to plunder her mouth with my demanding tongue.

My Angel grabs the table's edge for balance and gives in to me. Mewls meet my growls. A nip to her bottom lip makes her cry out. A lick, and she sighs.

When I've proven my point, I release my hold on her neck, and she collapses to her chair, staring at me with hooded eyes.

"Mine!" I rumble.

She shivers and responds, "Yes, Sir. Only you."

With a satisfied smirk, I spear another piece of bacon and pop it into my mouth.

My Naughty Girl watches me chew while her little pink tongue pokes out to taste her lower lip swollen from my passionate kiss. Her sorrel brown eyes glow. The front of her silk maxi dress can't hide the peaks of her nipples. She is so aroused.

Good.

The denial will be even sweeter.

"Eat up. I have plans for you," I tell her.

Her eyes widen with carnal want.

"Yes, Sir!" she says eagerly as she picks up her fork and dives in to Lucien's lobster frittata.

The moan that slips from her lips as she takes a healthy bite gets cut short when I raise my eyebrow and cock my head at her. She swallows thickly and attempts to assuage me with a tiny smile.

I chuckle darkly. Oh, my Naughty Girl.

"I'm sorry! Please, Sir! Forgive me!"

My poor Naughty Girl begs after multiple orgasms being denied. Her head hangs to her heaving chest pitifully.

Sweat drips from her forehead to between her luscious tits as she stands naked, blindfolded, and bound spread eagle to the posts at the foot of her bed. Rosy hued stripes tint the chestnut-colored skin of her heavy tits and her flat belly from the lashes of my suede flogger. Her pussy lips mimic the shade from the erotic caresses. Even her clit swelled as the tresses curled around the sensitive bud.

"Safeword?" I ask huskily.

I will push My Angel's limits beyond yellow. But I will never force her past red. Years as an Alpha Dom—and those I spent as a sub to learn both ends of the spectrum—provide me the experience to sense my sub's breaking point.

And My Angel is not there.

"No, Sir!" She responds.

Her head jerks up, as though horrified at the thought.

I smirk. Yeah, she wants to swing along the pendulum of erotic pain and pleasure some more.

I reach past her hip to pluck the Wartenberg wheel from the bed. Time for some sensory play.

A perk of being in the hospital with a spinal issue is access to the medical device used to test nerve reactions as it rolls systematically across the skin. The wheel has sharp pins evenly spaced and rotates with each stroke. One can't miss the sensation it causes under normal circumstances. It's heightened more on rosy stripes...

"ARGH!" My Angel yowls. "FUCK!!!"

"How pretty you look with my marks painting the canvas of your soft skin, Little One," I croon as I lean forward to lap at a welt on the underside of her tit re-sensitized from the Wartenberg wheel.

She hisses, then moans lustily when my mouth engulfs her tit, areole, and nipple at once.

I hum as her delicious milk drips down my throat.

The vibrations make her mewl.

Her nipple pops from my mouth, and her milk dribbles down my chin when she yanks back from the unexpected nip of the pins across her lower belly. She cries out.

Dutifully, I trail open-mouthed kisses from her tit, then down her belly to provide relief from the pain. I alternate the sensations until My Angel's legs quiver with her need for release.

I toss the toys to the floor and sit back in my wheelchair to survey her perfection.

"Cum for me, Little One," I murmur.

Instantly, she arches her back as she grips the white silks binding her wrists and throws her head back to let loose a wail as her climax overtakes her body. She convulses as it goes on and on, prolonged by the earlier denial.

Spent, she sags against her restraints.

I roll forward and untie her ankles, then pull the extra material hanging from her wrists to free the knots. I catch her as she collapses and hold her on my lap, pressed to my chest.

She curls into me and buries her face in my neck as I murmur words of love and stroke her back to soothe her. Lost in subspace, she sighs contentedly.

While she still flies, I roll to the side of the bed and carefully lay her on her side in a fetal position. Then I head to the bathroom for soft cloths dampened with water to cool her heated flesh and a tube of aloe vera gel to heal my marks.

No permanent damage to My Angel's flawless skin. My marks may fade by morning, but they're indelibly written on her psyche to remind her she's mine all mine.

"Hi, babe. How do you feel?"

I ask as she awakens from her sex-induced slumber.

My Angel does a feline stretch, then smiles up at me.

"Wonderful, Sir. Thank you," she purrs as she cuddles against my side as I rest against pillows on the headboard.

While she slept, I used the new overhead trapeze she had installed to help me in and out of the bed. The triangle bar hangs from the hook of a metal base attached to the floor behind the headboard. My Angel learned it has more than a medical purpose…

I give her a glass of cool water, and she gulps it gratefully. Then she finishes a second one, but declines a third with a shake of her head. Curls bounce around her face and shoulders.

I nuzzle the top of her head and kiss their silkiness. The citrus scent of her shampoo fills my senses.

"No more water; I'm about to pop now," she laughs as she rises from the bed.

I watch, entranced by the sway of her grip-worthy hips as she sashays to the bathroom.

"Malcolm!" She shouts.

What the fuck?!

I nearly fall out of the bed in my haste to reach her.

Seconds later, she rushes through the bathroom door. Her hands clasped between her tits.

"Malcolm! What is this?" She asks as she raises her hands to me.

Oh, that.

A smile broader than the Cheshire Cat spreads across my face.

"Your push present, of course," I respond triumphantly.

Her mouth drops open.

I crook my finger at her.

My Angel hurries to the bed and knees her way to me.

I kiss her lips until she's panting. Then I murmur against her them.

"The pink diamond pendant represents Selina, the blue for Elio. Their tear-drop shape represents the tears of joy you gave to me for having my babies. The diamond and platinum necklace represent the brightness of your star that lights my way, and the silver-white metal marks the three of you as Steeles. Mine."

I sit back and point to my chest, now bare.

My Angel studies my new tattoo, then brings her tear-filled eyes to mine.

"Oh, Malcolm. Thank you, my love," she whispers, overwhelmed.

# STARR

"Oh, Lola! This is the best idea ever! I miss our Girls' Getaways. And to have this one on Laucala Island where you and I met at my first international fitness retreat. Can you believe it's been four and a half years?! We've come so far. All of us."

I'm so excited about the surprise trip Lola planned. We're aboard a STEELE Gulfstream G700 heading from LAX to the luxury private island.

The ultra-plush jet easily accommodates us plus Slade, Sabrina, Stella, Leonie, Rodolphe, Gaspard, Daphne, Haley, Anita, her girls, Billie, Blair, our nannies, and the flight crew. The spacious, custom-built interior boasts the tallest, widest, and longest cabin of all private jets. Its size suits our needs and allows us to fly internationally without having to stop for fuel. At seventy-five-million-dollars it better be the best aircraft ever made!

"Yeah, well, some of us didn't get married and pop out babies!" Blair laughs.

Haley slaps a high five with Blair and says, "Exactly! Although I wouldn't mind being married…"

We gape at her since she rarely speaks about her relationship—at least we believe there's one—with Lachlan. I've tried to get tidbits out of her, but she remains mum. More than likely, Haley fears the wrath of her big brothers and doesn't want to risk Lola, Leonie, and me slipping up accidentally.

Hell, I don't blame her with those cavemen.

"No! I will not divulge a word," Haley declares, then turns to Slade. "Not even to you, Sweet Babboo. Your daddy is the absolute worse of the whole bunch. I feel right sorry for Sabrina and Stella."

We laugh and agree. Sebastian still can't get over his best friend with his baby sister.

"Anytime you care to share, let me know. I won't spill the beans!" Billie drawls in her Southern accent. "I promise those Steele men won't get a peep out of me, honey!"

Haley blows her a kiss as thanks.

The ten hours fly by as we catch up and make plans for our adventure in paradise. Anita and I will do yoga, meditation, and Pilates sessions. Lola suggests a hike, since she enjoyed the ones we did during the retreat. Billie claimed mixologist and rightfully so as she makes the best cocktails. Haley offers to put suntan oil on everyone's backs since she plans to stay on the beach all day!

As soon as my sandaled feet hit the tarmac, I close my eyes and inhale the tropical scent of frangipani flowers—the source of my signature perfume. Warm rays of the sun heat my skin exposed in my halter-top maxi dress. The sense of peace that fills me invigorates my soul. It's so good to be back on an island that means so much to me.

"Come on, slowpoke! Let's get going!" Lola urges as she waves at me from beside one of the Mercedes-Benz G-Wagens.

Nanny Patience smiles at me as we hurry to another SUV. We strap Selina and Elio into the backseat and climb in. The driver greets us after he finishes with our luggage.

We head from the airport in a caravan.

I shoot a text to Malcolm.

*Hi, my love. We landed and are riding to the villa. Miss you already... xoxo*

Immediately three dots appear as he writes his response.

*Hi, My Angel. I'm glad you're safe. I miss you more. XOXOXO*

I grin as I stare out of the window at the lush beauty of the island.

The sparkling, cyan-colored South Pacific Ocean reaches the horizon. The hues range from the darkest to the lightest blues and greens so varied in depth captivate me. Nearby verdant islands with rings of coral rise from the ocean.

Gulls and terns hover over the waves while shadows of fish schools appear below the crystal-clear surface. The birds swoop in and out of the water to catch their meals.

Soon the resort emerges, and the SUVs diverge to different paths leading to our villas. I opted to stay in the cliffside one Malcolm and I had when we were here over two years ago. It's spectacular, with breathtaking panoramic views of the ocean and the beaches below.

After the butler, chef, and maid greet us as we step from the SUV, I head inside. My priority to situate Selina and Elio. They were so easy for the entire flight: eating once and sleeping. Now they lie own their tummies surrounded by pillows on the bed watching while Nanny Patience and I put away their things. They laugh at the colorful toys I dangle in front of them. And I can't help but to join in their musical sounds.

My mobile rings with a call from Haley.

"Hey, almost ready? Remember to wear your new white string bikini and to put Mini Malcolms in their white rompers and matching sun hats. I'll swing by to pick you up in ten minutes," she says before ending the call.

I giggle to myself.

Haley cannot wait to get to the beach.

As promised, she waits for us in an SUV moments later. She helps me to buckle the babies into their car seats, then we're off.

"I love your sarong. The white on white floral patterns remind me of frangipani," I tell Haley.

"Thanks! I bought it in Bali when Lachlan and—"

She stops abruptly and peers at me.

I grin at her unintended revelation.

"You were saying?" I tease.

Haley waves her hand and ruffles Elio's ebony curls.

"And don't you look handsome, sweetheart," she coos. "Selina, darling, you are gorgeous!"

I let her slipup go and watch the foliage give way to the white-sand beach and the vibrant Pacific Ocean beyond.

"Where's everyone else?" I ask as we carry Mini Malcolms across the powdery sand. "And what's that tarp for?"

"Oh, darn!" Haley exclaims loudly. "I forgot my bag in the SUV. Starr, can you get it for me? Here, I'll hold Elio and your bag for you."

"Oookay…" I reply and hand him and my bag to her before I pivot on my heel.

"My Angel."

I stop, surprised to hear Malcolm's voice behind me. I miss him so much that I'm hearing him?

"Babe."

I whirl around to find the man himself sitting in his wheelchair, where only moments before Haley stood. My wide eyes scan the beach. She's no longer in sight. Only the tarp between two poles flutters with the breeze.

"Malcolm? What are you doing here?" I ask as I close the distance between us.

"You said you missed me," he chuckles and holds out his arms. "Here I am."

I giggle and wrap my arms around his neck as I slip on to his lap.

"It's a Girls' Getaway, you know," I tell him teasingly. "And here you are."

"And here I am, My Angel," he replies as he nuzzles my neck with his nose. "I promised I'd bring you back here before we left the last time. And I keep my promises."

I grin and kiss his full lips.

"Thank you, my love," I murmur.

"You know they say three times the charm, right?" He asks, then continues when I nod. "Well... This island represents firsts for us. It's where you held your international retreat and where we reignited our love. But I hope it will bring me luck for our third try at this... Marry me, Starr Knight."

Tears of joy fill my eyes, and I nod vigorously.

"Words, Little One. I will have your words," Malcolm commands.

"Yes, Sir!" I exclaim before I cover his mouth with mine. "A thousand times, YES!!!"

Malcolm smirks and pats my ass for me to rise.

I stand before him and tilt my head in question when he grips my hips and moves me backwards.

Then he stands from the wheelchair, strides to me, and kneels.

I cry out in disbelief, "Malcolm! You can walk!"

"I'd walk a thousand miles for you, My Angel," he grins.

Malcolm removes a little navy blue velvet box out of his white swim trunks pocket then opens it. A ginormous, flawless pear-cut diamond set in platinum glints in the sunlight.

My mouth drops open as he reaches for my left hand and places the stunning ring on my finger.

"It is a family heirloom given by one of my paternal great-grandfathers to the love of his life. They remained married for over sixty years. I chose it from the family's collection for that very reason. I want a long, happy life with you, My Angel," he explains its provenance reverently.

Tears stream down my face, overwhelmed by such love. It matches the diamonds of my push present—more happy tears.

He stands and wipes my face, even as his eyes glisten with unshed tears.

Suddenly the air fills with the opening chords for "By Your Side" followed by the soulful voice of Sade Adu.

I glance up to find the tarp gone to reveal the singer and her eponymous band with our family and our friends smiling at us dressed in all white beachwear.

Malcolm recreated his Bali proposal setting with a few additions.

The white gauzy canopy with its four posts covered in white hibiscus, frangipani, and orchards floats above the sand like a fragrant cloud where an officiant stands. Sebastian and Anton, with Lola and Adrienne holding Selina and Elio, flank the officiant.

Everyone else—my parents, the Steeles, the Jacksons, the Beaulieus, the Greens, Billie, Patrick, Blair, Luc, and Borya—stands beside canopy-covered round tables dressed in white linens and extravagant floral centerpieces. Chairs have more gauzy material drapes over them, with a bow in the back and a floral bouquet at its center. An aisle forms between them, lined with more flowers.

The tropical scent of the floral arrangements mingles with the aromas from the tantalizing dishes on white-linen-covered banquet tables manned by servers. Magnums of Krug Clos d'Ambonnay Champagne chill in silver tubs nestled in the sand.

Bamboo torches around the perimeter and white tapers

on the tables will provide lighting once the sun sets on the horizon. A bonfire to the side and more bamboo torches situated nearby, ready to be lit.

Further down the beach sits a white tent covered in gauzy material with white hibiscus, frangipani, and orchards entwined.

"For us later. I want to make love to my beautiful bride on the beach all. Night. Long."

Malcolm's husky whisper rouses me.

I turn to face him, surprised again.

"We're getting married now?" I ask.

"Absolutely! I will not waste another day without you as Mrs. Malcolm Steele," he growls in my ear, then nips the lobe.

I yelp just as my father touches my elbow.

"Starr, time to walk down the aisle, sweetheart," he says with a loving smile.

I glance around at Malcolm. But he's already striding to the ceremony canopy. Transfixed by the sight of his easy gait, my father has to nudge me to move. I take the beautiful bouquet of frangipani and Blue Sapphire orchids he hands to me and smile back at him.

We proceed down the aisle to the love of my life and our babies. Before he lets me go, my father pins Malcolm with an intense stare, then states he and my mother give this woman to be married to this man. He whispers, I love you, as he embraces me. I return the words with an extra squeeze to reassure him.

Lola takes my bouquet with a wink before I place my hands in Malcolm's outstretched palms.

We listen to the officiant, then recite our vows of everlasting love. Malcolm tears up, as do I when we each say I do.

But I squeal when Sebastian presses the clasp on a flat, blue velvet jewelry case. I thought my engagement ring was magnificent, but the enormous diamonds of the custom hand harness and an eternity band nearly blind me!

It's like Lola and Leonie's wedding jewelry.

The chain of diamonds connects to the eternity band on my middle finger by three pear-cut diamonds in a row that rest atop my hand attached to a diamond triple bracelet. My engagement ring sits on my ring finger. The harness is removable. So I can wear my band and ring together.

Malcolm slips the entire piece on me, and I gasp. My eyes fly to his, and he cocks his head as he raises his eyebrow.

"Three times the charm, remember? Now, you're marked as mine for all to see," he says with a smirk.

I lift my hand to admire the harness. Sparks fly from the flawless diamonds, making prisms on the white gauze covering the canopy.

I smirk and ask, "Where is your wedding band so I can claim you, Malcolm Steele?"

The gathering laughs, and he joins in.

Smiling, Sebastian hands a classic platinum band to me. I return his smile, then place the ring on Malcolm's finger. I hold his gaze and add, *"You're* my charm, my love."

The officiant pronounces us husband and wife.

Malcolm whoops and lifts me from the sand, then dips

me into a deep arc. He captures my mouth in a mind-blowing kiss. When he brings me back on my feet, I peer at him dazedly while he grins.

"Mine all Mine, Mrs. Malcolm Steele!" He says triumphantly. "And I will cherish you forever more, My Angel."

My heart bursts with joy. Ecstatic to complete our bond after almost four years of knowing each other and over three as a couple.

Malcolm leans down to whisper in my ear, "But your neck is bare... We will take care of that tonight when I put your collar back on, Little One."

A shiver races down my spine, and I bite my lower lip in anticipation of my Alpha Dom-turned-boyfriend now husband collars me his sub-turned-girlfriend now wife.

We lift Selina and Elio into our arms and make our way down the aisle as a family. A Photographer and a videographer I didn't notice before snaps shots and films. They direct us to another area for photos after Malcolm and I sign the marriage documents. The bridal party and our parents join us, along with the rest of the Steele clan.

"Congratulations, sweetheart!" My mother says as she hugs me, then Malcolm. "My son!"

Malcolm returns her embrace with a broad smile.

"Thank you, Mama Sun!" He beams.

Shelley pulls me close and exclaims, "Oh, Starr, honey, we're so happy to have you as part of our family forever!"

Malcolm and I receive more well wishes while we finish the photo shoot.

Before we sit at our table, Malcolm leads me to the

dance floor as Sade performs "Cherish the Day." I lose myself in his loving embrace as I bury my face against his powerful chest. His heart beats as fast as mine, quickened by our emotional moment. I lift my gaze to his, and we stare into each other's eyes until the last strands of music fade.

Malcolm kisses me softly, then takes my hand. We visit each table to speak with our guests, accepting their congratulatory remarks. Afterwards, we settle at our table with Lola, Sebastian, Adrienne, and Anton. Mini Malcolms sit nearby with the other children and their nannies.

The meal is delicious with local dishes using the flavors of the Fijian people. Lucien offers his approval of the fine fare and jokes how he'll have to open a restaurant featuring the specialties.

Following up on his teasing, Sebastian—the Best Man—rises.

"Friends and family, thank you for joining the Steele and the Knight families for the union of my bother Malcolm and my friend Starr. This day is a long time coming and marks the start of a wonderful life for them as a family with their adorable twins, Selina and Elio. Kindly raise your flutes in a toast to the newlyweds," he says.

Everyone drinks to our prosperity.

"Now, let me say this. Malcolm you are a rebel who has always done your own thing. And done it well I might add —even if unconventional, like your spectacular yet romantic bikini beach wedding. In Starr, you found your mate who shares your need to live as a free spirit on her own path. Thankfully, you are now one. *Namaste*, my brother and my sister," Sebastian ends with a bow.

Malcolm stands and pulls his older brother into a fierce hug. They murmur words only they can hear as Lola and I watch with tears in our eyes.

When they sit, she rises.

"Starr, on this very island, you put me back together again after I thought I could never love Sebastian Steele. You taught me a yogic piece of advice: *be equally thankful for what you perceive to be good and for what you perceive as bad. It all happens for a reason.* And today proves your point. Here we sit with the men we will love for all time despite any past missteps. Much love to you, my sister and my brother," Lola says as she raises her flute in a toast.

We hug and I thank her for her loving words. How right she is!

After we eat, Lola tells me to come with her.

We go to a tent where I change into a white bandeau top string bikini with a sarong. She hands a blue garter to me and giggles.

When we return to the gathering, a chair sits in the middle with Malcolm holding my bouquet beside it.

Ah, now I know why Lola giggled!

He crooks his finger at me, and I laugh as I make my way to my husband. He helps me to stand on it and hands my bouquet to me. I toss it over my shoulder to the single women.

Haley snatches it first and holds it high.

Malcolm helps me down to sit before he kneels and removes my garter with a flourish.

"Okay, boys! Who's next?" He calls out to the guys in front of us. "Catch!"

With ease, Lachlan grabs it from the air and twirls it around his finger.

Malcolm snarls, "Not you, Lachlan."

But I place my hand on his forearm. He glances down at me, and I give a shake of my head. He purses his lips but remains silent.

Lachlan takes Haley's hand and leads her to the chair.

We switch places with them.

When he touches Haley's leg, Malcolm issues a warning growl that Lachlan ignores. He slides the garter up Haley's leg and kisses her lips softly. Her face flushes prettily, and everyone claps—well, except for her brothers…

Staff changes the tables arrangement into an all-white lounge with the torches and the bonfire lit. Sade leave us for a DJ to spin. The night continues as we dance and party, sipping signature cocktails crafted by Billie.

As I'm shaking my grove thang to Zhané with my girls around me, firm hands grip my hips from behind and pull me flush against a rock-hard body.

Malcolm!

My pussy floods at the feel of his turgid length nestled between my ass cheeks.

He sways us to the beat as he nuzzles the sensitive juncture of my neck and shoulder. When the song blends into another, he nips my neck and murmurs for my ears only.

"Time to consummate our marriage, Mrs. Malcolm Steele."

# MALCOLM

*I* stalk towards my wife as she's shaking her ass, dancing with her girls.

If My Angel thinks she can taunt me all this time by changing into one tiny bikini after the other all night, she has another think coming. Or she won't cum on her wedding night…

It's been ten long months since I had her moaning and writhing beneath me, balls deep in her sweet, tight pussy. My aching cock's been hard from the moment she sat on my lap. Thank fuck, I can feel it now. I can feel everything.

After four months of intense therapy, I surpassed the expected stages set by the medical team. Dr. Stevens warned me results from the new treatment plan could take at least six months, if not more, with no guarantees of success.

I told him I would overcome every obstacle and walk again a hell of a lot sooner than his timeline.

And I did.

Two weeks ago, I awoke to immense pain radiating down my spine and into my legs, to the tips of my toes. My screams drew nurses to my bedroom. I could barely speak as nausea overtook me. My body was on fire. Sweat coated my skin as though I ran the New York City marathon.

The night doctor arrived and explained my nerves were reconnecting to my brain. Those simultaneous actions were overloading my system with the unexpected onslaught of synapses firing. The new trial neurostimulation therapy worked, he proclaimed excitedly.

Dr. Stevens arrived and conducted tests. The results confirmed my spinal injury was ninety percent healed. He was just as excited as the other doctor since their research paid off. The success will make the medical journals, he said proudly.

I told him I was happy to be the guinea pig and thanked the team profusely.

The weeks since were full of more testing, extensive therapy, and no-holds-barred sessions with Borya. Aside from him, only Baz knew I could walk. Even when I visited Starr and our babies, I used the wheelchair. I trusted the medical team, but I didn't want my family upset if my progress reversed.

Immediately, I asked Lola to arrange a Girls' Getaway as a ruse for getting My Angel to Laucala for a surprise wedding. My sister-in-law was more than happy to set it up. Once again, I enlisted the help of my mother and of Sun with the wedding arrangements. The family and our friends arrived yesterday to ensure all was in order and no one missed the big day.

The expressions on my parents' faces when I stood on the tarmac to greet them were priceless. I had the photographer and videographer document it as they did with My Angel—unbeknownst to her. My mother cried so hard I had to console her. When she found out it was weeks, she swatted me like a misbehaving toddler. My father teared up and nearly crushed me in his embrace. Roger and Harris understood and pulled me into a group hug.

My ability to walk again thrilled Peace and Sun as much as my family. The wedding had My Angel's parents pleased, but my recovery drove them to tears, too.

Before the wedding, Lola couldn't believe I didn't tell her and let Baz know she was none too pleased with him keeping it a secret. He spanked her ass, and she composed herself with a huff. I had to hear it from Haley and Leonie, too. Looks from Lachlan and Roger silenced them. I eyed Lachlan, and he smirked. Fucker.

The ultimate reaction was my wife's expression of pure gratitude for my healing. Her sorrel brown eyes glistened with tears as she murmured a silent prayer to, as she says, "thank God and every deity in every religion's pantheon."

I thank them too for bestowing me with the love of my life. Even if she's giving me blue balls, at least I can feel them again.

Once I stand behind her, shimmying to the music, I grip her hips firmly and pull her back flush against my front.

My wife gasps at the sensation of my no-longer-to-be-denied dick nestled between her round ass cheeks.

Without a word, I take control of her movements to set a sensual rhythm while I nuzzle the column of her swanlike neck down to her shoulder. Once the next song begins, my teeth graze her skin.

"Time to consummate our marriage, Mrs. Malcolm Steele," I murmur against the shell of her ear.

She shudders, and my cock thumps her ass.

I nod to her girls who titter as I scoop my wife into my arms like the bride she is and carry her away from our still-partying guests.

They hoot and holler—Harris the loudest with wolf whistles—as we make our way down the beach to the tent she spotted earlier.

My Angel laughs and waves then kisses cheek.

"I love you, caveman of mine," she sighs against my neck.

"I love you too, woman of mine," I answer, brushing my lips over her curls.

The music fades and the light of the reception bonfire gives way to the tranquil sound of the ocean lapping on the sand of the moonlit beach. Thousands of stars twinkle above us—as bright as My Angel covered in her diamonds. Ahead of us, smaller torches flank the entrance to the tent.

We're kicking off our honeymoon, so it's not just any old tent. We're glamping in a luxury, temperature-controlled one. The floor covered in colorful handwoven silk rugs and oversized silk pillows; the walls lined with delicate silk drapes; a large, round bed strewn with sumptuous white silk bedding takes up most of the interior space; flowers and flickering pillar candles surround it with a magnum of her favorite Krug Clos d'Ambonnay Champagne on ice and crystal flutes on a side table; soft music blends with the sounds of nature; a fully functional bathroom in a separate tent adjoins the main one.

As we step beyond the netting covering the entry, My Angel's mouth drops at the romantic sight. She squeals and kisses me passionately, murmuring words of love. I return her kiss just as zealously. Then set her on her feet and turn to untie the tent flaps.

"Alone at last, Mrs. Malcolm Steele!" I say as I pull her into my arms for another kiss.

"Yes, Mr. Malcolm Steele," she purrs with hooded eyes after I let her up for air. "Now, what are you going to do to me… Sir?"

My nostrils flare as my lips curl up in a smirk, and my eyes narrow on hers, dancing with mischief in the candlelight.

"I am putting another baby in your belly. In fact, two more for another set of twins. That is how much I am filling your womb with my seed, Mrs. Malcolm Steele," I growl low in my throat.

As expected, her pupils dilate, and she pants through parted lips. Her plump nipples strain against the one-shoulder bikini top, begging to be suckled. She shifts from one foot to the other as she rubs her thighs in earnest for some much-needed friction—friction only I will sate.

I spank my wife's ass cheeks in rapid succession.

"Still!" I command.

With stuttered breath, she complies.

I take her hand in mine and lead her to the vintage bathtub with fragrant flowers and essential oils in the warm water. More candles fill the bathroom with their sensuous glow and heady scent. A stack of white fluffy bath sheets rests on a table.

Once again, I kiss my wife until she whimpers in my mouth. Silently, I pull the ties of her bikini bottom to reveal her bare mons. I lick my lips, remembering her delicious juices on my tongue. My eyes drift up to the bikini top. Cupping her tits, I knead the lush flesh as I stroke her nipples with my the pads of my thumbs through the material. Not wanting to release my hold. I dip my head to nibble the string between my teeth. My lips brush her heated skin as I tug the tie slowly. I spin her around to face the tub and pull the last string on her top. It cascades to the floor atop her bottoms.

"Get in," I murmur in her ear.

She trembles from the caress of my warm breath. Then she takes my proffered hand and slides in to the water.

I kneel beside the tub and dampen the sponge, then squeeze the water on to her chest. Rivulets form around her mounds and drip from her pointed buds. Another dip of the sponge glides it along her inner thighs. They quiver beneath the surface, sending ripples through the water. Wanting to heighten the sensations, I skirt around her most sensitive areas as I bathe my bride from head to toe.

Her blissful sighs and moans surround us.

When I stop my erotic ministrations, she opens her eyes and parts her lips with a coo relaxed against the tub. She raises her arms to me.

"Your turn, my love," she whispers.

Unable to deny her anything, I stand and strip out of my swim trunks. My erect ten-inch cock—red and veiny—

points at her accusingly; its mushroom head drips pre-cum.

She kneels in the tub and swipes the evidence of my need for her with the tip of her tongue. She hums; I groan.

"Come," my wife demands.

I gaze down at her, confused she means for me to *cum*. But she shakes her head with a teasing smile and gestures for me to sit opposite her in the tub.

I smirk and comply.

Now I lose myself in the rhapsody of my bath. As if reminding me two can play that game, my wife touches every part of my body except for my hungry cock and heavy balls. Not having her patience, I wrap my arms around her and rise from the tub.

Thinking more clearly than me, she snags towels as we pass them.

I stand her beside the bed and dry her gently, then quickly take the other towel to myself. Patience at an end.

I toss her on to the bed, and she giggles as she bounces in the middle.

"Caveman!" My Angel teases as she swipes damp curls from her face.

I grunt as I drop to my hands and knees to prowl towards her.

She squeals when I grab her ankles and lift her legs onto my shoulders.

Open-mouthed kisses trail down her inner thighs until I reach their apex, glistening from evidence of *her need* in the glow from the candles. I blow warm air on to her seam; she whimpers.

"Shh... I know exactly what you need, My Angel. Let me give it to you," I murmur as I stare into her hooded eyes.

She bites her lower lip and nods. Then catches herself and responds verbally.

I chuckle as I lower myself between her thighs. My broad shoulders widen them to give me room to lie flat on the bed. I glance up the flat plane of her belly, over the rise of her tits to gaze into her eyes.

"Cum as much as you want, Mrs. Malcolm Steele," I tell her.

She lifts her hips and grips handfuls of my hair to urge me on.

I begin my meal with a nip to each leg and devour her until—after countless orgasms—she begs for me to stop while her legs tremble uncontrollably.

A kiss to each leg, and I plank my body over hers. Muscular arms and toes bear the weight as thighs and ass flex. My turgid length presses between us with the trail of hair leading to it tickling her lower belly; she squirms with need.

"Malcolm, baby, please... I need you inside of me," my wife cries as she digs her heels into my ass and her fingertips in my biceps.

"I will never deny you, My Angel," I rasp.

I lower to one forearm then reach between us to fist my ready cock and align it with her pussy. The tip brushes her soaked, swollen folds as it makes its way inside her greedy channel. My hands cradle her face as I roll my hips against her, filling my wife with my cock. I give her exactly what she needs.

We groan in unison as her tight pussy walls stretch to accommodate my ample girth, especially after months of being without.

She grips me with a stranglehold. Undoubtedly still vitalized even after giving birth from the Kegel exercises she loves so much. I hiss from the carnal pain.

Her cries for *harder and deeper* fuel me to shift from slow thrusts and drags to pistoning strokes. My heavy balls slap her ass with each brutal thrust. I change the angle to glide along her G-spot, making her scream with pleasure.

As My Angel's back bows, I latch onto her tit and suckle. Hard.

She wails and digs her nails in to my back as she meets me thrust for thrust.

Fuck yeah!

We hurtle unstoppable to simultaneous climaxes.

My thumb finds her puckered hole and presses against the ring of muscle as I plunder her pussy.

She howls in wild abandon as a last wave overtakes her spasming core.

I roar as my release follows hers.

As promised, I coat my wife's womb with copious amounts of my virile seed until it spills down her ass cheeks to pool beneath her. Mind blown, I collapse atop her. She welcomes my heavy weight, wrapping her arms and legs around me.

My wife soothes me with tender strokes to my sweaty

back as she clutches the back of my head, holding me to her neck.

Once our breathing evens out, I roll on to my back and pull her to my chest.

Sated, we lie stargazing through the top of the tent, clear so the stars shine brightly above us.

I take Starr's left hand adorned with my rings and harness in mine and kiss her open palm. She turns her gorgeous face towards me. Her sorrel brown eyes gleam as she smiles with a palpable intensity, mirroring my absolute love for her.

"I love you, Mr. Malcolm Steele," she coos.

"I love you, Mrs. Malcolm Steele," I rasp.

Then I kiss my Lucky Starr.

THE MORNING SUN filters through the tent's roof to dazzle my wife curled beside me. I brush a curl from her cheek and smile when her lips—still swollen from my kisses and my cock—turn up at my touch. So beautiful. So mine.

Even more so now that my collar readorns her neck. I kept her original ones—for day and for evening. Since it's our wedding, I chose to put the evening one on her. Handcrafted in an intricate platinum lacework covered in tiny sparkly diamonds. The sun glints off of it and the diamonds on her left hand as it rests on the pillow.

"Like what you see, Mr. Steele?"

Her laughter rouses me from my musings.

Then she squeals when I lift her from the bed, leave the

tent, and stride to the water where I dive in. She splutters when we breach the service and pushes at my chest.

"Good morning, Mrs. Steele!" I chuckle as I float beside her.

"You're so lucky I'm still recuperating from your exuberant lovemaking, or I'd 'good morning' you!" She huffs as she swipes water from her face.

I stand to tower over her and stroke my hard cock.

"Oh, so you're not up for some morning loving?" I taunt as I fist it.

My Angel attempts to hold back her smile but fails miserably. With a whoop, she throws herself at me and wraps her arms and legs around my torso.

I lift her hips and impale her on my cock. She rides me as the waves lap around us. We climax as one.

Back inside the tent, we bathe and dress for breakfast with our family and friends. A driver takes us to her parents' villa as I tease my wife in the backseat of the G-Wagen.

"So glad you can join us, Mr. and Mrs. Malcolm Steele!" Leonie teases when we walk on to the patio.

Laurent—the youngest Jackson and Harris' best friend—adds, "The newlyweds arrive! Cheers!"

Everyone greets us as we head to Selina and Elio, who sit between their grandmothers. We hug our twins close and kiss their cherub faces as they giggle.

Once we're settled at a table, I thank everyone for celebrating with us, then turn to my wife.

"Mrs. Malcolm Steele, for the next two months, we will remain on this special island for our honeymoon.

However, you never have to wonder when we can return. We may at any given moment, as it is my wedding gift to you. Laucala Island is yours, my love," I say, lifting my mimosa in the air.

She gapes at me with wide eyes.

I laugh and lean over to cover her open mouth with mine in a loving kiss.

She regains herself and kisses me back with enthusiasm as she bounces on her chair.

"Thank you, my love! Thank you so much!" My wife's sorrel brown eyes sparkle.

I grin, knowing I will keep her this happy and more for the rest of our lives.

# STARR

The warm rays of the tropical sun soak into my sweat-dampened skin as the sound of the waterfall mingles with my moans in an erotic symphony amongst the wild foliage of Laucala's rain forest. As I float face up to the cloudless cerulean blue sky—my arms bound behind my back and my knees bent with my ankles bound to my thighs—I cry out with each thrust of my husband's massive dick into my dripping pussy.

The jute rope drops from the palm tree above me to coil around my body like a snake capturing its prey. Each carefully crafted knot strategically placed to hold me firmly proves my husband has mastered the art of Shibari.

He knows it's my favorite form of play since the complicated yet beautiful knots restrict my movement, swaddling me with a sense of security, allowing my mind to just. Let. Go. Submit to him fully.

Over the past two months, my Alpha Dom husband has taken control of my mind, body, and soul to send me into the euphoria of subspace over and over. Each time we've done a scene, he's brought me to greater heights, proving he hasn't lost his mastery of my body.

And I love him even more for it.

"Are... you... still... with... me... Little One?"

His throaty growl with snapping hips that punctuate each word bring me back from my musings.

"Yes... Sir..." I pant breathlessly.

"Look at me!" My Alpha Dom demands. "I want to see your eyes as I fuck another orgasm out of your greedy, little pussy."

As if on cue, my core clenches on his hard length, and I keen through my climax.

"Aaaaaahhhhh... Yeessss..." I wail as my body convulses, jerking the dangling rope.

He continues to arc me through the air, swinging me back and forth like a pendulum to impale me on his thick cock. Corded muscles flex from his neck to his broad chest down along his eight-pack abs. Sweat drops onto my belly as he stares down at me with molten platinum eyes.

When my Alpha Dom bends his knees to thrust up at me on the next return arc, his Prince Albert piercing jewelry balls scrap my G-spot and the bottom of my channel.

"Arrrrhhhh..... Ffffuuuck!!!" I scream, throwing my head back as my eyes slam shut.

Too much.

Another climax rips down my spine to curl my fingers and my toes. My mind explodes with my pussy.

"Give it to me... Give it all to me!" He barks barbarically.

As I soar through subspace, my last sensation is of my husband's dick expanding, then jerking as he releases a torrent of his seed within the depths of my womb. In response, it spasms to coax every single drop from him. I shudder and feel no more.

"Welcome back, My Angel."

As my eyes flutter open, they alight on Malcolm's handsome face, so full of love. I lift my arms overhead and straighten my legs in a languorous stretch. It's then I notice I'm sitting on his lap across from the waterfall with the waves lapping at the tops of my breasts.

With a contented sigh, I wrap my arms around his neck and cover his mouth with mine.

Lazily, our tongues twine until he dominates the kiss. My breath hitches in the back of my throat as my husband nips at my bottom lip, then soothes it with a long, sensuous lick.

When he lets me up for air, I press my forehead to his and stare into his lust-filled eyes.

"You're insatiable, Mr. Steele," I purr.

He smirks, "And who's fault is that, Mrs. Malcolm Steele?"

In response, I circle my hips to drag my ass against his thick erection. It thumps.

"Mmmmm mmmm... What you do to me, wife," he groans and tightens his firm grip on my waist.

In one swift motion, he lifts me and lowers me onto his dick one inch at a time until my lips kiss his groin.

"Better, Mr. Steele?" I purr against his slack mouth.

He nods and kisses me as he guides my hips in the rhythm he prefers.

Our climaxes find us easily, and we rest on a colorful Hermès blanket, staring at the sky.

I roll over to face him and trail a fingernail down his powerful chest, bumping over his nipple.

"Ready for more, Mrs. Steele?" He rumbles.

I shake my head and sit up, gesturing around us.

"The island is so beautiful, and we've used so many areas of it for our playtime. I think others would enjoy its natural beauty and the privacy it affords for their playtime," I say.

Malcolm cocks an eyebrow at me and rises to an elbow. His flexing biceps distract me, and I stare, concentration broken. He tweaks my nipple.

"And?" He asks with a smirk.

I giggle and shake the carnal thought of jumping my husband's bones from my mind. For now.

"You and Lucien could convert the resort into LEVELS Laucala Island. BDSM on the Beach!" I say, grinning like the Cheshire Cat.

Before he can respond, I continue.

"And I can open Starr Light Fitness & Wellness Laucala Island to keep LEVELS LI members limber… However, we'll keep the other side of the island private for our family with the six villas. What say you, My Alpha Dom?"

He lays back down with his arms folded behind his

head—again with the bulging biceps and now the pecs and abs to mesmerize me. He ponders my idea in silence for a few moments.

The next, I'm flat on my back with all those tantalizing muscles on point above me. I giggle and squeeze his arms.

"Excellent idea, Little One! Another first for our island... Introducing LEVELS Laucala Island, exclusive members-only BDSM resort!" He proclaims.

My laughter turns into moans as he makes me soar once more.

* * *

"Now, you have my permanent mark, Mrs. Malcolm Steele."

I grin at my husband then at my left hand where three number threes interlock across my left ring finger to symbolize three's the charm forever.

"Yes, Mr. Malcolm Steele, indeed I do. Again!" I quip.

Sebastian may think Malcolm the rebel for having our wedding on the beach in bathing suits. But I loved it and wouldn't have it any other way. Even when Malcolm told me we could have the wedding of my dreams anywhere in the world. No thanks. Our family-only, beachfront wedding was absolutely perfect!

Elio must find my joke amusing as he laughs and waves his hands in the air. Selina joins in with her brother, and we laugh. So freaking cute!

The tattoo artist—the best in Asia—Malcolm flew over asks me if I'm ready.

Malcolm cocks his eyebrow, and I pat his cheek.

"Be back shortly," I smirk with a wink.

When I return, Malcolm stops playing with his babies and faces me questioningly, arms crossed over his broad chest. I saunter over to him and lower the v-neck of my shirt.

His eyes light up at the sight of a small heart with the letters MSS in the hallow between my breasts.

"Malcolm and Starr Steele?" He asks.

"Yes, my love," I confirm.

He jumps up and swoops me into his arms as he kisses me. Then he sets me on my feet and growls possessively.

"Did he see your tits?"

I throw my head back and laugh.

My Caveman!

# MALCOLM

"Damn, bro. If I knew I had to do manual labor in order to snag your Sunset Strip penthouse permanently, I would've bought another one. Give me a damn break already and hurry the fuck up!"

I chuckle and clock Harris upside the back of his head as he grumbles more under his breath.

We're in the new playroom I'm having installed in My Angel's—I mean our—Benedict Canyon Drive mansion. While we were on our honeymoon, my personal assistant and her PA organized the move of my stuff from my penthouse to here. This will serve as our West Coast residence while our beachfront mansion at Steele Southampton Village takes the place of my penthouse in The STEELE Tower as our East Coast residence. We'll use that home when we're in the city overnight. Otherwise, we'll take my Sikorsky S-92 Executive Helicopter to and from the compound.

When I tried to persuade My Angel to move in with me

at my New York City penthouse while we were dating, she declined. She told me she's a beach girl and prefers the Hamptons with access to the Atlantic Ocean. I couldn't even bribe her with an SLFW in the Flat Iron District—the Manhattan neighborhood renown for upscale fitness centers and retailers. She countered with SLFW Resorts at STEELE Southampton Village. She didn't want to enter the oversaturated Manhattan fitness scene. Her preference for incorporating her center with the bed-and-breakfast-style resort suits a more intimate setting. Fine by me.

Baz's words about *happy wife, happy life* come to my mind, and I chuckle.

"Really, Malcolm? You're standing there with a goofy AF grin on your gaga face with hearts circling your head while I'm holding this heavy cross?!"

Harris' reprimand yanks me from my pleasant little family thoughts to the playroom.

"Quit, your whining. I'm almost done," I smirk. "Didn't you say your one rep max bench press was 195? Maybe you need more time with Borya…"

Harris pulls his lips sideways and rolls his eyes while I finish mounting the St. Andrew's Cross to the wall. I had the rest of the heavy pieces installed, but the cross just arrived, and I want to surprise My Angel with a complete playroom tomorrow night.

Tonight we're going to LEVELS Beverly Hills for a party by a pair of my favorite members' collaring ceremony. We closed the Peepshow level for their private event. It promises to be a night of love and hedonistic bliss.

"Okay, what the fuck is this for, bro?"

I glance over my shoulder to find Harris holding a toy My Angel spotted when we made a stop in Hong Kong for some shopping on our way back from Laucala Island.

A pink glass dildo shaped to resemble an octopus' tentacle with a double row of suckers on top and ridges along its bottom, finished on one end with a loop for an easy grip. Perfect dipped into cool water or heated with my mouth. The stimulation it gave My Angel's channel drove her into sensory overload real quick.

"Put that down. Starr and I don't need your grimy paws on our toys," I scold him with a shake of my head.

Harris returns it to the drawer then leans on the chest with his arms folded across his chest.

"You and Baz with your Alpha Dom shit. Whatever happened to using what you got naturally to get what you want?" He asks as he pumps his hips.

I snort and throw the towel I was wiping my hands off with at him.

"You'll learn little, bro. Even Roger dips into the *other side* now and then…" I chuckle.

Although we're all Alpha Males and Global All Access Members of the four LEVELS clubs, he and Roger aren't Doms.

I grin when I recall helping Leonie to do a burlesque performance at LEVELS Paris as a wedding present for Roger. The next day, Lucien and I had hell to pay with him, despite the way his eyes lit up at the memory.

My Angel and I enjoy my clubs and make use of them regularly. But I like to have a playroom in my residence. Since Harris took over my Sunset Strip penthouse that has one in it, I had to design a new space here. And I cannot wait to play with my wife!

"You're still coming to the party tonight?" I ask Harris as we head downstairs to the entertainment floor.

I promised him a round of *Call of Duty: Black Ops Cold War* in exchange for his help.

"Me, miss a party? At LEVELS? Absolutely, I'll be there," he responds. Then goes on to tell me about a member he's had his eye on the past few times he's been at the club.

Before we get into the game, I shoot a text to My Angel to let her know I'm in the game room. She's with Leonie for a spa day while the nannies watch the babies. It's great everyone bought a house out here and created a new Steele compound.

"Oh, come on already, whipped boy..." Harris grumbles as he tosses the controller at me.

"Game on, bro!" I say, settling in for some fun time with my youngest brother.

Yeah. Family first.


"Congratulations on your marriage, Mr. Steele, Mrs. Steele."

My wife smiles and thanks the LEVELS Beverly Hills greeter while I tighten my grip on Mrs. Steele's hip.

It feels damn good to hear those outside of our clan refer to My Angel as Mrs. Steele. I grin to myself.

After our wedding, the press release went out to announce our marriage and Selina and Elio to the world. Our family prefers to remain low key in the media—

despite the hoopla around my accident and the trial—other than business-related activities. But marriages, births, and deaths warrant press releases.

We make our way through the double doors to Peepshow.

My chest swells with pride at another successful club filled with the crème de la crème of society. The club caters to the most wealthy and influential individuals. They prefer the relative safety that one can expect from the iron-clad nondisclosure agreement that LEVELS requires every member and their guests to sign.

LEVELS Beverly Hills is the fourth exclusive, luxury, members-only BDSM/dance club with Global and Local All Access Membership or Dine & Dance Membership. The layout mimics the other clubs. A main entry foyer has two sides with two greeter stations for access to Dine & Dance levels and BDSM levels, an All-Access member, can choose from any of the seven levels: $7^{th}$ Sky Lounge that offers a stunning view of the Hollywood Sign, a bar, restaurant by day dance club by night, coverable pool that's open for the summer, and a glass-retractable roof; $6^{th}$ and $5^{th}$ multilevel dance club with two bars and a lounge for food and drinks; $4^{th}$ Level 4 Restaurant and bar open for breakfast, lunch, and dinner; $3^{rd}$ has twelve private suites for members to continue their pleasure apart from the BDSM levels; $2^{nd}$ Peepshow for BDSM with seating alcoves, main stage, performance rooms, and a bar that serves non-alcoholic mocktails; below ground the Cellar BDSM dungeon with mocktails bar. The Dine/Dance members only have access to the party levels—Sky Lounge, Dance Club, and Level 4 Restaurant.

"Ah, Malcolm, you married a real beauty, mate."

I glance to my left to find an Australian actor with the latest box office hit action movie grinning at my wife. A growl rumbles deep in my chest.

Of course she's beautiful and oozing sexy in her Swarovski crystal embellished sheer floor-length gown with a slit to her crotch covered by a minuscule G-string. Her tan accentuated by the whiteness of the beading. Fuck-me mules make her toned legs go on for miles. Her upswept hair reveals her evening collar while her left hand glitters with her full wedding jewelry.

I bring it to my lips and kiss her rings as I eye the actor.

"Yes, and all mine, *mate*," I smirk.

I give zero fucks he's a member; she's my wife!

"Hey, there's a woman eye fucking you," Harris interjects and turns the actor toward some fictitious fan.

He bites the lure and hurries off without a backwards glance.

My Angel giggles and says, "Okay, My Caveman! Let's find the happy couple."

"Good idea," Harris chuckles. Then adds with a wink, "I'll see you guys around."

My Angel kisses his cheek, and he laughs at whatever she whispered to him.

I arch my eyebrow in question, and she shrugs.

"He saved you from acting possessive because of a member, Mr. Steele," she says, then tugs my arm. "Now, come on."

I spank her ass and murmur in her ear, "So you think you are in control, Naughty Girl. When the ceremony ends, I will remind you who is the Dom and who is the sub."

My wife shudders and bites her plump lower lip with downcast eyes.

I chuckle darkly and place my hand on her hip to guide her through the guests.

"You cheated, Malcolm! You're supposed to go around the *outside* of the buoy, and you know that, big cheater!"

Haley shouts as she storms towards me already on the beach, having left my Jetski on the sand.

We've been on Baz and Lola's Bougainvillea Cay—their private island in the Bahamas—for a couple of days. It's our first Thanksgiving as a family with My Angel and her parents since my accident prevented our gathering last year.

More specifically, it's an island within the chain of the Exuma Cays known as the yachting, sailing, and fishing paradise of the Bahamas. The location offers an ideal spot for relaxation and fun activities.

The forty-million-dollar investment of Bougainvillea Cay lies in one of the most beautiful parts of the Bahamas. It features over five hundred acres of lush, tropical land with a network of paths and walkways. Surrounded by crystal clear turquoise waters, it boasts many white sandy beaches, three inner lakes, and different elevations for stunning views. An airstrip for us to fly in and out with ease makes it perfect for quick getaways. Another plus is its proximity to STEELE Exumas should we wish to use the recreational, spa, or dining facilities.

Two properties round out the island. A palatial two-story, ten-bedroom beachfront villa with saltwater pool, four guest cabanas, and a caretaker's house and an actual castle built by an Englishman in the 1930s. With Leonie doing the design through her STEELE division, they rebuilt it into a spot for the kids to take over. The perfect solution as they grow into teenagers and want their space apart from the adults.

Our parents and the rest of us siblings built our villas along the coastline that features natural coves for privacy. With his STEELE division, Roger created a clubhouse on the largest beach for our family to gather. They added docks with lifts for sailboats, Jetskis, and other water toys.

Bougainvillea Cay is the Steele Caribbean retreat. A spectacular place for our family to gather for Thanksgiving and during the winters, as we do at Steele Southampton in the summers and *Chalet de la Joie* for the holidays. Laucala Island will host Memorial Day and anytime our family—Steele, Knight, Beaulieu—needs a tropical respite.

I race towards Haley and lift her off her feet before she can duck away. Spinning her in the air, I tease her about being my little sister and to respect her elders.

Haley huffs, but giggles when I tickle her silly.

I drape my arm over her shoulders, and we walk back to the others gathered on the sand. My eyes meet Lach-

Ian's, and I arch my eyebrow at him in challenge. My little sister, fucker.

She squirms from my embrace and hustles to him.

He smirks over her head at me, and I curl my lip in warning.

"Who's ready for some grilled lobster and shrimp?" My father calls out from the pit we dug for cooking on the beach.

Sun made her famous potato salad, and Josy baked her equally loved double-chocolate soufflés. Not to be outdone, Lola made delicious fried chicken. They teased Leonie was best left with tossing the green salad since she's famous for burning water.

"Hey, babe, go get your food. I'll watch Mini Malcolms," I tell My Angel as I drop onto the oversized blanket beside her.

"Thanks, my love. I'll make you a plate, too," she says before she kisses my lips.

I've noticed she's been hungry lately but can't seem to hold down her food. I know how much she loves lobster, so I hope she can enjoy it.

Elio crawls towards the red sock puppet as I dangle in front of them as they laugh with drool dripping down their chins. Selina's first tooth popped up a week before Elio's. At seven months, they amaze us with their growth and development every day.

"Oh, so you want to play, do you?" I coo at them when Selina rolls to her belly and follows her brother. "Well, come and get it."

We play until My Angel returns with our plates and my mother with bottles of water.

"Here, your father and I will watch our grandbabies while you eat. He's been nibbling on the food while he grilled, and I already ate," my mother offers with a smile.

"Thanks, Mom," I say as My Angel nods around a mouthful of food.

After she finishes, I clear our plates and cheek on Mini Malcolms. They're being spoiled by both sets of their grandparents who shoo me away.

"Come on, My Angel. Let's go for a walk on the beach," I tell her when I return to the blanket.

"Good idea! I'm stuffed!" She giggles, patting her belly, then takes my proffered hand.

We stroll along the shoreline as the waves of the Caribbean Sea lap around our feet. The white-powered sand scrunches beneath our feet with each step.

I tilt my head back with my eyes closed to revel in the warmth of the sun's rays on my face. When I open my eyes, my gaze lands on My Angel.

She stares at me with such blatant love, my heart stutters in my chest. Then she smiles, and her beauty outdoes the surrounding nature. She's brighter than the sun could ever be.

I scoop her flush to my body, not wanting an inch of space between us. My mouth slants over hers as I kiss her passionately. We remain locked together until we need to catch our breath.

My wife cups my face and brushes her thumb over my bottom lip, just as swollen as her from our kiss.

"I love you beyond words," she whispers.

A lump forms in my throat, and I bury my face in her neck as my heart races.

She tangles her fingers in my hair while she soothes me with more words of love.

Once I regain my ability to speak coherently, I lift my eyes to hers.

"I love you so much it hurts sometimes, and I can't express myself with words. Thank you for loving me, My Angel. For giving me Selina and Elio. This is the best Thanksgiving of my life," I confess.

Tears fill her eyes. Now, it's her turn to bury her face in my neck, too overcome for words.

I hold My Angel in my loving embrace as the breeze carries the sounds of our family's laughter to us.

Family first.

# STARR

*And* here I thought I would always be the doula and never the mama. I am eternally grateful for Selina and Elio. But another set of twins? So soon?! Mini Malcolms are eight months barely. Dear God and every deity in every religion's pantheon: help me.

I nod when Dr. Sánchez confirms my inkling I may be pregnant again. Then I nearly fall off of the examination table after she points to two little blips on the ultrasound monitor. She turns up the sound, and their heartbeats fill the room.

Then fill my heart with immense love.

A mama of four, I think as I trace their shapes with my fingertip on the screen. Growing up, I wanted siblings.

Now my children will each other—not to mention their six cousins. And Haley and Harris haven't even begun their families. The Steele grandkids will be as abundant as the family's billions!

"You know the routine, Starr. Not much has changed with the process in eight months," Dr. Sánchez teases.

I smirk and take the images she printed for me. Instinctively, my hand caresses my slightly raised belly—goop and all.

Dr. Sánchez leaves me to clean up before I join her in the office.

I tell her I'll have to schedule my follow-up appointments for after Malcolm and I return from Europe and New York City. With my parents and Mini Malcolms, we fly to Verbier for Christmas and New Year's tonight. Then we plan to stay overseas for business while my parents return home.

I assure Dr. Sánchez I'll ask Leonie's OB-GYN to see me when we get to Paris. On the way back to the West Coast, we're stopping in the City for more business and to move into our East Coast residences. If necessary, I can see Lola's doctor.

Dr. Sánchez laughs at the OB-GYN in every city and tells me to get adequate rest. Then she laughs again when I tell her Malcolm will probably put me in a bubble with my feet up all day!

If I'm not ready for another unexpected pregnancy, I won't blame him if he's not, I giggle as I drive home in my Tesla. During the ride, an idea forms on just how to tell Malcolm the good news. I make a stop at the craft store and smile when the clerk gives my bundle to me.

\* \* \*

I CAN BARELY CONTAIN my excitement as our family gathers in the great room of *Chalet de la Joie*—Leonie and Roger's multimillion-dollar chalet in Verbier, Switzerland—for Christmas Eve.

Verbs, as the in-the-know jet-set call it, is a town in the Swiss Alps. A part of the Valais canton in the southwest of Switzerland, France borders Verbier to the west with Italy to the south. It's the most exclusive ski destination in the world.

It's the winter version of Monaco, with the difference being people who go to Monaco want to watch or be watched. Whereas Verbier has an understated style where wealth is glamorous, stylish, and tasteful. People are here for the reasons one goes to a ski resort—the superb skiing. Not to mention the phenomenal bars and restaurants; the après-ski is perfect for party lovers. Verbier is a glamorous winter playground.

The luxury chalets occupy the area south of the Médran lift. They're slightly away from town along Rue de Médran, where the extra space means they are rarely overlooked and have a private, exclusive vibe. The residential compound is opposite to the STEELE Verbier that's closer to the heart of the village square. The concept is for the STEELE Verbier Chalets to access the resort for its five-star amenities. The most important include the luxury thermal bath spa and the three Jackson Corporation restaurants headed by *The Sexy Chef*.

The massive chalet fits right in with its comfy and chic custom build featuring all the top amenities and accoutrements expected by a posh family. Five stories, twelve bedrooms, sixteen bathrooms, four fireplaces, an oversized ski room, and the usual entertainment rooms including a sixteen-person cinema room, game room, gym, and wine-tasting cellar. The indoor-outdoor heated pool pavilion with spa is an added bonus. Staff quarters are above the six-vehicle garage.

We just finished le *Réveillon de Noël* for the Christmas meal: the dishes included Beluga caviar, foie gras, oysters, lobster, scallops, fresh truffles, roast goose, venison, and cheeses. We ended with the paramount French Christmas dessert *la bûche de Noël*—the Yule log. All the while, a selection of wines and champagne pleased our palates—well, everyone but me.

To continue with French tradition from Leonie's French upbringing, we're about to exchange our first gifts. The beautifully decorated eighteen-foot tree has a vast number of gifts beneath and around its base. The colorful boxes of all shapes and sizes fill the space.

Mariah Carey's "All I Want for Christmas Is You" plays in the background from Leonie's favorite Christmas playlist. The classic songs of Nat King Cole, Johnny Mathis, Céline Dion, Gladys Knight and the Pips, Frank Sinatra, and, of course, the Trans-Siberian Orchestra who performed at her Winter Wonderland Wedding. The sizable stone hearth has a blazing fire and Christmas stockings for each child.

My grin widens as I hand Malcolm's present to him.

"Thank you, My Angel," he says with twinkling eyes.

He holds up two mini red stockings and frowns, glancing towards the fireplace.

"Selina and Elio have stockings already on the mantle," Malcolm says, perplexed. "And these have MM III and MM IV written on them. Why did you—"

A shriek comes from Haley.

Everyone turns in surprise.

She's bouncing and clapping her hands. Her dove gray eyes shine with jubilance. Then Lola and Leonie clap as they grin knowingly.

A slow smile of dawning spreads across Malcolm's face. He drops the stockings in the box as he jumps up and kneels before me. Tentatively, he places his hand on my lower belly, then gazes at me as he bites his full lower lip.

I nod and put my hand over his.

He lets out a whoop and pulls me onto his lap, covering my mouth with his.

The room erupts with shouts from our family and with barks from The Twins' Bichon Frises and Slade's Siberian Huskies.

"Hold on a minute. Two stockings, Starr?" My father asks.

Malcolm jerks back from our kiss and stares gobsmacked at me.

I nod and whisper, "Merry Christmas, baby."

His chiseled jaw drops to the floor.

"Holy shit, Malcolm! Super Sperm Man!" Harris chortles.

"Yeah, you win, bro!" Sebastian snorts. "Hands down, the winner!"

"Absolutely!" Roger guffaws. "Always doing it your way!"

I worry my lower lip with my teeth, nervous about Malcolm's silence.

"Don't hate the playa; hate the game, my brothers!" He quips gleefully.

Then he cups my chin and murmurs, "The best Christmas gift ever, My Angel. Thank you."

"Oh, sweetheart, that's amazing!" My mother says as she dabs her eyes with my father's handkerchief.

He rubs her back and exclaims, "Indeed! Excellent news!"

Shelley and Morgan add their congratulations and hugs.

"This calls for some Champagne, *non?*" Guy asks as he strides to the bar.

We toast—me with sparkling water in my flute—to more grandbabies, as Shelley says.

"When did you find out?" Malcolm asks as he caresses my belly, lying in bed later that night.

He stares down at me as he leans on his elbow. Platinum grays search my sorrel browns.

I stroke his cheek with my thumb. So gorgeous my husband.

"The afternoon before we left. I've been experiencing pregnancy symptoms but wanted my doctor to confirm. I wasn't sure how you'd feel so soon after having Selina and Elio and getting married…" I trail off.

Malcolm puts his fingertips over my mouth to hush me and shakes his head.

"My Angel, I know I behaved like an ass when you told me about being pregnant the first time. And I will forever kick *my ass* for my abysmal behavior and pray you forgive me truly"—he presses his fingertips when I open my mouth —"However, never feel you cannot come to me about anything. Especially about being pregnant. I'm grateful for all the children you will give me, my love."

I try to blame the raging hormones for the tears that spill from my eyes. But they're really because of his beautiful words.

"Shush, baby. Happy tears, I hope?" He asks.

I nod.

"Words, wife. I will have your words," Malcolm admonishes me with a smirk.

"Yes, husband… *Daddy*," I add coyly, knowing how the moniker turns him on.

Malcolm growls and pulls me beneath his hard body. His kisses increase in ferociousness as his arousal amplifies. His knee drives my thighs apart as he fists his turgid length directing it to my weeping pussy.

We groan as one when one demanding thrust breaches my folds to wedge him deep inside of me.

I cry out in passion, and Malcolm stiffens.

"Oh, fuck! Did I hurt you?" He asks with panicky eyes. "Damn! I didn't mean to be so rough. Did… Did I hurt the babies?"

I would laugh if he weren't so alarmed. Instead, I reach between us to angle his bulbous tip to my seam.

"No, you feel wonderful, my love. I'm not fragile, and

the babies are safe within my womb. No need to worry," I reassure him. "Now, fuck me, Mr. Steele!"

Hesitantly, he slides inside inch by tortuous inch.

The pace nearly kills me, so I grip his firm butt cheeks to drive him forward as my hips thrust up. I stare into his wide eyes, then throw my head back on a moan as I impale myself on his ginormous dick. My chest heaves as my back bows from the bed.

"Oh, Malcolm! Fuck. Me. Hard!" I demand. "I need you!"

He blinks, then shifts to his knees as he grasps my ass, lifting my lower half from the bed. I wrap my legs around his hips and offer another plea.

Malcolm bites his lower lip. The veins in his neck strain as he withdraws to his tip. One snap of his hips and he impales me again with a grunt. He pauses to gauge my reaction, and I throw my arms—crossed at the wrists—over my head to grip the headboard.

"Ride me, Mr. Steele... Fuck. Me. Raw. Now..." I grit out as I pin him with my eyes.

He narrows his and tightens his grip.

"Take it, Mrs. Steele! Every fucking inch!" He growls.

I cry out in wild abandon with a white-knuckle grip on the slats as my head tosses side to side, and my heavy tits bounce with each brutal thrust.

"YES! YES! YES!" I cry each time Malcolm re-enters my pussy.

He grunts and growls, shifting positions to increase his penetration, determined to obey my command. His primal roar of release sparks another spasm of my inner walls around his thick girth, sucking him in deeper.

Soon I spiral into erotic bliss from the countless orgasms Malcolm demands from my ravaged pussy. As I float, my thanks go to the architect for his foresight to put soundproof walls in each bedroom suite!

"Hello there, Demanding Mama."

I grin as my eyes flutter to Malcolm's handsome face hovering over me.

"I thought I was going to need to resuscitate you. Feel better?" He smirks.

I stretch and purr, relishing in the ache in my well-used pussy and our combined wetness between my thighs.

"I didn't clean you off because it pleases me to see my seed drip from your pussy. Reminds me of how I put my babies inside of you… Again," Malcolm says as he trails his fingertip along my swollen seam.

He collects some of our juices and places his finger against my lips.

A moan slips from between them when I lick his digit into my mouth. Then I suck it greedily.

"Good, girl," Malcolm croons with hooded eyes.

I smack my lips and grin.

"You do realize you made good on your promise to"—I tilt my head to the side pretending to ponder—"How did you say it? Ah yes, *put another baby in your belly. In fact, two more for another set of twins.*"

Malcolm snorts and falls onto his back.

I lean up, then straddle his hips and place his sizable hands on my belly.

"According to the timeline, you most certainly did!" I giggle.

He strokes my babies bump and smiles.

"I am a man of my word, My Angel. And this time you'll get sick of me. That's how attentive I'm going to be to you," he vows.

I roll my eyes, remembering what I told Dr. Sánchez about the bubble. Then I gasp as Malcolm rolls us over and makes good on his attention, too. A true man of his word…

# MALCOLM

"Out of the way! Coming through!"

Haley's tinkling laughter trails behind her as she zips past me on the black diamond piste, her fleeting figure a blur on her Rossignol skis.

The sunlight glints off of her silver helmet as she zooms by in an all-white Moncler Grenoble two-piece ski suit with her eyes covered by gray Dragon googles and matching helmet. Haley's long, toned legs help her carve through the fresh powder. She moves with ease and grace down the expert slope since she's skied from the time she could walk.

It's New Year's Eve morning and we're out en masse for an early morning run. The entire Steele clan, Knights, Beaulieus, and Lachlan—fucker—make our way from the top of the mountain piste to the base lodge. It's a popular time to come out, so other skiers bob and weave around us.

And of course Lachlan isn't far behind my little sister. He salutes me as he schusses past on silent skis—emerald green eyes covered by mirrored googles. He and the rest of the Jackson clan along with Lydie's boyfriend Chase flew in two days ago after spending Christmas at their family seat in Scotland. They purchased a residence at STEELE Verbier Chalets last year, close to Roger and Leonie's.

Once we make it to the bottom of the mountain, we'll have brunch on the deck of the base lodge.

"I'm sorry, baby. I don't know how my boot buckle opened. Thanks for fixing it for me."

My Angel's words draw my attention up to her face as I kneel before her, adjusting the catch. With a snap, I rise and let my hands roam over her lush curves—long legs; rounded hips; nipped-in waist; swell of full tits. The black Cordova retro ski suit with contouring white stripes on the sides fits her trim figure in a mouthwatering way. Or rather, in a cock-thickening way...

"My absolute pleasure, Hot Mama," I murmur against her lips before I swipe my tongue inside her mouth for a toe-curling kiss.

I swallow her moans as I tip her head for the best angle to devour My Angel whole.

"Get a damn room, man!" Lucien shouts, as he flies by us.

Our passionate kiss breaks with My Angel's giggles.

"Come on. Let's go," she says as she pulls from my embrace. "No shows on the mountain today!"

When she turns to step into her skis, I slide my hands around her flanks to rest on her lower belly. Despite my insistence she not ski, My Angel reminded me she's perfectly fine and has skied her entire life. When I quipped *not pregnant*, she boxed me upside the head.

"Are you sure you don't want to take a less risky piste?" I ask for the thousandth time. "I'll go down on you—I mean with you…"

She snorts and leans back against my chest, placing her hands on top of mine.

"Slip of the tongue, Mr. Steele?" She asks coyly.

I grind my groin above the swell of her ass. Just the talk of fucking my horny wife makes me hard AF.

"I have a slip of the tongue for you, Mrs. Steele. Would you like to feel it?" I rejoin.

The click of her boot into the ski binding precedes her slipping from my arms. A wave over her shoulder, and my pregnant wife picks up speed.

Fuck!

I step into my bindings and pursue her down the mountain.

Part of my determination to heal was to get back into my extreme sports: heli-boarding; base jumping; fighter-jet flying; name it, I did it. I would not let that ex-psycho-sub keep me from my favorite pastime since I was a teenager.

But marriage and fatherhood have a way of realigning one's priorities. I can't put myself in a position with the chance of danger or to harm myself where I can't care for mine. And with another set of twins due… No fucking way!

I'll stick to the simpler—if you will—extreme sports including cave diving, motocross; MMA; and the like. No more tempting fate with my life.

My Angel... While I know she would never ever put herself in harm's way, I'd rather she hangs out at the chalet or the base lodge... I swear, if I have to rope her up to keep her still, I will!

To assuage my concerns, we had a video conference call with her OB-GYN. Dr. Sánchez confirmed My Angel's perfectly healthy state and ability to take part in any activities that do not cause her discomfort. I thanked the doctor, then proceeded to spank My Angel to test the boundaries of her discomfort...

With little effort I reach her side and wag my finger at her.

She grins and tightens into a tuck, zipping away.

Dammit!

We play cat and mouse as we maneuver around other skiers down the mountain. Breathless, we come to a stop in front of the lodge. Our ski butlers help us remove our equipment and hand us our heated après-ski hats, sunglasses, and footwear.

"Real cute you are, Naughty Girl," I growl in her ear as my warm breath fans across her cheek flushed from our race and the crisp wind. "It must be time for another discomfort test, hmm?"

I add emphasis with a few pats to her round ass.

She shudders and bites her plump lower lip.

My wicked chuckles follow her as we enter the lodge. I place my hand on her lower back and guide her through the great room to the deck, kept warm by heat lamps.

We stop and chat with a few friends and acquaintances, also in Verbs for the holidays. The opening of the STEELE properties attracts many of our social circle. Including those who enjoy their LEVELS memberships. A Verbier location —as suggested by Harris—is in the pipeline. We're awaiting approvals for a location atop the mountain for spectacular views to take the Mile High Club to another level....

Pride swells in my chest when I introduce My Angel as my wife to those unfamiliar with our nuptials. Some eyes appraise her while others try to hide jealousy behind syrupy smiles.

One woman I may have fucked in the distant past dares to whisper how she misses my cock when My Angel greets a friend of hers. I glare at the hussy and slip my arm around My Angel to get us the fuck out of there. Tine to join our family. Pronto.

We settle between Lydie seated with Chase and Baz next to Lola at the table laden with delicious food and steaming beverages. One by one, everyone arrives. Our hunger spurred on by the challenging run.

"So what's next on the agenda, Papa Griswold?" Leonie asks, referring to Roger as Clark Griswold from *National Lampoon's Christmas Vacation*.

Everyone laughs at the running joke, knowing Roger and his planned-down-to-the-minute activities for our time in Verbier.

"Hardy har har, Mama Griswold," he responds, not at all bothered by her teasing. "After this deluxe meal, time for a walk through town. And if you are good... we'll spend the afternoon soaking in the thermal baths at Lavey-les-Bains. *Bien?*"

"Ah, *oui, Mon Cœur!*" Leonie exclaims, clapping her hands and doing a shimmy in her chair.

"Spa Time!" Lydie laughs. "Now I can definitely get on board with that agenda item!"

The girls—including our mothers—chatter on about the benefits of the baths and the beauty products they prefer. The guys turn to talk about the sporting activities Roger has on the list. I'm all for the snowmobiling but decline the off-piste run. Priorities!

The sounds of shouts reach us from the front of the lodge. As the hullabaloo intensifies, people gather at the railings of the deck to get a better view. Whispers of a major crash and an intensive injury make me rise from my seat to get more information.

"They say she hit a patch of ice and flew off the trail headlong—"

"—only the tree stopped her from—"

"*C'est horrible!*"

"I hear she damaged her spine—"

Fuck. Me.

A shudder rips through me as memories of me flying over the embankment on my Ducati. Then the spinal injury followed by the coma bombards my mind.

"Pray she makes it—"

I shake my head to clear the fog, then continue to the entry of the lodge. A helicopter appears from the left, heading towards the medics surrounding the rescue snowmobile. Covers over the sled attached at the back obscure the injured woman. Nearby, a man gestures wildly while he speaks into his mobile. Another man comforts a woman who cries in his arms.

My body jerks at the unexpected touch of a small hand on my back. I glance over my shoulder to find My Angel watching me with empathetic eyes. I slide my arms over her shoulders and pull her close to my chest, resting my chin on the top of her head.

Eyes squeezed shut against the images; I let her rock me as she strokes my back and whispers comforting words.

Wind from the helicopter blades buffets us and blows loose snow at our feet.

"Come, my love. Let's get back inside," My Angel says as she circles my waist with one arm while her opposite hand rests on my stomach.

"Wait," I tell her, then turn to watch the helicopter lift off.

The couple hurries away—presumably to the hospital. I take My Angel's hand and rush after them, calling out to get their attention. They pause and face us.

"Excuse us. I'm Malcolm Steele and this is my wife, Starr. I'm sorry about your friend," I start as they nod. "Recently I was in an accident with extensive spinal injuries and a subsequent coma. I can give you the contact information for my lead doctor—Dr. Clint Stevens. He's the best spinal specialist in the world."

They thank me for the doctor's contact information, and we offer our prayers for the woman.

Before we return to the lodge, I sent a text message to Dr. Stevens to apprise him of the situation. He responds in moments and promises to reach out to the spinal specialist at the hospital nearby. With their permission, he can assist in the woman's case. I thank Dr. Stevens and ask him to let me know if he has any difficulties. My heart goes out to the woman. I don't want anyone to not have the best medical help possible.

"You are a good man, Malcolm."

My Angel's soft words reel my drifting mind back to the present. I attempt a smile, but my thoughts are in overdrive.

"What happened?" Baz asks as he approaches us with Roger at his side.

I fill them in, and they agree it was good of me to offer the couple Dr. Stevens' information. Since they helped my father to organize the best team in the world for me, they know the importance of getting the right doctors in place at the onset of a spinal injury.

As we rejoin the others, my mind continues to work out the situation. A thought niggles that begs me to suss it out. While we fill everyone in, my mobile vibrates with a text message: Dr. Stevens confirms he's in touch with the family and will help them.

I close my eyes to offer a silent prayer of thanks for the doctor and of healing for the woman.

Roger's intense stare meets mine when I open my eyes. *The Responsible* cocks his eyebrow questioningly. As the middle child, he's always been sensitive to his siblings, and the need to make sure we're okay resonates within him as much as it does within Baz.

I smile and incline my head.

Roger nods in understanding. Then he claps his hands for everyone's attention.

"Time to move to the next item on our New Year's Day agenda, folks. Right this way!" Roger announces with a smirk as like a tour guide, he directs us to leave the lodge.

We laugh at his antics and head to the G-Wagens for a stop at the chalets before we go to the thermal baths.

Yeah, time for some much-needed relaxation in the idyllic setting surrounded by fragrant pine trees and the snow-capped Swiss Alps that Lavey-led-Bains offers.

\* \* \*

"WHAT'S ON YOUR MIND, SON?"

Morgan, my mother, Baz, Roger, My Angel, and her parents sit with me in the study, eager to learn the reason I called a meeting the morning of New Year's Day.

At the ring of midnight, I kissed my adorable babies, then left the party to make love to my beautiful wife. Afterwards, my mind returned to the puzzle, yet to be solved. The niggle from earlier demanded I figure it out.

So while My Angel slept in a sex-induced coma, I let my mind do its thing. The pieces fell in to place little by little until the 1000-piece puzzle completed itself.

"STEELE Spine."

I allow the name of my new foundation to roll off of my tongue, pleased with the sound. My eyes make contact with each pair, staring at me quizzically.

Okay, so the puzzle—framed and hung on the wall—sits prominently in my mind but not in theirs. Yet.

"STEELE Spine is my new foundation dedicated to spinal research, technological advancement, and treatment with a division to support people who suffer from injuries and cannot afford the best medical care," I pronounce.

Then I shift on the sofa to face my father.

"Dad, you did an incredible thing when you organized the best doctors, researchers, and physical therapists from around the world to heal me. The section of the hospital you had them design a custom facility dedicated to me and to my recovery has the latest equipment and treatments. Even after the initial setup, prototypes arrived and with the team having the freedom to explore their ideas, I was able to be their tester. Hell, the trial neurostimulation therapy the medical team created was an undeniable game changer!" I tell him.

Standing, I raise my arms out to the sides and spin in a circle.

"Look at me! Who would have thought I'd ever recover? It's because of you, Dad. And all of you with your prayers and support,"—I sit and clasp My Angel's hands in mine—"Without you I wouldn't be here now. I want to pay it forward. Give others a second chance at life… at love."

She sobs as tears roll down her cheeks.

I smooth them with the pad of my thumb and tuck her into my side as I face the others.

Even their eyes shine with tears.

"Excellent idea, Malcolm," Peace says in the silence. "So many people can benefit from STEELE Spine. Case in point, the woman injured yesterday. You put her family in touch with Dr. Stevens. Once your foundation goes live, more people will have access to his team's brilliance."

My father crosses the room to pull me into a fierce hug.

"Yes, son. Your mother and I are proud of you and of the thought you put behind STEELE Spine. We will support you in every way," he says gruffly when he releases me.

Everyone adds their impressions of my foundation and volunteer their time and resources.

"I'd be happy to arrange a meeting with STEELE Foundation's team to guide the creation of STEELE Spine. Perhaps while you're in New York?" my mother asks when she hugs me. Her organizational skills and experience rise to the forefront.

I smile down at her and respond, "Thanks, Mom. You have the most knowledge of foundations. So any help you can give to me will be appreciated greatly."

She returns my smile and agrees to be my guru.

We chat some more then everyone goes about their day.

I place a hand on My Angel's elbow to stop her as she walks towards the door.

"Hey, babe, I hope you don't mind I didn't speak with you about the foundation first. I wanted to surprise you with the rest of our family," I tell her earnestly.

She wraps her arms around my waist, squeezing tight and buries her face in my chest. Her warmth seeps through my cashmere turtleneck as I pull her close. Coconut and frangipani fill my lungs as I breathe in her tantalizing fragrance.

"My love, you amaze me with your resilience, perseverance, and thoughtfulness. I sensed you had something on your mind, but I knew you would share it with me when you were ready. So, no, I'm not upset with you at all. In face the exact opposite. STEELE Spine—Strength in its Support," she says as she beams at me.

My heart thumps against my ribcage. My Angel gets me always. I should have known not knowing first wouldn't bother my free-spirited wife.

I nuzzle the tip of my nose to hers.

"Thank you, my love. And you created the slogan!" I chuckle.

She giggles and says, "I know you didn't just marry me for my pussy, Mr. Steele!"

Now my cock thumps against the zipper of my jeans...

# STARR

"Wiggle your fingers. Wiggle your toes. Allow your awareness of your surroundings to return as you lift to a comfortable sitting position slowly; eyes remain closed. Bring your palms together at heart center; repeat the sound of the Earth with me three times. Aum... Aum... Aum... Bow your head; Namaste."

"Namaste," I return as I bow to the divine in Anita.

"And cut!" The video director proclaims. "Great shots today, ladies!"

Anita finished teaching a prenatal yoga session to me for our program collaboration in her private studio at Norman Green's Elite Training Facility Paris—her husband's luxury gym in partnership with STEELE International.

Over eleven years ago, Roger met Norman in Las Vegas at a party at STEELE LV after his final KO match. He told Roger he promised his girlfriend, now wife Anita, he would stop with that fight. He was at the top of his game with no more to prove. Norman said it's better to leave on high than get carted away low.

Roger offered him the opportunity to open his chains of branded gyms globally through STEELE's Entertainment Properties Division. One for underprivileged youth and another as exclusive elite training facilities for the über-wealthy and star athletes. Anita has her eponymous full-service yoga studios in each Facility location besides the food services in both chains.

Now she includes Starr Light Fitness and Wellness locations and fitness retreats as her client handling our cafés, offering meal plan delivery service to clients, and cooking demonstrations at the retreats. Our clients rave about Anita's skills gained through her culinary training at acclaimed Le Cordon Bleu in Paris.

And after a morning of recording sessions, I can't wait to have lunch. Mini Malcolms 2.0 need sustenance!

"Well, that's it for today, Starr. You did amazing, and I'm sure our subscribers will enjoy part two of our prenatal program! You're moving well with excellent coordination and balance. How do you feel now that we finished?" Anita asks. Her chocolate velvet brown eyes study me like the doula she is for me.

I rub my babies bump and grin. Our subscribers loved what Anita and I thought would be a one-off prenatal yoga program they could stream at home. She thought of the collaboration while I was pregnant the last time to increase our viewer bases. And really, to keep me busy after Malcolm told me he needed space…

A shake of my head dispels those negative thoughts.

Then I glance at my engagement ring and wedding band as I cradle Mini Malcolms 2.0. That was in the past. We have an unimaginable present and a future filled with more happiness ahead of us. We're determined to focus on the positive.

"Fantastic! As always, your sequences flow so well. Our Zoom sessions are fine, but nothing beats time with you in person. Especially in your gorgeous studio. I love coming here," I respond, spreading my arms to encompass the room.

Anita's studio reminds me of the tranquil ones at my ashram in Rishikesh, India, where I've gone since I was a teenager. The interior's natural materials of stone, wood, and bamboo, warm ambient lighting, and bright yet sophisticated pops of color for the mats and accessories set the peaceful mood. As you enter the space, you forget we're in the still in Paris' bustling business district instantly.

"Good, since we have two more days of shooting! The preliminary footage looks great. After lunch, we'll review what the editor sent for our approval," Anita says as we leave her studio.

After the holidays, Malcolm and I decided to use Paris as our base for business in Europe. He's traveling to Germany, Spain, Italy, and Montenegro to check on his Entertainment Division's projects. I'm staying put while I partner with Anita and meet with Anton and his development team on the status of SLFW's expansion. Since I'll go on maternity leave—again—I want to get as much done as possible now.

Hence the back-to-back filming days for the yoga streaming program.

Anita and I head to the locker room for quick showers before we go upstairs to the rooftop bistro for lunch. It's clear and sunny; a perfect crisp winter's day. In the summer, the staff withdraws the retractable glass roof into its casing. Now the sun filters in through the panes.

"Ciao, *mes sœurs*! How was your filming?" Leonie greets us with double kisses and hugs. "You're as bad as I was working while pregnant with twins, Starr Steele! How does your husband feel about that? Not good, *non*? Roger drove me crazy! So I can imagine Malcolm most definitely..."

I give Leonie an extra squeeze as my heart swells with love for her calling us her sisters affectionately. And for knowing her brother-in-law so well. Who has told me to slow down or else he'll bind me to our bed until I give birth. I giggle at the thought. I could prove promising...

Over the years, along with Lola and Haley, the five of us have grown from friends to the sisters we never had and always wanted. It reminds me of Shelley's sisterhood with Lucie, the Jackson Matriarch. They met as young women in New York City and became fast friends before they married their billionaire husbands and had children who went on to consider themselves cousins. As they say, not sharing DNA doesn't keep their families from being a close-knit group. And that's how my girls and I are now.

"Well, after the night Malcolm and I had at LEVELS Paris, I needed to limber up my sore muscles and re-center my mind... that he blew!" I laugh, mimicking my head exploding.

Leonie and Anita—both members with their husbands—nod knowingly.

"Ah, yes, the post-coital yoga session will fix you every time. I need to add a class to the schedule!" Anita quips.

"*Oui!* And it'll book up fast for instant gratification!" Leonie giggles, then snorts until tears spill from her glowing amber eyes.

Anita and I join in her infectious laughter.

After the server takes our orders of mixed greens and grilled chicken or salmon, we return to more serious topics.

"So, what do you think of my latest Lola's Coterie prenatal designs?" Leonie asks. "Your boobs look amazing in this bra. It's from the collection, *non?*"

While she was pregnant with The Twins, Lola asked her to create exclusive prenatal and postnatal collections of sexy yet functional lingerie and loungewear. Leonie has been the face of the brand since its inception, thanks to Luc's introduction of the two women. *The Lion* megamodel brought her fashion credibility to the company and helped Lola to catapult it into the realms of much sought after high-end retailers.

For the last few years, Leonie's collections sell out as soon as they're put on preorder. I'm just as hooked as the others. I love every single piece!

"Thanks to you! The balconette gives my boobies an extra boost, and the front closure makes it easy to breast-feed Mini Malcolms," I respond. "Plus, Malcolm enjoys the easy access!"

Anita giggles and shakes her head while Leonie sits back smugly.

"*Voilà!* Mission accomplished," she smirks.

The rest of our conversation turns to our children and SLFW's upcoming fitness retreats. With me preggie, Anita plans to guest co-host the events with Adrienne like she did for me last time. I cannot wait to get back on the road. It's been too long since I led a retreat. They're my favorite part of being an instructor. I get to interact with people beyond my studio on Beverly Hills. It's great!

Leonie and I bid Anita goodbye after we review the yoga program film footage in her office. My sister-in-law and I head to Lola's atelier for dress up. Really for work, as I try on more of Leonie's creations for my feedback and her adjustments before the collection goes to the manufacturing stage.

Later we're having dinner with Malcolm and Roger at the three star Michelin restaurant, Kei. Mini Malcolms 2.0 demand delicious Japanese food tonight!

\* \* \*

WARM OLIVE OIL drizzles over my sun-kissed golden brown skin as I lie propped against a nest of pillows on the oversized Hermès towel beneath the trees filled with the ripe fruit. Their fragrant aroma blends with the salty air of the Aegean Sea. Nearby waves lap at the rocky shoreline in a lazy rhythm.

I stretch languorously as Malcolm's big hands massage the oil into my flesh with a sensuous touch.

He trails his long fingers along my flanks; the tips brush the side curve of my breasts, making my nipples pebble tighter. The pressure of his calloused pads form goosebumps in their wake. He skims my butt cheeks with a feather-light touch.

A brief moment for more olive oil to drip over my body.

Then Malcolm spreads his fingers wide as he drags them along the backs of my thighs. The taut muscles sigh in relief as I relax deeper into the pillow pile. With a gentle touch, he circles the erogenous zone behind my knees. Warm air from his mouth blows across the sensitive area.

I moan softly.

He chuckles wickedly.

Knuckles knead my calves and the soles of my feet to loosen the knots in the overused muscles. The unexpected pain makes me groan. But Malcolm's lips pressed to my heel, followed by the tip of his tongue gliding up the middle of my foot to suck on my big toe sends a shudder through me.

"Mmm... mmm... Malcolm," I murmur, eyes closed in carnal pleasure.

The skin-on-skin connection as he covers my back with his front cocoons me while his hands glide along my arms to the tips of my fingers. More oil coats my skin as he massages the tight muscles of my triceps. Then he planks over me as he laces his fingers with mine and rubs his nose along the side of my neck.

I nearly climax.

"Feel better now, My Angel?" Malcolm rumbles against the shell of my ear.

His massive dick thumps my ass as though seeking entry.

"Even better if you'd make love to me," I purr, turning my head to capture his full lips with mine.

No further invitation needed, Malcolm pours olive oil on to his thick length. I watch over my shoulder impatiently as he rubs it in from root to tip, slowly. His corded forearms flex as his eight-pack abs tighten. The veins on his cock snake around his girth as pre-cum mingles with the fragrant oil. His Prince Albert piercing jewelry balls glint in the sunlight.

"Like what you see, My Angel?" Malcolm asks gruffly.

I lick my lips and nod.

"Such an enticing sight. Help me up, I want to taste you," I respond.

A predatory gleam fills Malcolm's platinum gray eyes as he lifts me into a kneeling position before him. He stands—feet wide apart, muscular thighs flexed, abs taut—ready for me to engulf his turgid dick in my warm, wet mouth.

I brace my hands on his thick thighs and part my lips when he taps the mushroom tip to them. They wrap around his girth as I bring my nose closer to his groin. My gag reflex flutters, but I breathe through my nose and take him deeper down my throat. When his pubic hair brushes my nose, I hum in carnal satisfaction at the feel of every ridge, every vein, and every inch of him.

"Awww…. Fuuuck… Feel… so… good…" Malcolm groans.

His dick lies heavy on my tongue as I roll it around, then withdraw to the tip. I set a steady pace as my head bobs, determined to give him absolute erotic pleasure. It's his turn for bliss. I peek up at him through my lashes when my lips touch his groin again.

Our eyes meet, and Malcolm sucks in a jagged breath.

When I swallow and hum around his girth, his eyes roll back in rhapsody. Unable to relinquish control for long, his firm hand dives into the loose curls, tumbling down my back to guide my pace for his satisfaction. His hips snap as his release draws near, precipitated by the thickening of his impossibly hard dick.

"Fuuuck, Starr!!!" Malcolm's roar punches the balmy air.

A torrent of his hot, salty seed spews down my throat as he grips me by the back of my head to his groin. His massive dick pulses on my tongue with each jet of cum. I swallow every. Single. Drop.

With a feral groan, Malcolm squats before me and cups my flushed face. Wild eyes stare into mine, then he covers my mouth in a savage kiss. His tongue pushes past my teeth and sweeps every corner of my mouth to taste and to conquer. He ends the possessive kiss with nips and licks. Then he sucks his way down my throat and breastbone, leaving his mark.

My back bows when he pulls a peaked nipple into his mouth and worries the sensitive tip with his teeth. He suckles and swallows the milk with zeal as he moans. Two thick fingers tease my swollen clit.

An orgasm builds at the base of my spine. I can already tell it's going to be mind-blowing.

When he drives his fingers deep inside of my pussy, my climax crests, and I ride his digits to the end like the surfers on the Aegean Sea. My screams of passion could shake the olive trees to their roots. Then middle Earth itself as they reach a fevered pitch from the brutal thrust of Malcolm's ginormous dick into my throbbing pussy.

"Uh. Uh. Uh. Uh," I cry out in wild abandon as our flesh smacks together.

"Cum for me, woman. Cum for me now!" Malcolm demands fervently.

He bites my shoulder as he fills me with his seed again. The hot cum drips down my sticky thighs.

Triggered by his release—with a howl—I come undone for my man.

We collapse in a tangle of arms and legs on the blanket, sweaty and panting. Once our labored breathing returns to normal, Malcolm lifts me in his arms effortlessly. He strides through the orchard to the water's edge.

The sparking sea greets us with its cool and refreshing temperature. Sea gulls cry out in the distance—the only witnesses to our skinny dipping. Even so, Malcolm angles my naked body towards his chest until I'm neck deep in the turquoise water. Then he turns me to face out—away from the Greek private island's shoreline.

He surprised me with a trip here for Valentine's Day after we finished our business in Europe. It coincides with our six-month wedding anniversary. I was beyond thrilled.

The secluded, fifteen-acre island features a four-bedroom, six-bath main house, an open-plan beach house, a private church on one end and a Venetian watchtower on the other, a boathouse with piers, and a staff house. The fertile land allows more than just olive trees.

Pistachio trees, a variety of fruit trees including pomegranates, apricots, peaches, almonds, plums, and figs offer tasty morsels. Sturdy pine and cypress trees around the perimeter of the island, as well as hundreds of ornamental bushes of oleanders, bougainvillea, hibiscus, and geraniums add to its unspoiled beauty.

A sated smile spreads across my face as I tip my head back to rest against his chest. The sun blankets us with its warmth. And Malcolm envelopes me with his powerful embrace.

"Happy Valentine's Day, my love," I whisper as our eyes meet.

His sparkle with joy as he brushes his lips on mine and murmurs, "Happy Valentine's Day, My Angel. I love you so much."

# MALCOLM

"Listen, take my advice… It's best to leave the women to their activities than to involve yourself in them. And before you ask, no, they won't appreciate your 'help' in any way whatsoever. As the longest married of us, trust me on this one, bro."

"Amen, brother. I couldn't agree more. So newlywed, heed the knowledge of the more experienced of us. Stay out of their way."

"Thank fuck I don't have to worry about this crap…"

My brothers and I chuckle at Harris' response to Baz's advice seconded by Roger on me leaving My Angel and her sisters to their plans for her move into my penthouse at The STEELE Tower. We arrived from Greece two days ago to boxes of her belongings in one of the guest suites. Clothes, shoes, handbags, makeup, the whole kit and caboodle. Not to mention new items for Selina and Elio and Mini Malcolms 2.0.

Instead of freaking out at the vast amount of boxes and

the need to put everything in their places, my laid-back wife merely shrugged. Then she called Lola, Leonie, and Haley to give her a hand. They were more than willing to help her. Even my mother and Sun offered to organize the nursery. Leonie reconfigured Selina and Elio's nursery into one for our new twins and converted two guest suites into rooms for our one year olds. Of course she impressed us with her designs—all shades of pinks and cream. My Angel's squeals of delight scared the shit out of me.

We decided to make New York City our primary residence and waited until we arrived here for My Angel to meet with Lola's OB-GYN—Dr. Oscar Rice—for Mini Malcolms 2.0's sex scan. I was more nervous than My Angel. When the doctor announced two girls, it shocked me speechless. Four women at once? Talk about karma…

She must have sensed my surprise because My Angel squeezed my hand and graced me with the most beatific smile. My heart stuttered in my chest. Then tears filled my eyes when Doctor Rice handed the images from the scan to me.

I made a silent vow to never let a man near my three girls until they were forty years old. Take that karma!

Baz also warned me I'd want to rip Dr. Rice's eyes out when he examined My Angel. And boy, was he right. I could barely contain myself. Meanwhile, she was completely blasé about his head between her spread thighs, with his eyes on my pussy. You'd think we were in the Cellar at LEVELS New York and I strapped her to a bench and not an examination table.

So I sit back and clink bottles with each of my brothers

as we hang out on the expansive terrace of my penthouse, while My Angel and her sisters handle things.

The spectacular unobstructed view encompasses Central Park to the north, the Hudson River to the west, the East River opposite. The STEELE Tower's remarkable gray-tinted glass mixed-use skyscraper on Fifth Avenue and Fifty-seventh Street stands in the heart of Billionaires' Row. It serves as our family's residences on the fiftieth through fifty-seventh floors.

My parents live in their duplex penthouse on the fifty-seventh and fifty-sixth floors. Baz and Lola are below in their duplex. The rest of us have floor-through penthouses with mine on fifty-three. Our private family elevator connects our residences to STEELE International's executive floor on twenty-nine.

Our headquarters are on the nineteenth through twenty-ninth floors. The rest of The Tower has commercial and retail spaces and residential properties.

"And the same thing applies when Starr gets out to Steele Southampton. Let her run the show. Give her control or you'll be sorry..." Baz continues with his sage advice.

Again Roger nods and takes a sip of his beer.

"Exactly. When I asked Leonie if she wanted to make changes to our mansion, she was all no, no. The moment she walked in the door, she went on and on about how this would look better like that and that would look better there," Roger shakes his head. "Thanks to Baz's advice, I gave her carte blanche to do as she wished. In the end, all was right in our world. Yup."

"Thank you, oh wise ones," Harris quips.

At the same time, Baz, Roger, and I answer.

"Oh, just you wait and see, Harris!"

"Give it time, bro!"

"You say that now. Just you wait and see. When you least expect it… Whammo!"

He grunts and finishes his beer with a cocky smirk.

I chuckle to myself. We'll see.

\* \* \*

"So, Mr. Steele, we would be grateful for the opportunity to handle STEELE Spine for you. We hope you will allow us the opportunity to bring your extraordinary vision to life and to aid those who can most benefit from the medical care and support STEELE Spine offers."

I turn to my mother to gauge her opinion on this team's ability to manage my new foundation.

We're in the conference room of my offices at STEELE International, Inc. to meet with potential teams to determine the best fit. With my duties at the company, I need the help of capable people to run the foundation. I will remain hands on, but the day-to-day operations will require a dedicated staff.

My mother arranged interviews with several people after she and I met with STEELE Foundation's leaders the other day. They offered sound advice and put us in touch with recruiters who have excellent candidates for the various positions we require. After days of meetings, we've narrowed the finalists to three.

With an imperceptible nod of her head, my mother lets me know the ones before us impress her. I give in to her experience with foundation staff and tell them we'll be in touch shortly. Miles Crawford—my assistant—escorts them to the elevator after we shake hands.

"I believe they will make a good fit for your needs, Malcolm, sweetheart," my mother says when the doors to my conference room close.

"I agree. They appear well informed and have the experience we seek. Do you prefer them over the other two?" I ask.

We spend some time reviewing the three dossiers before we break for lunch. My mom—just like My Angel—doesn't need fancy things, although they enjoy them. So we order delivery from the corner deli. As we nosh on sandwiches and potato chips, we decide to hire the last team.

I'll ask Miles to send them the offer letters. Just in case, we hold the first team on deck should our offer fall through. When Miles leaves us, my mother turns to me.

"Malcolm, I am so proud of you, sweetheart. To take a setback and turn it into an opportunity to help others is commendable," she says, then flicks her shoulders. "Your father and I raised you right!"

We laugh.

But I know she's correct. Never did she allow her children to behave like spoiled, rich kids. We interned at our family's business each summer and during school breaks to learn from the ground up. She and our father made sure we deserved the titles and responsibilities we have now.

And both being philanthropists, they encouraged us to give back, too.

I'm the first to establish a foundation outside of STEELE Foundation. Even though each of us has causes we support, SF remains the top priority. Now STEELE Spine. And I'm excited to make a difference in others' lives who experience injuries similar to mine.

"Yes, Mom. You certainly did. And then some," I grin. "Now I have another huge ask of you."

She leans forward with inquisitive dark brown eyes and an arched eyebrow.

"I want to host a fundraising gala at the end of September weeks after your Labor Day event for STEELE Foundation. So no conflict with the dates. I'd love for you to organize the Spine gala, too. Pretty please with sugar on top?" I ask like I did as a kid when I knew I was pushing it with my parents.

Shelley sits back and tilts her head as she considers my request.

Our mother is an exceptional party planner, and if anyone can juggle two major events within weeks of each other, she can. Her two assistants and the vendors she uses ease the burdens for her. After a few minutes, she reaches for her mobile.

"Tabitha, kindly come to Malcolm's offices with Sharon. We have another fundraising gala to plan," Shelley says as she eyes me.

It won't take long for her assistants to arrive. They're upstairs in her home office. If one considers three generously sized rooms an office. An anteroom for two assistants' desks, a sitting area, and a bathroom, a conference room, and her inner sanctum with en suite bathroom comprise Shelley's version of a home office. She runs her private activities from there and her foundation work from that office on the executive floor of the STEELE International corporate office.

"Thanks so much, Mom," I say as I kiss her cheek.

"Well, you know I'll do anything for my babies," she responds with a grin. "Now we get down to business."

I throw my head back and laugh at her abrupt change from motherly to sergeant.

Once her assistants arrive, we discuss my vision and the timeline. My mother thinks a masquerade theme will make a night to generate donations more fun than the typical dinner dance event. Similar to her choice of a Labor Day White Party in Southampton Village culminating in a fireworks display to attract guests. They confirm the gala will meet my end of September date even with only five months to plan. We'll have it at STEELE42 one of our award-winning entertainment venues. It specializes in weddings, parties, and galas for society's best both in the United States and abroad.

I thank my new gala coordinators. Then my mother and I take my car to the West 30$^{th}$ Street Heliport to fly out to our Hamptons' beach compound. My Angel and her sisters are moving her in to my mansion and she's checking on SLFW Resorts at STEELE Southampton Village's progress. My father and her parents are there too. I'm eager to arrive so I can help—if she lets me. Otherwise, I'll give Nanny Patience the day off and spend Daddy

Time with my babies. Well, toddlers since they're one-year-old.

Tomorrow we're celebrating Selina and Elio's birthday. The rest of the family flies in tonight for the festivities. I still can't believe how much Mini Malcolms 1.0 have grown. I used to scoff at parents bemoaning time flying. Now, I understand completely. All the more reason for Daddy Time.

"VERY GOOD, Selina. You're doing well, Elio."

They may do well, but I sure as hell feel sick to my stomach despite their swimming instructors' words of encouragement.

I'm sitting on the bench with a white-knuckle grip on the edge as I watch Mini Malcolms 1.0 during their first lesson at the club's pool. Roger *The Responsible* is alert, but at ease while Rodolphe and Gaspard have their lesson with the two-year-olds. Other parents sit and chat all nonchalant while I can't keep my eyes off of my babies.

And the women can't keep their eyes off of my brother and me. Cue the giant eye roll.

Mothers or nannies, married or single, stare at us openly while they whisper amongst themselves. The sight of two of the STEELE Quaternity—in swim trunks and t-shirts no less—proves too much for the gawkers. When we entered the indoor pool area, silence descended. Then a buzz rose. After a nod in greeting, Roger and I took seats and focused on our kids.

Who the fuck has time to leer and gossip when your

babies are in water deeper than their height?! Give me a break. I have no time.

"*Papa! Papa! Regarde moi!*" Gaspard calls out when he spies Roger.

He beams as he strides to the edge.

"*Excellent travail, Gaspard!*" He says as he claps proudly. "*Et toi aussi, Rodolphe!*"

Although identical twins, we can tell them apart by their personalities. Rodolphe has the seriousness of his father, while Gaspard has the playful spirit of his mother. One's eyes watch you with intensity while the others shine with mirth. And we adore them equally!

Frantic splashing draws my attention from my brother and my nephews.

Elio! Fuck!

I run and jump in to the pool as he flounders between two instructors. His head goes under a second time just as I snatch him by the waist. I glare at the two dummies with my son clutched to my chest.

"What the—"

"Malcolm!"

I pivot with a scowl to face Roger, who's standing at the edge of the pool. He shakes his head.

"That's normal. No need to worry," he says calmly, knowing I'm about to go ballistic. "Elio is fine. The Twins behaved the same during their first lessons. Let them finish."

Not placated, I glance around to find Selina. She's watching me from the arms of another instructor. When she waves her little hand and flashes a two-tooth smile at me, my anger subsides. Still carrying her brother, I wade to her and pull her into my arms. I plant kisses on their chubby, golden cheeks and sigh in relief.

My babies are safe and sound.

Thank fuck!

I apologize to the instructors for disrupting the lessons and return Selina and Elio to them, then climb out of the pool.

Roger claps me on the shoulder and smirks.

"You're gonna have gray hair to match your eyes if you stress out like this all the time," he teases.

I grab the wet t-shirt at the back of my neck and yank it off. My arm muscles and my abs flex from the movement. The sound of a gasp makes my eyes jerk in that direction. A brunette gapes at me as her gaze travels from my head to my toes, pausing at my crotch where the wet swim trunks cling to my ample package. The piercing stands out in bas-relief.

Oh, give me a damn break. They must starve these women of a good fuck. I'm off the market. So good luck with that...

Roger snickers as we take our seats again.

I can feel their gazes burning my back as they take in my tattoo. But I ignore them and return to my vigil. I have more important matters to attend to than these horny housewives.

* * *

"We closed on the Sutton Place duplex in Lola's building. The proximity to the East River gives us the water view we love. It's a sunny, spacious penthouse in a magnificent, Rosario Candela designed building. Leonie agreed to handle the redesign, including a nursery and two bedrooms for Selina and Elio," Sun says as we eat birthday cake in the living room of my parents' beach house.

"Yes, and the seven-block drive across Fifty-seventh Street from Sutton Place to Fifth Avenue makes for a quick trip to you at The STEELE Tower. We'll be able to take our grandchildren to the zoo in Central Park easily," Peace adds.

Since My Angel and I will live here mostly, her parents decided to become bicoastal. They arranged to work out of their offices in Knight & Knight LLP New York. Their search for a residence took more time given they wanted a penthouse on Sutton Place and those properties come on market rarely.

However, Lola learned of one in her building where she maintains her penthouse, even though she and Baz live in The STEELE Tower. Her realtor keeps her informed of other opportunities in case Lola wants to expand. This residence is on the top two floors and has been owned by one family since the developer erected the building.

"*Oui!* And don't forget Southampton Village. I cannot wait to get started!" Leonie gushes.

"Of course! It was a stroke of luck the family next to the Steele compound moved to Florida and had to sell quickly. Their beachfront property has just the right sized mansion and a caretaker's cottage on it. So our favorite interior designer will handle the gut rehab. Peace and I took a suite at STEELE Southampton for the season or until our renovation completes," Sun tells us.

My Angel leans up from where she's nestled against my side, with Elio on her lap and Selina on mine.

"Mom, you can stay with us. We have plenty of guest suites in our home. Right, Malcolm?" She asks as she glances over at me.

I nod and add, "Certainly. No need for you to stay at the bed-and-breakfast."

Peace shakes his head and presses his palms together at his heart center with a bow.

"Thank you for the offer. But Sun and I don't want to intrude on your new little family. We're fine with our accommodations," he replies.

"Know that you are always welcome," I say as I bow to the light in him.

My father raises his flute of Champagne for a toast.

"Here's to our family being together with East Coast and West Coast homes!" He exclaims as he nods at Peace.

The patriarchs have become friends along with Guy. We're thankful for the growth of our family clan.

# MALCOLM

"*Ugh! This is when I always get the least attractive. My belly looks like a giant beach ball. My legs tingle and my back aches. Everything is just so damn uncomfortable! On top of that, I'm tired again. And stop looking at me like that, Malcolm Steele! Argh!*"

Okay, so Roger and Baz warned me about the third trimester. But damn... My Angel is not having it. At. All.

She refused the nightly massage I give her. She pretty much told me to buzz off and dozed off to sleep curled in a fetal position. When I spooned behind her, she stiffened, then relaxed when I didn't make any sexual advances. Which surprised me since she's been insatiable from the start of our pregnancy.

But hey, I'll take it, especially since I missed being there for her with Mini Malcolms 1.0.

After consulting with my brothers, they informed me My Angel and I are almost overdue for our babymoon.

Roger took Leonie to Lucien's Villa die Fiori in Capri at nineteen weeks for seven days, then bought it for her. At twenty-six weeks, Baz surprised Lola with a fourteen-day trip to Bougainvillea Cay he bought for her.

So I knew my game plan: take My Angel some place warm and secluded on the East Coast easily accessible to major hospitals just in case. She can relax without thinking bad about her body changes and the stress of moving, expanding SLFW, raising Selina and Elio, being a new wife, none of the headaches.

I want to give her joy. See her dazzling smile on her gorgeous face. She'll always be a beauty to me!

Now My Angel rests her head on my shoulder as we fly on our Gulfstream G650 bound for STEELE Little Palm Island off the Florida Keys. Within fifteen minutes of take-off, she asked me to join her in the bedroom.

At first I thought she meant for some Mile High action, but she slipped out of her maxi dress and under the covers. As enticing as her round ass in a black lace thong and her grip-worthy hips appeared bent over the bed, I squashed my lascivious thoughts and held her in my arms. Blue balls be damned...

She slept soundly, finally at ease.

I hate to wake her, but we land in ten minutes. She's bound to need to use the restroom and freshen up before we deplane for the brief ride on the resort's water shuttle. I didn't tell her about our destination, only to dress comfortably. I asked Lola and Leonie to shop for her bikinis, sundresses, and sandals. She won't need much else.

"Babe, time to wake up," I murmur as I stroke her soft cheek.

After a bit of coaxing, My Angel wakes and readies herself. When she sits beside me and peeps out the window, a smile spreads across her face.

"The Florida Keys?" She asks.

Of course, being a world traveler, she'd recognize the islands. I nod and she shimmies in her seat.

When we arrive at the resort and spa, the driver takes us to the only beachfront three-bedroom villa on the opposite end of the island to the main property. There's the reception, bar, and restaurant pavilion; close to it is the spa facilities in another pavilion; a pool with a restaurant and a bar next to the general beach. Ten one- and two-bedroom bungalows stand along the shoreline. STEELE Little Palm Island is a boutique property that caters to the affluent who don't have private islands of their own but want the experience.

As the golf cart travels along the paths, My Angel chats with him about the activities and the spa. He's as enthralled by her as me.

I wrap my arm around her shoulder and hold her hand, content to bask in her glory. I won't begrudge him his five minutes. Especially when My Angel glances up at me and kisses my lips. Her sorrel brown eyes dance.

Our single-story villa sits on its private beach with an infinity edge pool, chaise lounges, and a hammock. Palm trees and fragrant flowering shrubs hide it from the rest of the guests. A butler, chef, and a maid greet us. The butler gives us a tour while the maid unpacks our bags and the chef plates our lunch of fresh grilled seafood and vegetables.

By the time we step on to the deck, My Angel seems one hundred percent better. I send a silent prayer of thanks for my sage brothers.

"Oh, Malcolm! This is fantastic! I can't believe you had the girls shop for me! This bandeau bikini is fierce. I don't seem like such a blimp, only sexy!" She exclaims.

My eyes roam over her body. Bouncy silky curls cascading down her back. Lush tits still heavy from breastfeeding and to prepare for Mini Malcolms 2.0. Long, toned legs ending with fire-engine red toenails. My Angel looks good!

While I take in my fill of her beauty, she chatters on about the spa amenities, going for a swim, tonight's salsa dance party, and yoga on the beach in the morning. I grin and nod, equally enthused. We have an entire week to do whatever her heart desires. And I will be sure to fulfill each and every one of them—to the max.

\* \* \*

"Ssssss... Mmmm mmmm... Fuck..."

Slowly, my senses dawn. What I thought was a dream becomes my reality. Hooded eyes open to reveal My Angel astride me, lowering her hot, wet pussy onto my morning wood. Her voluptuous curves steal my breath. Her head thrown back, eyes squeezed shut, mouth slack.

Damn.

I reach for her hips to guide her down my engorged shaft. Each inch draws another hiss from my parted lips.

My Angel feels so damn good…

This is the second morning I've awoken to her taking advantage of my sleeping form but erect cock. And she'll get no complaints from me. No ma'am!

Over the days we've been on our babymoon, My Angel has returned to her usual carefree self. The shadows beneath her sorrel brown eyes have disappeared. The raised shoulders—hunched from stress—lowered after day three. Instead of frowning at the full-length mirror in the bathroom, she grins at it and takes her daily pregnancy selfie. Her prenatal glow adds to her innate beauty.

We've done the entire list of her desires and have a day to spare. She left the agenda blank. But I guess making love to her husband tops the list.

Yessss!!!

"Oh, Malcolm… right there…" My Angel moans as I swivel my hips.

We continue our slow erotic dance melded as one until she can take no more orgasms and I can no longer hold back my release. With one last upward thrust as I hold her still, I erupt deep inside of her greedy pussy. Then pull a sated My Angel into my arms.

THE BRILLIANT SUN glints off of the turquoise waters of the Straits of Florida as the waves lap onto the white sand beach before us. We finished a yoga session and took a dip in the warm water before our couples' massage. The masseuses just set up our tables when we arrived on the deck from a shower—and a steamy romp.

I reach over and skim my fingertips along My Angel's arm. She turns her head and smiles at me as she twines our fingers.

"Hey, baby," she murmurs.

"Hey, My Angel," I respond as I kiss her knuckles. "How do you and my babies feel? You're not uncomfortable, right?"

She yawns, then glances at me sheepishly.

"I take that as your super comfy, yes?" I chuckle.

"Yes, indeed. So good and so serene," she giggles. "This table fits around my babies bump perfectly."

When I made the appointment, the spa manager assure me they could accommodate a pregnant woman's shape and offer a prenatal massage approved by OB-GYNs. I scheduled more treatments from a body scrub to a facial and even a scalp massage to pamper my wife. So today is just the beginning.

"Good. You have a whole lineup of treatments over the next few days. So get ready for some major indulgences," I tell her.

My Angel nods and sighs as her eyes drift closed.

Absolutely serene. Mission accomplished.

"This is just what I needed! Thank you, my love!"

My Angel's excited peals of laughter make my heart soar. Her dewy, sun-kissed face beams as our bodies grind to the rhythms of the bongos, horns, and guitars blended with the sultry vocals of the live Calypso band.

When she told me she wanted to dance to the Afro-Caribbean music, I called in a favor for the most popular group in Trinidad to fly up and play for us. The resort staff decorated our private beach with bamboo torches, fragrant flowers, a candlelit table set for a delicious seafood dinner, and a stage. It's our last night in paradise, and I want to make it more than memorable.

So I told My Angel to glam it up for the grown and sexy. And boy, did she deliver in spades.

Luxuriant curly hair caught up in a messy bun lengthens her neck where my evening collar, along with her full wedding jewelry on her hand, sparkle in the torchlight. Makeup-free with pouty glossed lips begging to wrap around my more than willing cock. A gold, strapless tube mini dress clings to every one of her bountiful curves with her babies bump on display proudly. So excited by the music, she kicked off her gold strappy sandals to dance in the sand barefoot. My Angel is a stunning vision who rivals any woman on the planet—far from how unattractive she bemoaned before our babymoon.

I'm one lucky man.

"You're welcome, babe. I only want to see you smile, not upset with yourself. Promise?" I ask with a cocked eyebrow.

My Angel lifts her arms around my neck and gyrates her plump ass against the tops of my thighs. I bend my knees to press my hardened cock to the cleft of her ass cheeks and match her erotic rhythm. We continue to sway as we lose ourselves in the other.

Between sets, the singers invite My Angel to the mic. She joins them for an impromptu serenade that makes me want to snatch her from the stage and ravage her. Instead, a cocky smirk spreads across my face.

Yeah, that's my Hot Mama!

# STARR

"Well, I am always one for business before pleasure. *Da, khlopushka?*"

Anton smirks at Adrienne, then chuckles wickedly when she sputters her sip of Château Lafite Rothschild Pauillac. He wipes the errant droplets of wine from her lips with his thumb, sucks the digit into his mouth, and licks his lips, never taking his glacial blue eyes from her green feline ones.

The seductive gesture darkens Adrienne's complexion from a buttery pecan to a rosy pink from her hairline to her décolletage. She gapes at Anton, then snaps her lips together as she glares at him while dabbing the rest of the wine with her linen napkin.

"*Udovol'stviye sub"yektivno, da?*" She replies in Russian fluently before translating for me. *"Pleasure is subjective, yes. It appears as though Anton forgets his table manners…"*

Malcolm covers his chuckle with a sip of his wine as his eyes flit between the pair.

Anton throws his head back and laughs uproariously.

"*Mne nravitsya, kogda ty srazhayesh'sya so mnoy, khlopushka,*" he says, then leans to her ear and continues in a whisper. "*YA delayu menya tverdym, kak skala.*"

Malcolm chokes on his wine and puts his glass down on the table with a clatter. His eyes bulge, and he speaks something to Anton in Russian.

"My apologies, Starr, I meant no offense to you," he tells me with contriteness. "You, *khlopushka*, know how true my statement is, *da?*"

The last question he smirks at Adrienne, and she shakes her head with pursed lips.

"I'm sure whatever you two are up to makes me no never mind! You can settle the matter later in one of the rooms in the Cellar," I respond, giggling.

Adrienne turns crimson, and Anton guffaws again. Other patrons glance in our direction.

The four of us came to LEVELS New York for dinner at LEVELS 4 Restaurant—business—and for a bit of pleasure later. Even after experiencing the other club locations, the flagship ranks as my favorite still.

Situated in Manhattan's Meatpacking District, Malcolm told me he and Lucien chose the historic location as a play on the area's name. Put a club where men pack their meat into willing women and willing men allow women to pack them with their toys. The theme for the lobby is minimal and industrial. The fixtures and furniture that appear well worn are high-end, modern replicas used to add authenticity without the grime of old pieces.

On the third floor, the bar bustles as usual with the

crème de la crème of society. They hobnob with top-shelf drinks. Seating ranges from the leather and black metal stools at the long, reclaimed-wood-covered bar to the dozen high-top tables styled to match. The bar along the right wall features a floor-to-ceiling mirrored wall of shelves of only the best spirits and wines—most are from the Jackson labels. The bartenders serve signature cocktails. Tables on the left complete the layout of the open-plan room. A path between the two areas leads to the restaurant's maître d' station.

Patrons eat delicious meals prepared by chefs trained by Lucien. The menu offers the expected fare typical of Continental cuisine of pastas, meat, and steaks with favorable sauces. *The Sexy Chef* complements the usual dishes with appealing specials that change daily to keep the choices fresh and habitual guests from getting bored.

Plus the client care is impeccable. Model-perfect and well-groomed servers wear spotless, all-black uniforms of a long-sleeved shirt, pants, butcher apron, and shiny Oxford shoes or heels—the de rigueur fashion for LEVELS employees. They provide top-notch professionalism and knowledge of the dishes and wine selections.

Just as with the lobby and the bar, the décor stays true to the original use of the warehouse. Clean lines and antique pieces for the decor: floor-to-ceiling mullion windows allow natural light to filter through to the room during the day, now dimly lit for dinner; light fixtures hang from the ceiling where the dark metal duct work and copper pipes are visible; exposed brick walls; the floor poured concrete; the well-heeled patrons sit on antique leather chairs at wooden tables. The guys really did a great job with their enterprise. Few can pull off and maintain a high-end, respectable establishment, especially one that's a combo BDSM/dance club with a restaurant.

I shake my head and take a bite of my Steak Frites. Delicious, I moan to myself as the succulent meat melts in my mouth.

"Yes, Anton, keep your sexcapades to the other levels and away from my wife's ears," Malcolm rumbles as he spears an asparagus with his fork.

Adrienne cocks her head to dare Anton to respond, then huffs when he winks at her.

I rub Malcolm's muscular thigh beneath the table to soothe my caveman and brush my lips against his ear.

"As long as we keep ours in the Cellar… Sir," I purr, so only he can hear me.

He turns to me with platinum gray eyes darkened to coal by lust and a wicked smirk.

He leans over to bring his full lips against my ear and murmurs, "That I promise, Little One."

My body quivers as his warm breath fans across my cheek. Malcolm never ceases to arouse me, even with a simple vow of pleasure. I trail my fingernail along the growing length of his dick, then tug a ball on his piercing. His dick jumps as he groans softly.

"Naughty Girl," he admonishes me as his sizable hand covers mine.

"Business first, remember?" Anton smirks pointedly.

Malcolm inclines his head in acknowledgement and says, "Touché, my friend."

"Well then, may I have your attention?" I ask, then continue when everyone nods. "Adrienne, you have been my best friend since Stanford B-School and my CMO and general manager of Starr Light Fitness & Wellness Beverly Hills for nine years. From the beginning when SLFW was my dream to the expansion with the international retreats and the resorts you never failed to stand by my side and make SLFW flourish."

I pause to dab the tears in my eyes—damn hormones.

Malcolm rubs my back and kisses my cheek.

"Starr, do not tell me something is wrong with you!" Adrienne exclaims as she reaches for my hand across the table.

I shake my head and clear my throat.

"Oh no, I'm fine! Ignore the hormonal waterworks," I laugh, squeezing her hand. "With Selina and Elio and now Mini Malcolms 2.0 on the way plus more expansion plans for SLFW, I realize I cannot go on as the CEO alone."

I raise my glass of iced lemon ginger tea and continue, "So this decision was a straightforward decision. Adrienne, I would like to offer you a partnership and the position of co-CEO!"

She gasps while Malcolm and Anton clap, then raise their wine glasses in a toast.

"You deserve it, Adrienne!"

"Congratulations, *khlopushka*!"

After a few moments, I quiet them down and raise my eyebrow at a silent Adrienne who sits back staring at me.

"Do you accept?" I ask, hoping she answers in the affirmative. "I mean, just don't leave a preggie lady hanging, no pressure!"

She jumps up and gives me a hug as she agrees wholeheartedly. Servers appear with chilled bottles of Krug Clos d'Ambonnay Champagne and a variety of decadent desserts.

"We'll drink for you, Starr!" Anton teases.

Adrienne adds, "We know it's your favorite bubbly, but oh well, partner!"

"Awww... Don't tease My Angel. Although I must say you are missing out, babe!" Malcolm chuckles.

I laugh and sip my tea, still in a pretty crystal glass.

"And... since I'm based in Southampton Village, you can head the Western Division and I'll head the Eastern Division. Malcolm and I will still be bicoastal. But this way I won't have to travel as much—especially with a brood of four babies! Sounds good to you, Adrienne?" I ask.

She grins and nods.

"Absolutely! It makes the most sense. What about Márcia?" She asks.

Márcia Souza—my administrative assistant and a yoga substitute teacher—acts as another integral part of SLFW. I spoke with her earlier today, and she agreed to move to the Hamptons wanting a change in scenery. She told me as long as she's near the water, she's fine. Since she grew up in Rio de Janeiro, then moved to LA, she prefers to be close to the ocean like me.

She's a Brazilian petite spitfire who says the crazy New York City streets won't frighten her since she's the Queen of Capoeira. I laughed and told her she won't have to worry about that out on the Island!

I recall my conversation with her to the others, and they agree she can handle herself with her defensive moves. Márcia even impressed Borya *The War Defende*r MMA champion.

We spend the rest of the time chatting and enjoying one another as we indulge in the tasty morsels and sip Champagne—well, and tea. The boys discuss the merits of various martial arts while Adrienne and I talk about an upcoming retreat in Marbella she's leading with Anita.

I have to admit I'm a tad bit jealous of them enjoying the beauty of Spain's Costa del Sol. Adrienne promises to send photos and videos to make me feel as though I'm with them and the clients. Then I promise her I'll back as soon as Mini Malcolms 2.0 can travel internationally!

So engrossed in our conversation, we startle when Malcolm and Anton rise from the table. We glance up at the men towering over us.

They have determined expressions on their handsome faces. Fierce, hooded eyes stare down at their prey as they place hands on our chairs.

Adrienne and I turn to each other and giggle as they help us rise. Then we shiver when the Alpha Doms murmur their vows of carnal pleasure in our ears.

The night proves full of vows to keep…

"You look divine tied to my cross, Little One. All trussed up and ready for your Dom to use you well…"

After we left the restaurant, we walked through Peepshow and down the stairs to the double doors of the Cellar.

Each time I enter the BDSM dungeon, I'm awed by the expansive, grand hall, austere in design. A multi-beamed high ceiling; cobblestone floors; brick walls; lighting that resembles flickering torches in brackets on the walls and in metal stands scattered around the room; an assortment of what looks like Medieval torture devices placed in clusters.

My gaze bounced from one area to another. An older man in one of the several hanging bondage stockades, his head thrown back in pure ecstasy. His engorged dick eagerly sucked by a younger man on his knees. A blindfolded woman in a swing, her thighs glistening with her pussy juices, and stretched wide to accommodate the large man standing between them, aligning her core to his massive cock. Several men and women attached to hooks hanging from the ceiling in varied positions, being whipped by Doms and Dommes with canes, floggers, and paddles extending from their hands. Still others led naked subs by leashes while they crawled on their hands and knees to one of the partitioned rooms for a bit of privacy. Here and there voyeurs stood watching, mesmerized by the decadent sexual activities.

Adrienne and Anton stopped at the bar for mocktails while Malcolm guided me towards the back.

We're in one of the Cellar's alcoves separated from the main hall by heavy blood-red velvet curtains held by metal links suspended from the ceiling. Within each alcove, a multitude of BDSM toys and equipment offer various levels of pleasure and pain. Malcolm chose an alcove with my favorite piece—the St. Andrew's Cross.

The standing wooden cross has red, suede-lined leather cuffs on the four corners for wrists and ankles dominates the area; a leather bench is along the stone wall; an antique wooden chest sits beside the bench; various whips, crops, and a few paddles hang from hooks. Some paddles are smooth wood, while others have holes or studs on their surfaces. The sizes vary from as large as a cricket bat to as small as an oven mitt.

A glance over my shoulder reveals My Alpha Dom chose a flogger with a woven leather shaft and multiple soft leather tails ending in tiny knots. I shudder and flex my pussy walls in anticipation of its erotic bite on my heated skin. My head drops with a breathy moan as my mind creates visuals of what's to come.

"Tell me your safewords, Little One."

My Alpha Dom's command jolts me back to the alcove.

"Green to continue; yellow for a moment; red to stop all play at once, Sir," I pant.

The unexpected soft caress of the flogger on my hip makes me gasp.

"We will push your limits, so be sure to choose the appropriate safeword. I will respect your wishes. Remember, the sub holds all the power, not the Dom. Do you understand, Little One?" He croons in my ear.

I nod.

Then yelp.

"Words, Little One. I will have your words," my Alpha Dom demands with another flick of his wrist.

The tails slip around my inner thigh while the knots find my wet pussy lips.

"Fuck!" I cry out as my back bows, and I pull at the restraints. "Yes, Sir!"

He chuckles wickedly and murmurs, "Happy to have your full attention, Naughty Girl. Now. Hold. Your. Position."

With experienced snaps of his wrist, the flogger punctuates each word as the tails and knots land on the top curve of my ass precisely. My Alpha Dom continues to warm my body up with increasing stings in a pattern that traces my back, ass, and thighs. Even my calves get a taste.

I concentrate on keeping still, but my engorged clit needs relief. Tears prick my eyes, more from the carnal ache than from the pain. I cry out to beg for permission to cum.

The blows stop, and I sag with the belief he will reward me for maintaining form. But my head jerks up when I hear the clipped strides of his A. Testoni Oxfords carry him across the alcove. Another glance over my shoulder reveals him rummaging through the chest. With a satisfied grunt, he rises and returns to stand behind me.

I squeal when three of My Alpha Dom's fingers smack my pussy lips and the tips catch my sensitive clit. Seconds later, a large, ribbed dildo breaches my soaked folds in one thrust.

"Cum," he growls.

My head falls back as my eyes roll up. A guttural scream pours from my mouth as my pussy creams on the toy fucking me with wild abandon. Wave after wave rocks through me. Shameful squelching sounds along with the musky scent of my arousal fill the air around us.

The dildo drops to the floor, and the flogger resumes.

Stunned by the sudden change, I flinch.

"Ah, ah, ah, Naughty Girl. Hold your position or safeword," My Alpha Dom reprimands as the butt of the flogger traces my ass crack enticingly. "The choice is yours."

I clench my fists, determined to go on and my butt cheeks for more ass play.

"Green, Sir," I grit out, head high.

He chuckles wickedly.

Ten more minutes of tortuous shifts between erotic pain and pleasure kept on the edge with not one more orgasm. And I'm ready to explode. Face wet from tears and skin reddened with his marks, My Alpha Dom removes my feet then my wrists from the cuffs.

My climax-starved body drops limp into his powerful arms as he cradles me to his bare chest. Questions swirl as I wonder when he disrobed and where is he taking me. But they're shoved aside when he lays me in a fetal position on the leather bench. With a sigh, I sink into oblivion as his strong fingers smooth a cool gel onto my heated back, buttocks, thighs, and calves.

"Promise kept, Little One," he murmurs against my ear.

Even in subspace, my body quivers in response to My Alpha Dom.

# STARR

*I* toss and turn all night. No matter the position, I cannot get comfortable. The restlessness drives me crazy. Malcolm tried to comfort me, but I wasn't having it. At. All.

It became so bad, he moved to the sofa in the sitting room of the primary bedroom in our penthouse at The STEELE Tower. I tried to persuade him to stay in bed with me. But he didn't want to disturb the bits of sleep that I got. Well... I realize I can't sleep if he's not lying next to me. His presence comforts me. But not him holding me right now.

As I pace back and forth past the double doors to the sitting room, I glimpse Malcolm asleep on the sofa. His long limbs are not at all comfortable as he flips from one side to the other. At one point, his blanket falls off. I pause mid-stride to see if he will reach for it. But he doesn't. So I waddle over to pick it up and drape it back over his sleeping form.

I sit on the chair opposite the sofa and watch him for a moment. I must have dozed off because I awake in bed, and Malcolm is no longer on the sofa. With a groan from the pain in my achy back, I get up gingerly and follow the sound of water to our en suite bathroom.

Malcolm stands at his vanity, shaving two-day stubble from his handsome face. I lean on the doorjamb and watch my man. Even doing banal tasks, he's sexy as fuck. When he nicks his chin for the second time, I go to him.

"Hey, babe. I didn't know you were awake. It's early, you need to go back to sleep"—he raises his hand to stop me from speaking—"And the chair is no place for you to get your rest, Hot Mama. You and Mini Malcolms 2.0 need to go back to bed. Now."

He cocks his head and raises his eyebrow at me, and I mimic his actions with a pout.

"Nor is the sofa for you, Mr. Steele. You need your rest, too."

I take the razor from his hand and move him back from the sink. I squeeze my babies bump between him and my ass against the counter.

Malcolm lifts me and settles me on top of it with ease. I smile at how strong he is again and say a silent pray of gratitude for his recovery. Then refocus on my task.

"Now, allow me, Mr. Steele," I say as I shave his face, careful not to nick his skin.

Malcolm closes his eyes and rests his hands on either side of my hips.

Silently, with a steady hand, I remove the stubble from his cheeks and chin. I rinse the razor and apply fresh shaving cream each time. When I shave all the hair, I put a warm wet cloth over his face. After I'm done, I pat it and kiss the tip of his nose.

Malcolm rinses the rest of the cream off his face and kisses me on the tip of my nose in return.

"Thank you, Mrs. Steele," he says with a warm smile, his gray eyes shine like liquid platinum in his gorgeous face.

I cup his chin and pull his lips to mine, not satisfied with a mere peck. No, Sir!

Malcolm covers my mouth with his and takes control of the kiss as he tilts my head for the best angle. Our tongues dance, and I moan in appreciation. The hormones rage and demand much more.

"What do you want, Little One?" He asks huskily with eyes now darkened by desire.

"You, my love, I want you," I purr, tilting my neck to give him better access as he trails open-mouthed kisses from my ear to my collarbone.

"Mmmmmm... Then you shall have me, Little One," he growls.

Malcolm grips my hips and slides my ass closer to the edge of the vanity. He skims his hands up my spread thighs, taking my silk negligee with him. He lowers his mouth to my puckered nipple and suckles it hard until I writhe on the counter.

He chuckles wickedly against my heated skin.

"Needy, are you?"

I growl and put my fingers in his hair to pull his mouth back to my sensitive bud. Then I groan when he nips it into his wet mouth.

"Yeeesss," I hiss as I drop my head back and lean on my other hand, still cradling him to my breast.

Malcolm continues to lavish attention on each one, driving my carnal lust through the stratosphere and higher.

My pussy clenches on air with each tug. I need more! I sit forward and cup his heavy balls in the palm of my hand, kneading them.

He growls and snaps his hips in sync with my erotic massage. Malcolm loosens the tie on his black silk pajama bottoms, and they slip down his hips to puddle on the floor. He takes the base of his erect dick in hand and shifts me forward until he impales me on his ginormous shaft.

We groan in unison as he breaches my carnal core. Then take a few breaths as my pussy stretches to accommodate his girth.

Our rhythm is slow and deep. We allow our bodies to connect and to speak for us. Only our moans fill the air, along with the musky scent of our lovemaking.

Malcolm's cock swells, and I squeeze my inner muscles to draw out his release. With a shout he cums, and I follow right behind him with a strangled cry hampered by my teeth on his shoulder. After the intensity of our release, I need to ground myself or float away.

"I love you, My Angel," he murmurs against my damp neck.

I shiver from his breath and bury my face in his silky hair.

. . .

"Are you sure you're okay alone with Selina and Elio? Why don't you let me call my mother or Anita to spend the day with you? You've been out of sorts since last night."

Malcolm's concerned eyes peer at me as I wait with him for the private elevator to take him to his offices downstairs.

I wave my hand at him and smile.

"Don't worry, my love! I am fine; I promise. Go conquer the world, hotshot," I tease as the elevator doors ping open.

Malcolm shakes his head and strides inside. He gives me one final questioning look before the doors close.

With a sigh, I shut the front door and lean against it for a moment. I'm not due for another three days, so I chalk the tiredness up to being ready to give birth soon.

We're staying in the city until Mini Malcolms 2.0 make their appearance. Then we'll go to the Southampton Village compound. Everyone is in the city to await their arrival—my parents, the Steele clan, the Beaulieus, the Greens, and Blair. Adrienne and Billie will fly in together from the West Coast once I go into labor. I love how they circle around to support Malcolm and me. Our family and friends are the best!

I make my way back to the playroom and place the monitor on the table when I enter.

"Mama!"

"Mama!"

Selina and Elio greet me as they toddle over with arms raised.

"Hello, my little loves! You missed me that much?

Wow!" I exclaim as they hug my legs. "Well, I missed you even more, sweethearts!"

The morning passes quickly with a few calls from Malcolm, our mothers, and Anita. Lola and Leonie stopped by before they went to a photoshoot for Lola's Coterie. Obviously, Malcolm put the word out to check in on me throughout the day. That man of mine, I laughed to myself each time a call came in.

"Ready for lunch, Selina and Elio?" I ask as I stand from the glider and reach for their hands.

They clap and babble as we make our way to the kitchen. I settle them at the banquette and head to the pantry. As I reach for the bread, a sharp pain stabs my lower back and radiates down my legs. A pitiful whimper escapes my mouth. I clutch my belly with one hand and grapple at the wall with the other when I realize I'm falling.

I drop to my knees with a pained cry. The bracelet on my wrist beeps. A second later, my mobile rings in the pocket of my sweater.

Malcolm. Thank God.

Harris—the tech wiz—created a monitor to track vitals, particularly for erratic or elevated heart rates that deviate from the norm. Plus, it has a fall detection and a GPS tracker for location of the wearer. He gave one to me. The app connects to the monitor, then alerts Malcolm, Harris, Anita, and my OB-GYN Dr. Rice.

I shift to sit on my butt and accept the call on my mobile.

"Starr! What's happening?!" Malcolm demands over the speakerphone.

I start to speak, but another cramp hits me and knocks the breath from my lungs. Instead, a pitiful moan spills from my lips as I grimace.

All morning my back continued to bother me, but I just assumed it was just my body getting ready for birth. So I ignored the pangs.

Wrong.

"I'm on my way up!!" Malcolm shouts and disconnects the call.

Elio appears at the pantry door followed by Selina. They stare at me, then toddle over to hug me as though they sense my distress. I cradle them to myself and try to hold back the tears from the pain.

"STARR!!!"

My head jerks up to find Malcolm, Anita, and Shelley bustling into the pantry. Malcolm's face blanches.

"What… What's wrong?" I ask as my eyes flit among them.

"Selina, Elio, come with grandmommy, sweethearts. We'll read your favorite books in the playroom," Shelley says as she takes their hands, then looks at me and the floor beneath me. "You'll be okay, Starr, honey."

My heart flips and I gasp when I see red-tinged fluid staining the seat of my white leggings.

Everything fades: Malcolm barking into his mobile; Selina and Elio crying as Shelley leads them away; Harris appearing behind Malcolm.

"Starr! Snap out of it!"

I turn my head to Anita.

"Starr, listen. We have to move you. The babies are coming. Now."

"WHAAAT?!?!?!"

"NO FUCKING WAY, DUDE!!!"

A blur of activity ensues as Anita wraps tea towels like a diaper on me, then directs Malcolm and Harris to carry me to a guest suite down the hall. Once inside, they lay me on the bed gingerly, and Anita begins to undress me. Harris leaves the room yelling orders into his mobile. Malcolm gets more towels from the linen closet and brings them to the bed.

"It's going to be all right, My Angel. Dr. Rice is on his way with his labor team. Don't you worry. Okay?" Malcolm says.

Despite his attempt to remain calm, his panicky eyes dart around as he takes in the scene.

"AARGH!!!" I cry out when another contraction wracks my body.

Malcolm jolts and reaches for my hand. Then he winces when I squeeze it during the next contraction.

They're coming faster, and I know what that means.

"Starr, you're going into labor. You can do this. Malcolm and I will help you. Ready?" Anita tells me.

I pant and nod.

Malcolm curses under his breath.

"It'll be okay," I assure my panicked husband as I squeeze his hand.

He peeks over at me and leans in to kiss my lips softly.

"I'm right here with you, My Angel. All the way," he responds with a loving smile.

. . .

AND HE WAS HERE for me, from my yells of this being his fault to the cutting of first one, then the other umbilical cord to helping Anita clean our babies. The two of them did it all—well, aside from the labor—before Dr. Rice and his team arrived thirty minutes later.

It surprised them to find me sitting up in bed with Mini Malcolms 2.0 feeding at my breasts. The pediatricians took them for a checkup while Dr. Rice examined me. He commended Anita on a birthing well done and Malcolm on his nursing skills. We laughed at his jokes and sighed with relief when they declared the three of us healthy and able to remain at home. The girls weighing 5.0 and 4.9 pounds.

Then the nurses bathed me and changed me into a nightgown and robe before the EMTs put me on a stretcher to take me to the primary bedroom. Malcolm and my mother carried Mini Malcolms 2.0 along to the bedroom and placed them in the bassinets until later.

Now, I turn to watch Malcolm holding Selina and Elio in his arms as he introduces them to their baby sisters. The sight so poignant tears slip down my cheeks. When a sob sneaks out, Malcolm glances over his shoulder at me.

"Babe, what's wrong? Do you feel all right?" He asks as he strides over to the bed.

I nod, dabbing my eyes with the pads of my fingers.

"I'm just so happy and grateful for you and our babies," I respond. "You're so good to me and a good father, my love."

Tears fill his eyes and a beatific smile spreads across his handsome face. Elio wipes one of Malcolm's cheeks while Selina plants a sloppy kiss on the other.

We laugh at their methods of comfort.

A soft knock on the door draws our attention.

"You're ready for the fam?" Malcolm asks. "They've been pretty patience, My Angel."

"Absolutely! Let them in to see their newest family members," I exclaim.

Malcolm grins and calls for them to come in.

My mother enters first, followed by Shelley close behind.

"We want to check on all of you before we let the others in," Sun says as she hurries to my side.

Shelley nods and asks, "How are you doing, sweetheart? You gave us a fright going into labor alone! Thank God for Harris and his gadgets!"

"We're well! And I know. Plus, if it wasn't for Malcolm and Anita, I don't know what I would have done," I respond, then turn to Malcolm. "You were right, my love. I should have asked Shelley or Anita to spend the day with me—"

"No. Let's focus on the positive, My Angel. You and our babies are healthy, period," he cuts me off with a firm shake of his head.

Our mothers nod in agreement.

"Now, let's get everyone in here so we can name Mini Malcolms 2.0," he finishes.

Once our family and friends gather around us, Malcolm turns to me. Selina and Elio sit on the bed between us while we hold our twin girls.

"My Angel will do the honor of revealing our daughters' names to you," he says before he kisses my forehead.

I close my eyes and breath in his strength. Then open them refreshed.

"Malcolm and I introduce you to Dione and to Iris," I announce.

"Still in keeping with the Knight tradition. Dione is Greek for child of Heaven, My Angel, and of Earth, me since I ground her. Iris is the Greek goddess for rainbow and the messenger of Zeus and Hera who rode a multicolored bridge between Heaven to Earth," Malcolm adds proudly.

"So beautiful."

"Awww, I love it!"

"How clever!"

"They're gorgeous, just like their Hot Mama!"

Everyone congratulates us and welcome Dione and Iris to the family.

LATER, when we're alone, I watch my husband with his babies.

"Hi, Sexy Papa."

Malcolm lifts his platinum gray eyes from staring into the same ones of his youngest daughters. The three of them with their ebony-haired heads close together as they lie on the bed beside me.

Once again, the Steele traits win. Our children resemble their father with my curly hair instead of his waves. As they say, the apples don't fall far from the Steele family tree.

"Hi, Hot Mama," Malcolm replies. Then he raises his

eyebrow and adds, "Keep looking at me like that, and I will fill your belly with another two babies right now."

I giggle at his joke, but stop abruptly when he doesn't join in. My eyes scan his face.

"Oh my God! You're serious?!" I exclaim.

Malcolm shrugs.

"You are one *very* Hot Mama, Starr Steele…"

# STARR

"Oh, Starr! Elio looks like a Mini Malcolm most definitely. And his sisters are beautiful female versions of your sexy AF man! Damn, girl, I don't see a glimmer of you in your own children! Poor thing."

Billie's laughter rings out in the pergola on the ocean-facing deck of Malcolm and my Steele Southampton Village beach mansion. She's holding Iris dressed in a pink polka-dot-print onesie on her lap while we chat with the girls.

The morning after Dione and Iris were born, we drove out to the Hamptons in a caravan of Mercedes-Benz Sprinters. I didn't want to spend an extra minute in the city with our babies. It's been four weeks since we arrived. And we couldn't be more delighted.

My parents moved into their mansion on the property next to ours earlier than expected. The first two weeks they worked from home to be near their grandchildren on a daily basis. Now they commute via helicopter for the weekends, leaving the City on Thursday evenings.

Shelley and Morgan cannot spend enough time with all ten of their grandchildren. Normally they would go to the Mediterranean either to their Villa Sogno in Positano or aboard their megayacht *Serendipity*. Now, they want to be near their grandbabies. They bounce from house to house in the compound to visit, or they have the kids over for babysitting at their mansion. They can't get over how in sync the births are allowing for the children to grow up together around the same ages.

Both sets of grandparents spoil the grandchildren. Toys —all developmental—books, tricycles, clothes, you name it; they have them. We've given up trying to stop them. And when Nanny Grace—an early childhood development specialist—confirmed no harm would come of the abundance, the grands went buck wild with more things!

Malcolm took paternity leave from STEELE International for the rest of the summer through September. On occasion, he works from his home office or takes the helicopter into the City for face-to-face meetings. Sebastian and Roger handle the bulk of his responsibilities, similar to the way they stepped up during his recovery. I'm glad he's here with us.

And then there are my girls.

Anita stayed for two weeks before she, Norman, and their girls returned to Paris. I couldn't thank her enough for delivering Dione and Iris for me. She saved us truly. The best doula ever! Malcolm told them they could have use of any STEELE property anywhere in the world for as long as they want whenever they want, and a company jet to transport them. Norman laughed and said he'd be sure Anita was available for all future births. We laughed, but Malcolm stared at me all smugly. He thinks more babies? Not!

Adrienne and Billie landed hours after I gave birth to Dione and Iris. My girls came straight to the penthouse and traveled with us to the Hamptons. For a week they stayed at Anton's and Patrick's mansions before they had to return to the West Coast for business. Two days ago they came back to stay through Labor Day for the STEELE Foundation fundraiser.

Haley and Blair stay in the City to work, then come out on Thursdays with my parents to spend the weekend here. Haley's desire for a baby makes me wonder what's happening between her and Lachlan. We still can't get her to admit much on their relationship... Blair can't get enough of being with all the kids. She gets a giggle out of them calling her Auntie! And what does Luc think about it?

Lola, Leonie, and I spend every day together since they took off August through the week of Labor Day. I'm thrilled since they have a wealth of knowledge they impart on me from their firsthand experience as moms, and especially Leonie as a mother of twins. Even as a doula, I didn't have the physical experience they had until Selina and Elio. So it's great to learn and to share with them: what to do about swollen ankles; the best oils for breast massages; how to soothe teething gums. My sisters help me tremendously.

Now I giggle at Billie and respond, "I know, right!

Malcolm struts around like a proud Sexy Papa all day long! He can't get enough of his babies. He only bemoans with Elio about them being the only males…"

Lola joins in the laughter as she nuzzles against Stella's soft ebony curls.

"Tell me about it! You cannot keep Baz from claiming his babies either," she says.

Leonie nods and adds how Roger does not differ from his older brothers.

"I wonder who's next to pop one out…" I say as my gaze bounces among the singles.

Adrienne studies her red-polished fingernails; Billie skims through her iPhone; Blair goes to refill her citrus-infused water; Haley stares wistfully across the sand to the Atlantic Ocean.

Mmmmhmmm.

"Well, don't everyone speak at once!" Lola laughs. "You can hear a pin drop in the middle of the ocean after that comment!"

Leonie pokes Billie and adds, "You don't know what you're missing, *chérie*! We still bring home the bacon, have someone else cook it, and get tied up for dessert! *C'est la vie!*"

The three of us laugh so hard we snort as tears spill down our cheeks. Leonie cracks us up.

"Okay, so what did I miss?"

We shift on the chaise lounges to find Márcia behind us. Her waist-length hair so jet black it appears inky blue in the sunlight. She arches a perfectly shaped eyebrow above one obsidian eye.

"Oooh! She may be the one! A giant Russian!" I laugh.

"Good grief, could you imagine getting a baby by him out of your little—"

"Whaaat?!?!?" Márcia screeches over Lola.

Yeah, and then there's that Russian pair…

We fill her in on our conversation, and she goes mum just like Haley.

We share more fun times before we have lunch. I call for the nannies to come and take all of our babies for their naps along with their dogs. The rest of the afternoon, my girls and I go for a swim, lay out on beach blankets sipping refreshing iced tea, and relax. Nothing beats Girls' Time.

BLAIR REMEMBERED how I kept a journal to document my pregnancy with Selina and Elio. So she gave a set of beautiful leather-bound journals to me as one of her baby shower gifts for Dione and Iris. The first one has my notes, sketches, and my musings on nearly every page. Each day I update their growth and development: when they first lifted their heads; their sleep patterns; feeding schedule. I even doodle little drawings of them sleeping or with Malcolm and their older siblings.

I love to go back to the first page and read through. Malcolm often joins me to marvel at their progress. Since Selina and Elio, he's become a professional photographer and can't wait to snap shots of his family.

He's kitted out with the top-of-the-line digital camera, various lenses, flashes, you name it. During my first pregnancy, he used his mobile to take pics. Before Dione and Iris were born, Malcolm had a BDSM photographer friend of his who's a member of LEVELS advise him on "nothing but the best equipment." Now Malcolm takes so many shots of us, I feel as though we need to be camera ready all day and all night long!

Not only still shots, but video, too. "It's important to mark milestones and to record our family like my parents did with my siblings and me, My Angel!" He insists each time the camera clicks or starts.

I have to admit I love his enthusiasm and the time we spend going through his many libraries categorized by theme. We have memories we'll cherish forever. He's an amazing father.

My thoughts drift back to our first morning here.

*The sunlight streams through the windows and glows like orange fire behind my closed eyelids, still heavy from sleep. For a moment, I lie there. Through the open balcony doors, the squawks of the seagulls as they soar above the ocean in search of their breakfast filters inside. The breaking waves splash onto the private beach in a soothing rhythm that lulls me to sleep once again.*

*I'm beyond tired and rest some more before I rise for the day.*

*My attention returns to our suite as I listen for sounds within our primary bedroom and en suite bathroom. The first things I notice are the loss of Malcolm's warm body wrapped around mine and the lack of breathing from his side of the bed. I crack one eye open to glance towards his pillow. An indentation serves as proof he slept beside me. I reach my hand out to touch the rumpled bedding. Cold.*

*I lift onto my elbows and scan the empty room for a clue to his whereabouts. The sound of his gentle baritone over the latest version of the fancy-schmancy baby monitor Harris created for Leonie originally is the third thing I notice. I pick it up off of the night table and place it on my breasts—heavy with milk—as I lean back against the headboard with a contented sigh.*

*My husband is with his twin daughters and Selina and Elio.*

"—understand your situation... Absolutely... But your Mommy needs her rest, Iris... You and Dione kept us awake all of last night. But that's okay. You realize why?... Because we love you so very, very much, my beautiful daughters. You are two more gifts for us, along with your older siblings Selina and Elio. Right, guys?"

*Their responses of dada, dada followed by the rustle of material and the coos of the babies float over the monitor. He's in the nursery next to our suite, with Selina and Elio's rooms on the other side.*

*I imagine Malcolm changing his baby daughters' diapers or getting them dressed for the day. He's better at coaxing his baby girls into their diaper than I by a long shot!*

"Now, you have to feel better, Stinky Butt Monsters..."

*I giggle at the nickname Malcolm gave to Selina and Elio and now uses for Dione and Iris. When Malcolm changed his son's first diaper, he gagged and ran out of the room, holding his hand over his mouth. I laugh harder and snort at the comical memory.*

*Not one to back done from a challenge, Malcolm now aces the diaper and dressing routine. The night prior, he selects their outfits for the next day and lays them out on their dressing tables. His attire varies based on the activity: walking on the beach or visiting their grandparents or resting at home.*

*Again, I crack up at my silly man.*

*"I appreciate you're hungry, Dione... Yes, okay... We'll sit on the window seat this morning and watch the seagulls eat their breakfast while you eat yours. Deal, Iris?... Good girls... Yes, Selina, you'll eat too. Don't any of you worry about Daddy taking care of his babies. You and your mother are mine and my responsibility. Understand?... Excellent, my little loves!"*

*Over the last four weeks, we found schedules and routines that work well—and some that were abysmal. The one I recognize Baz treasures the most is his morning time with his babies. A time father and his children can bond alone.*

*And a time for Mommy to sleep in bed longer. I roll over to my side and place the monitor beside Malcolm's pillow. The hushed cadence of his voice lulls me back to slumber again. My eyes drift shut, and I rest just as my husband knows I need.*

I close my journal for today and go in search of Malcolm and our babies.

We have to get ready for our one-year wedding anniversary dinner. Since Dione and Iris cannot fly yet, we decided to have a sunset dinner on the beach—a traditional New England Clambake—with our family, Jacksons, and friends tonight. When they turn three-months old, we'll go to Laucala Island to celebrate as our little family. A week later, the rest of the clan and our friends will join us.

And I cannot wait for perfectly steamed clams, lobsters, potatoes, and corn on the cob topped with melted butter and paired with local beer and white wine make for a scrumptious meal. Dessert options of warm blueberry and apple pies with vanilla ice cream to round out the dinner. Yummy!

I walk outside to the beach and spot the group further along in front of Shelley and Morgan's mansion. My mobile rings in my pocket—Malcolm's ringtone. I smile as I accept the call.

"Hi, my love. I'm on my way now. See, look towards our home," I say, then wave when a figure turns in my direction.

"Oh, good. I thought I'd have to come rescue you, or you ran away from me and the brood I gave to you," he chuckles.

Even though he can't see me at this distance, I shake my head vehemently. No way would I ever abandon our little family. Malcolm and I worked too hard to get this far for us to part, ever. Hell to the no!

"Absolutely not, Mr. Steele! You are stuck with me for eternity," I vow.

Silence descends on the line. I pull the iPhone from my ear to check the call is still live—it is.

"Malcolm? Are you there?" I ask, concerned.

A soft snuffle comes over the line.

Aaaw... He's emotional.

"Oh, my love. You don't have to say a word, I know. I love you so much it hurts. We will never be apart, no matter what may come. You are my soul mate, the love of my life. As I am yours. Let's enjoy our anniversary today and always," I tell him equally emotional.

"I love you, My Angel. Now and forever," Malcolm replies quietly but with conviction.

My heart swells as I make my way to my man and our family.

# MALCOLM

"Hot damn, Hot Mama! Am I one lucky man or what? Give me a twirl, Mrs. Steele."

I can't control my reaction to My Angel and follow up my exclamation with a sharp wolf whistle. It pierces the air as I lean with my hands in my tuxedo trousers pockets against the doorjamb of her dressing room at our penthouse at The STEELE Tower.

A celestial goddess stands in front of the room's center island putting her pear-shaped diamond earrings on—a stone at her ear and one dangling below. The giant gems sparkle, along with her wedding jewelry and evening collar with a matching bracelet. She peers over her shoulder at me. Dressed in a white long-sleeved gown that clings to her curvaceous ass and hips to skim her thighs and drape loosely at her knees until the hem pools on the floor.

A sensuous smile spreads across her face as her sorrel brown eyes shine brighter than her jewels. She skims her hands along her hips and down her thighs. More to tempt me than to smooth the silk-jersey material. Wordlessly, she turns in a circle, and her red-polished toenails with a glimpse of Swarovski crystal embellished straps peek out from beneath the hem of her gown.

Fuck. Me.

The front of her dress makes my jaw hit the floor.

A wide vee-neck dips to above her belly button to expose an expanse of chestnut-colored skin from her delicate collarbones to the inner curves of her lush tits, down to her toned abs. The vee ends in a circular diamond-crusted white-gold brooch with two dragon heads holding pearls in their mouths. A cutout at the left side of her waist forms a mock belt to hint at more skin.

Curly hair slicked straight and pulled back in a low bun at the nape draws attention to her flawless face with natural makeup and blood-red matte lipstick.

My Angel stuns me speechless.

"My... My... My... look who we have here..." she purrs as she prowls towards me with a glint in her predatory eyes. "Mr. Steele looking every inch the powerful Alpha Dom billionaire in his custom black tuxedo and patent leather dress shoes. He's leaning against the doorframe with his hands in his pockets, smirking at me. A sexy devil, might I add."

As she steps into my personal space, My Angel runs her nude-polished fingernail along my clean-shaven jaw to stroke across my lips. A purr escapes hers as she leans up on her toes to brush her lips over mine.

I hiss in a breath and nip at her lower lip, trying to take

back control. With a shake of my head, I refocus and pat her ass.

"Keep that up, Mrs. Steele, and we will not make it to our fundraiser gala," I warn in my most dominant Alpha Dom voice, despite my cock roaring to life at the feel of her melded to my body.

With a coy shrug, she saunters towards the dressing table and throws over her shoulder, "As you wish... Sir."

That earns my temptress another swat on her ass. My cock strains at the back of the zipper as her flesh jiggles against my palm.

Did I say, Fuck. Me. Already?

My Angel tsks at me and rubs the spot, making me want to bend her over the silk-covered chaise lounge and mount her like a feral beast.

Instead, I watch as she slides a zebra wood box from a top drawer of the center island. She ghosts her fingertips over the elegant box, then turns to me with a smile.

"Malcolm, my love, I am so very proud of you and your achievement of STEELE Spine. I want to commemorate the official start of your foundation with a gift that will always remind you of this incredible evening," My Angel says as she presents the box to me.

"Babe, you didn't have to—"

She shushes me with a finger to my lips and with a shake of her head.

I oblige her and press the emblem for the most-coveted watch brand in the world: Patek Philippe.

The click of the closure reveals an extraordinary piece of craftsmanship. My mouth falls open and instinctively I reach out to gingerly touch the watch. And not just any old watch or even any old Patek Philippe.

This beauty is the rare Sky Moon Tourbillon 6002G without a doubt one of the most widely recognized watches the horologist ever made. With its astonishingly intricate engravings adorning its eighteen-carat white gold case, sapphire blue faces and matching crocodile band, the watch elevates the collection to another level. It also features the most complicated wristwatch movement they make. The front displays the time, perpetual calendar with retrograde date, and the phase of the moon. While the dial on the back has a stellar illustration of the northern sky along with indications for sidereal time on a twenty-four-hour scale, time of meridian passage of Sirius and of the moon, plus the angular progression and the phase of the moon. At $2.5 million, it better...

"For you, my love. Allow me," My Angel says as she hands the box to me and removes my Grandmaster Chime 6300A-010—another pricey Patek Philippe at eight-figures—then replaces it with her gift. "When I accompanied Lola to a Phillips auction and saw this piece, I knew it was meant for you, like the meanings of our babies' and my names. You'll think of us each time you check the time, too."

I tilt her face up to look into her eyes, so radiant with her love for me.

"Thank you, My Angel"—I lean down to press my lips to hers—"You and my babies make each second of every day and every evening incredible. I love you dearly."

. . .

Our Bentley Mulsanne Duo-tone in platinum and black pulls up to the front of STEELE42, one of our award-winning entertainment venues. It specializes in weddings, parties, and galas for society's best both in the United States and abroad. A buzz surrounds the area with paparazzi and news crews angling for the best shots and interviews on the red carpet. The energy is high and reaches into the luxury sedan, drawing us out as a valet opens My Angel's door and my driver Oscar Carrera opens mine.

The red carpet is bustling with photographers, television crews, and international glitterati. Lights flash and the photographers yell my name to turn my head in their direction.

As I reach My Angel, I can't help but smile at her radiance. She looks spectacular with the lightbulbs flashing off of her diamond jewelry, particularly her hand harness, engagement ring, and wedding band prove to all the world she is mine. I will have the best-dressed woman on my arm tonight.

My Angel smiles as her hand wraps around my forearm and like a pro saunters along the red carpet. When the paps call for her to pose, as a good sub should, she looks to me for approval, then poses like the best supermodel or movie star. My dick weeps for her.

The paps call for me to join her for a few shots. I loop my arm around her waist and settle my fingers on her hip. Then bend down and softly kiss her lips. The paparazzi go wild and scream our names.

I squeeze her hand and put it into the crook of my

elbow, pressing it close to my side as we make our way down the carpet, posing for pictures and chatting with reporters.

Leonie and Roger are just ahead of us. When Leonie hears them calling our names, she turns and makes her way back down the carpet towards My Angel and me. Roger grins and strides along with her.

"*Chéri*, this is your night!" She gushes as she double kisses my cheeks.

The megamodel-turned-interior-designer looks fantastic in a gold, silk satin strapless floor-length gown. Her long legs play peek-a-boo with the thigh-high slit. Her smile is as dazzling as the diamonds adorning her body. Leonie tosses her waist-length hair and twinkles her amber eyes as she hugs me close. The paparazzi reach a frenzied peak and thousands of flashbulbs pop.

Baz appears in a classic tuxedo cut perfectly to emphasize his height and muscular frame. He, too, hugs me and congratulates me on my success. Ours, I correct him with a smile. Lola—in a form-fitting black satin one-shoulder gown—gushes with My Angel and Leonie. No one would believe these Hot Mamas have ten babies among them!

Soon the rest of our clan arrives—including Lachlan with Haley, fucker. All of us pose for the cameras. The rarity of all the Steele siblings in one frame will make for excellent social media posts and traditional media coverage. After several minutes, we walk through the doors of STEELE42.

. . .

Once we arrive inside, we place our masquerade masks over our faces before we chat with other attendees. I introduce My Angel to key guests and mention her Starr Light Fitness & Wellness locations and international retreats. Women and men want to be at their peak performance and can appreciate access to a notable fitness brand. Some of whom are already familiar with their offerings and have attended sessions or retreats, even streamed them. Their excitement to meet the founder palpable. The men as expected nonchalantly check out My Angel, and I struggle not to flip someone on their ass.

"Oh, Malcolm, this is a beautiful venue. All the STEELE properties are so refined!" My Angel says, looking up at the vaulted ceiling where the constellations twinkle in the dim lighting.

I want to lave her throat and suck on it until I leave my bright red mark as a warning to others to back the fuck off.

"Not as refined and gorgeous as you, though," I reply instead. "But this is one of my favorites. It was a bank and when we refurbished it, we strove to keep the integrity of the space. We kept the original ceiling, columns, teller windows on the sides, the vault, and more original details."

"It's impressive," she murmurs.

Further inside STEELE42, I spot my father deep in conversation with some prominent businessmen with my mother engaged in conversation with their wives. They exemplify a power couple I hope to replicate with My Angel.

"Mr. Steele, you have news crews to speak with," my

assistant Miles says as he steps behind us with the team for STEELE Spine.

"Thank you, Miles," I respond, then turn to My Angel. "Will you join me?"

She smiles and nods as she slips her hand around the crook of my elbow.

We finish the interviews that interspersed questions on my accident and the trial to details on the foundation's mission. The team and I answer the business-related questions with gusto. But deftly avoided substantial responses on my personal life. We keep it simple with I'm thankful for the opportunity to pay it forward and hope to make a positive impact on the wellbeing of others.

The less fodder given to the media, the better. As with most old money families, the Steeles like media coverage to further our business gains, but prefer intimate aspects to remain private.

"Sweethearts, how do you like the gala? Are you pleased?"

My mother materializes next to me, holding her elaborate feathered mask by its silk ribbon-covered handle. I smile down at her and wrap my arm around her shoulders. She's the same height as My Angel and fits under my chin with her heels on.

"I love it! You and your team did a superb job. Thanks so much, Mom," I squeeze her close. "It's even greater than I expected."

"Well, we had to be sure everything is perfect for your new foundation! Your father and I are very proud of you."

She pauses as her eyes mist with tears. She takes a deep breath and I squeeze her again. Her words make even the Alpha Dom in me blink back tears. I strive to make my parents proud of me. It's so good to hear it from both of them.

"Oh, Shelley, this is awesome!" My Angel adds as she takes over the embrace. "I told Malcolm he has a lot to be proud of!"

The most important women in my live chat some more before we spend the evening mingling during the cocktail hour, speaking with potential donors. We place bids on a few interesting items from the silent auction. Then, eating a fantastic dinner—Lucien's catering division handles the food and drink.

Miles appears beside me to let me know it's time for my speech. I turn to My Angel, and she places a light kiss on my lips before she whispers good luck. Then I nod to the other guests at our table and excuse myself.

As I stride to the stage, several guests greet me, and I take a few moments to thank them for coming. When I arrive on the dais, the new head of the foundation introduces me. A round of applause rings out. I wait for the guests to settle before I speak.

"Thank you for joining my family and me for the inaugural STEELE Spine Annual Fundraiser Gala. Before I impress you with our mission to dazzle you for your hefty donations," I pause for their ensuing laughter. "Kindly allow me the opportunity to thank the most important person in my life—my wife of one glorious year with many, many more to come—Starr Steele. Without her unwavering love and support I would not stand before you today."

A spotlight highlights My Angel at our table. Her eyes widen when our family and friends stand and clap for her. She covers her mouth with her hand and fans her face with the other to hold back the tears. Then she stands and inclines her head to me as she claps.

In a clear voice that carries across the space she responds, "Our love and the love of our family will forever strengthen us. We are grateful for you and your vision for STEELE Spine, my only love."

Then she blows me a kiss and re-takes her seat, indicating for the others to do the same.

My heart clenches at her words. When she gives me a thumbs up, I grin and launch into my speech with gusto. And sure enough, by the end of the night we raise over $40 million.

"Well done, Mr. Steele."

My Angel tips her head back to gaze into my eyes as we glide across the dance floor to the music of the live band.

I tighten my hold on her and kiss her full lips.

"Thank you, Mrs. Steele," I murmur against them.

"Shelley enlisted me to help next year since I was too preggie to work with the team this time. I told her I'd love to help my man in any way whatsoever," My Angel says. Then she winks at me, "But what I didn't tell her was there's a fee…"

I cock my head and raise my eyebrow in question.

"As long as you play doctor to my patient at LEVELS New York for a night, I'll consider my services paid in full… Sir," she says as she bites her plump lower lip.

I growl and cover her mouth with mine, drawing the succulent flesh between my teeth for a nip.

She trembles from the erotic pain then mewls when I lap at the bite with the flat of my tongue.

"Consider that a tasty down payment, Naughty Girl," I rumble.

# MALCOLM

"Ready to take this jump with me, My Angel? With our responsibilities, we don't have to do this, you know. The choice is yours as always, babe."

She slips her googles over her eyes that glow with excitement, then tightens the strap on her helmet. Once again, she gives me a thumbs up and grins.

"I'll jump with you anytime and anyplace, my love. Let's do this like Brutus!" She high fives with me.

I whoop and pump my fist.

This will be my first extreme sport since before the accident. I stopped them; being a father and a husband, not wanting to risk my life when I have theirs to care for. My top priorities. But My Angel surprised me with a skydiving session for our second morning on Laucala Island.

We arrived yesterday afternoon with our babies and Nanny Patience. In a week, our family and friends will join us for the renewal of our vows on the beach. I want to include all of our little ones as we claim our love as a family forever.

But first My Angel and I jump!

A crew member opens the door of the skydiving plane. We're flying over the spectacular Fiji Islands with the Pacific Ocean glittering in various shades of turquoise. Bright blue sky and wispy clouds surround us.

The adrenaline pumps through my veins as I check first My Angel's safety gear then mine. We may enjoy a good thrill, but I will not allow us to take avoidable risks.

The guide gives us last instructions. Then we line up to exit the plane one after the other for the drop zone 300 feet above sea level.

My Angel glances over her shoulder at me and waves. Even though it's not her first jump, my heart still lurches when she leaps from the plane with a gleeful shout.

Her excitement sparks my own.

Up next, I go through my ritual to give thanks for my fearless wife, love to our family, and our safe finish. It's what I do before any of my extreme activities, even when I was a pain-in-the-ass teen. My rebel spirit still exists, but it's alongside my duty to family and self.

A thumbs up to the guide, and I take my jump.

"Whoohoo, baby! Time to rock and roll!" I yell before I follow her out the door with a somersault in the air.

My laughter floats behind me as I soar through the stratosphere. The air rushes past as I hurtle through the clouds. My blood races through my veins as my heart pumps with exhilaration. Damn, I missed this!

I watch My Angel below me and hear her faint laughter carried on the wind.

A shit-eating grin stays plastered on my face as I free fall through the sky at 120 miles per hour. I take in the pristine beauty of the South Pacific. The twenty-thousand feet give me eighty-five seconds to view it all.

I pull on my cords and float safely to the ground under my parachute. Years of experience allow me to land on my feet at a run.

Damn! That's what I'm talking about! I am back!

The ground team rushes over to help me wrangle my open parachute. They relieve me of the harness, then my helmet and goggles as I remove them. I scan the area for My Angel.

Once I spot her, I thank the team for their help and jog to reach her side. I scoop her in my arms and spin in a circle. Her long, toned legs wrap around my waist as she devours my mouth with hers. I give the passionate kiss back to her in spades.

Our tongues entwine and our teeth gnash. The adrenaline makes us ferocious, starved for the other. My cock hardens to steel and presses against her fiery core through the layers of our cargo pants.

She moans and grinds her pussy to my groin. Then her moist lips blaze a trail to my ear.

"Take me back and fuck me raw, Mr. Steele. It's been twelve long weeks since I had your colossal cock inside of me. And. I. Will. Wait. No. Longer!" She punctuates each word with a snap of her hips.

I damn near cum in my pants. The friction against my aching dick proves too much.

Fuck. Me.

Without delay, I carry her to the awaiting Sikorsky S-92 Executive Helicopter. It'll make for a quick trip back to our side of Laucala island. My long strides eat up the distance, and I climb in the cabin without breaking our contact. I sit on a back seat, and she squirms on my lap, purposefully teasing my cock. It thumps against her pussy, and she mewls in my mouth. I gobble the erotic sound like a starved man.

I untie her pants to slip my fingers between her wet and puffy folds. My thumb strokes her needy little clit. The calloused pads of two fingers brush just inside of her pussy to skim her G-spot. I apply enough pressure to cause her juices to flow into my palm, but not enough to elicit an orgasm.

As she moans pitifully with her face buried in my neck, I keep her on the edge for the duration of the ten-minute flight. We'll both explode soon enough.

Before the rotor blades stop, I carry My Angel to the door, impatient for the crew to open it. With a brief word of thanks, I step down and stride to the golf cart.

My Angel protests when I sit her on the seat beside me. Then a mischievous gleam fills her sorrel brown eyes. With a smirk she ghosts her hand over my giant bulge. The outline of my ten inches clear along my thigh from the thick root to the mushroom head Prince Albert's piercing jewelry balls.

I grab her wrist and shake my head.

"We do not want a knee-jerk reaction now do we, Naughty Girl?" I reprimand her.

She sits back with a huff and pouts, arms crossed over her tits and eyes forward.

I chuckle wickedly.

The ride is short, and I chase her into the villa and to our primary bedroom. Fortunately, Nanny Pierce has the babies at her cottage for the rest of the morning.

My Angel squeals when I catch and toss her onto the bed. She bounces, then shifts to her knees. She rips her t-shirt over her head and yanks at the tie of her cargo pants. Standing in the middle of the mattress, she shimmies them with her red lace G-string past her hips. She kicks them to land in a pile with her crumbled t-shirt on the floor. She crooks her finger at me as I stand transfixed by the temptress.

"Come here, Sir," she commands me. "Let me help you with all of those pesky clothes."

I nearly trip over my own feet in my haste to reach her.

She giggles and drops to her knees. Equally frantic to remove the offensive garments as she did hers. My Angel tugs my long-sleeved t-shirt from my pants and over my head. Nimble fingers unbutton and lower the zipper on my fly with ease. She bites her bottom lip when she catches sight of my cock's angry red tip poking up from the waistband of my boxer briefs to my navel. Pre-cum drips from the hungry boy.

Her delay breaks my resolve. I grip her shoulders and

lower her to the bed. Legs go up on my shoulders as I plank over her with one hand by her head and the other fists around my throbbing dick. So ready and wet for me, I slam home in one brutal thrust.

She screams and arcs her back as she claws the bedding.

I hiss and flex my ass cheeks, bending my knees to increase the penetration.

So fucking tight; her pussy like a vice.

I dig my heels into the floor and wrap my hand around her throat to hold her in place. Thoughts of making sweet love to my wife for the first time since she gave birth dissipate as a red veil of carnal lust drops before my eyes.

Her full tits topped by pebbled brown nipples bounce with each insistent snap of my hips as I drill her into the mattress. Wild cries of carnal pleasure burst from her slack mouth. Head—with mussed curls a halo around it—thrown back. Eyes squeezed shut.

My mind tells me to fuck her until I can't walk. And then some more. Relentless. Possessive. Claiming. Mine.

And you know why?

Because I'm the rebel; the bad boy billionaire playboy of the STEELE family who in the end always knew I would get what I wanted. And I wanted the brown-eyed beauty. Starr Steele—My Angel—is mine all mine to cherish.

Forever.

***

**Malcolm & Starr's Story Concludes For Now...**

**Turn the page for the Steele Family, Author's Note, and the next series in the STEELE World: STEELE International, Inc. - Jackson Corporation Crossover Series Book 1**

*Tempt My Desires Lachlan & Haley Part I*

# THE STEELE FAMILY

## STEELE INTERNATIONAL, INC

Multigenerational, multibillion-dollar business luxury real estate development and management corporation

Headquarters & Family's Primary Residences:

The STEELE Tower, New York City

A modern, gray-tinted glass fifty-seven story mixed-use skyscraper on southwest corner of Fifty-Seventh Street and Fifth Avenue within Billionaires' Row

Global Offices:

- The United States of America (New York City, New Jersey, Chicago, California, Miami, Las Vegas)
- The Caribbean (St. Maarten, St. Barth's, St. Lucia)
- The French & Italian Rivieras (Nice, Cannes, Positano, Capri)
- Monaco (Monte Carlo)
- The United Arab Emirates (Abu Dhabi, Dubai)

## STEELE FOUNDATION: A STRONG AND SUPPORTIVE HOUSE

Builds and manages attractive, affordable housing for urban, lower-income families

Available for download at **bit.ly/STEELEFamily**

## Author's Note

Thank you for reading Part III of Malcolm and Starr's sexy, sizzling romance! I hope you enjoyed the Happy For Now conclusion of their written-in-the-stars love affair. If so, I'd love to hear your thoughts, please share a review at **bit.ly/CLBooksSI9Review** and tell your friends.

**Wait! What's up with Lachlan and Haley or Billie and Patrick or Blair and Luc?! The STEELE International, Inc. Series gave lots of hints at what's brewing for these lovers...**

**Click below for the answers to one steamy story featuring forbidden lovers Alpha Dom Lachlan Jackson and shy, tech wiz Haley Steele as their scintillating trilogy introduces the next series in the STEELE World with STEELE International, Inc. - Jackson Corporation A Billionaires Romance Series Crossover Book 1:**

*Tempt My Desires Lachlan & Haley Part I Click Here*

At **CharmaineLouise.com** take the *Four types of lovers. Which are you?* **Quiz** to match your Sexy Fantasy: sub, Voyeur, Dominatrix, or Dominatrix sub Switch.

**Follow me on social media including my CLBooks Coterie Fan Club below** or on your favorite channels below and subscribe to my newsletter at **bit.ly/CLBooksNewsletter** for a **Free Book**.

Fulfill Your Desires.
xoxo
Charmaine Louise

- bookbub.com/authors/charmaine-louise-shelton
- facebook.com/CharmaineLouiseBooks
- instagram.com/charmainelouisebooks
- goodreads.com/charmainelouisebooks

**STEELE International, Inc. - Jackson Corporation
A Billionaires Romance Series Crossover**

*Tempt My Desires Lachlan & Haley Part I*

Click on the link below or visit books2read.com/u/4DPzve to get your copy.

**Tempt My Desires Lachlan & Haley Part I**

## Books in the Series:

Tempt My Desires Lachlan & Haley Part I

Tease My Desires Lachlan & Haley Part II

Grant My Desires Lachlan & Haley Part III

Intrigue My Desires Harris & Kat Part I

Decode My Desires Harris & Kat Part II

Honor My Desires Harris & Kat Patt III

A Trilogy of Desires Lachlan & Haley Parts I-III

A Trilogy of Desires Harris & Kat Parts I-III

Series Extras

Series Playlist

# COMING NEXT: TEMPT MY DESIRES LACHLAN & HALEY PART I STEELE INTERNATIONAL, INC. - JACKSON CORPORATION A BILLIONAIRES ROMANCE SERIES CROSSOVER BOOK 1

# 1
*3 Years Ago — Southampton Village, NY*

Haley — 16

"Hi, Sebastian!"
"Oh hi, Malcolm!"
"Hi, Roger!"
"Hey there, Harris!"
"*Hello* to you guys, too!!"

Shall I hurl now or later?
Cue the biggest eye roll in history!
If I'd known my friends would go gaga over my older brothers and my cousins, I would've told the girls we'd

hang out at one of their beach houses instead of at mine. Give me a freaking break already...

Eyes batting; duck lips in full effect; cheeks flushed; bouncing on their blankets with uncontainable excitement.

Is this what I have to look forward to all summer???

Gag. Gag. Gag some more. Did I say... gag (all caps)?!

"Uh, hi, girls," Sebastian says followed by similarly surprised greetings from the rest of the boys as they stride past in various board shorts, fit physiques on blast.

My eldest brother tosses the football to Roger—my third older brother after Malcolm—then ruffles my jet black, mid-back-length hair that matches the rest of my siblings. Our signature gray eyes—in me are soulful, set in my heart-shaped face with cheeks that display dimples when I smile or laugh—shine with brotherly affection.

"Hey, little sis. Where's your one-piece?" Sebastian asks with a frown at my new hot pink, triangle string bikini. "What's with theses bits of material, huh?"

Before I can respond, my fraternal twin chimes in.

"Oh, she went *shopping* the other day, Baz," Harris says with a smirk. "Who are you trying to impress, little Haley?"

I scowl in consternation at both of them. But once again, I'm cut off before I can even open my mouth.

"Leave her alone, Harris. I think you look nice, Haley. Who says you have to follow the rules?" Malcolm demands, glaring at Baz.

I smile at my rebel brother Malcolm, also known as *The Enforcer*.

He and Baz used to go at it all the time. Malcolm hated they resembled one another from their muscular six-feet-four-inch frames to the stubble on their chins and their dominant personalities. Plus Malcolm felt he had to follow in our eldest brother's footsteps, being a year younger and the second son. At twenty-three and twenty-two, many people confuse them or assume they're twins. Not good at all.

I know how Malcolm feels since I'm the youngest of the Steele clan at sixteen. The *baby* of the family, as Harris likes to point out since he was born a few minutes before me. We are the double surprise for our parents, who had not planned on having more children. Then a twofer to boot. Roger is three years older and had been the baby of the family until Harris and I popped up.

"Shall we play football or bug Haley?" Roger asks, tossing the ball back to Baz as he winks at me.

Roger *The Responsible* takes his role as the middle child seriously. We can always depend on him to keep peace and order under his intense gaze.

I wink back at my savior, but swallow my words around the nervous butterflies that fill my belly suddenly.

"Yeah, leave Baby Girl alone, Baz, and get ready to have your ass handed to you, cuz!"

Lachlan.

O... M... G! Lachlan!

The second oldest of the Jackson clan at twenty—he's two years younger than their eldest sibling Lydie—and Baz's best friend.

My heart skips a beat when he flashes his movie-star smile at me. Everyone says he resembles Cary Grant with his rugged masculinity and gorgeous looks.

His fit, six-foot-four-inch well-formed frame topped by a face so incredible it takes your breath away. Blazing green eyes lock in on you as your gaze takes in his thick, dark brown hair slicked back from his chiseled cheekbones and strong jawline. The cleft chin adds to his heartthrob persona.

"Screw you, Lach! *You* are going down, man!" Malcolm jeers.

Can Lachlan go down on me?

Oops, what??? Where the heck did that thought come from, Haley Steele! I admonish myself as a hot, crimson flush spreads from my hairline to the tops of my newly developed breasts. I duck my head to avoid my brothers noticing my reaction to Lachlan—especially Baz.

"Yeah, right, Malcolm! We'll see about that, *cuz!*" Lucien retorts as he snatches the ball from Baz and tosses it to his younger brother Laurent, who laughs and shoulders past Harris.

They're the third and fourth of the Jackson siblings at nineteen and sixteen and best friends with Malcolm and Harris, respectively. And just like Lachlan, they share the Jackson family traits of emerald green eyes, dark brown hair, and six-plus feet in height.

I hear the girls whispering about his hint of a Scottish accent—*He's so James Bond, OMG!!!*—and cover up a gag with a cough. An unstoppable eye roll happens behind my glasses, though. I push them up the bridge of my nose.

Yeah, our cousins spend most of the year—and their lives—in Scotland where their family's company is based in Aberdeen at the Jackson Town House. Like the Steeles, they have a multigenerational, multibillion-dollar company. Jackson Corporation's repertoire is fine dining, distilleries, and vineyards worldwide. Their Irish and Scottish family created the finest single malt Scotch Whiskey and became billionaires years ago.

STEELE International, Inc. is my family's luxury real estate development and management corporation based in New York City in The STEELE Tower with offices and properties around the globe. The Tower is also our family's residence on the top three floors of the fifty-seven-story building. Morgan, our father, is the CEO and Chairman of the Board. In time, each of us will take on a leadership role within the company. For now, we intern during our school breaks to learn our family's business from the ground up.

Our mother Michelle—known by friends as Shelley—insists we do more than as she calls it "lounge around the pool working on our tans" in Southampton Village during the summers. As the head of STEELE Foundation, she contributes through our philanthropic arm that builds and manages attractive, affordable housing for urban, lower-income families. My siblings and I help to construct some properties, too.

She and her best friend Lucinda—aka Lucie and the Jackson Matriarch—spent most of their adult lives together, forming a closer bond than they have with their blood siblings and relatives. Incredibly, our mothers met our fathers while working as a shopgirl in a STEELE retail space and as a bartender in one of the Jackson pubs. Both families became super close even without sharing DNA.

Hence our cousin relationship and Aunt Lucie and Uncle Connor.

Not that I desire for Lachlan to be my *cuz* or for him to consider me a *Baby Girl*...

While my brothers and I are at our family's private beachfront compound in the Hamptons, our cousins came over from Aberdeen for the last half of the summer. They'll intern at Jackson Corporation's New York City offices while we're at STEELE International. Aunt Lucie uses the same playbook as our mother.

Baz and Malcolm and Roger are on break from Harvard University Business School and Harvard University, respectively. Harris and I are still in high school at Collegiate School and its sister school, The Brearley School. They're all the Steele family's legacy schools.

Lydie starts her first year at Saïd Business School at the University of Oxford in the fall. Lachlan is in his third year and Lucien in his second at Pembroke College at the University of Oxford. Laurent attends Gordonstoun School. All are the Jackson family's legacy schools.

Tradition ranks high for our families.

"Haley, who is that fine specimen of a man?!"

My best friend Natasha Bond's question and nudge draws me from my musings.

I sigh inwardly and plaster on a smile before I glance over at her.

She's all gorgeous face, long blonde hair, big blue eyes, and willowy figure compared to my only now forming curves and gawky self. She's tall like me, more so since she's two years older at eighteen and not from my genetics.

At first it shocked me the most popular girl at school wanted to be friends with me this past year. Oddly enough, others started asking me to hang out for lunch or sleepovers. I'd always been a bit of a loner, so it took me a moment to get used to their constant attention.

"Which one?" I ask with a hint of sarcasm.

My tone goes over Natasha's head.

Did I mention she's not the brightest lightbulb in the box...?

She elbows me with a giggle, and her big boobs almost pop out of her minuscule bikini top—I went with her shopping for my new bathing suits.

"The movie star one with the sexy Scottish accent, that's who!" She giggles as she tilts her chin towards the boys playing near the surf.

I scowl.

My Lachlan.

Could this situation get any worse?!

I choose to ignore her question—rude, yes, but oh well—and rise to get a bottled water from the cooler.

Is Natasha serious with me right now?!

I uncap the bottle and let my gaze drift from my brothers and cousins—including my man Lachlan—to my friends, who whisper amongst themselves as they point at the sweaty boys and giggle.

With a harrumph, I gulp down half of the bottle.

It's just not fair Lachlan only sees me as a baby girl and not someone he's attracted to, like he's eyeballing Natasha. She's grinning at him all coy like as she adjusts her breasts in her bikini top.

Why can't she back up off of him?!

Since I was little, I used to follow Baz and Lachlan around like a little stray puppy, just wanting to be around my eldest brother, who I've always admired. Until recently when I realized I wasn't just following them to see what they were up to, rather to be near to Lachlan as much as possible. When he returned this summer, something just clicked inside of me. Suddenly, I wanted him to pay attention to me as more than his little cousin or *Baby Girl*.

I even picked out this bikini in hopes he'd see my new curves and want me.

Is it too much to ask for???

Lachlan — *20*

Even while we play football, my gaze keeps going to the sexy as fuck blonde who all but drops her top for me. Baz sacked me good a minute ago when her feminine wiles distracted me, and I ended up on my ass in the sand.

It's not like I don't get laid whenever I want. Hell, girls —and women I might add—throw themselves at me. A Jackson male with billions in the bank and a more than willing ten-inch cock. Not that I'm interested in settling down with one female at the moment. No, ma'am!

Like my father Connor tells us, "Live life to the fullest, boys. But do not bring home any unexpected bundles…"

Yeah, not something he says to our eldest sibling, Lydie. He's never hidden his intention to marry her off to improve Jackson Corporation's business with some type of alliance. Can you say old-fashioned?

Even though Lydie is older than me and should be the heir to the family's business, our father wants me to take over when he retires. My loyalty lies with my sister. So, we'll see...

But this bird here.

No question. I would shag her in a heartbeat.

But she's Haley's friend, so she can't be of age despite her banging body.

"Pay attention, Lach You dolt!!"

Laurent's fierce growl and shove to my chest returns me to the football game at hand. Right.

"Okay, damn!" I retort, wiping the sand from my hands.

We play some more, and I remain focused despite the wolf whistles from our impromptu cheerleading squad. The Jackson clan wins, and we do a victory dance before both teams dive into the cool Atlantic Ocean.

When I come up for air, the blonde appears and wraps her arms and legs around me like a starfish.

"I knew you'd win!" She exclaims as she covers my mouth with her full lips in a passionate, no-holds-barred kiss.

Well, damn.

I cup her ass and kiss her silly. Not once do I hide the burgeoning erection of my thick cock from her eager, hot snatch. Nor does she try to deny me access to her greedy core. Her hips pump to their own beat.

It's good being a Jackson.

I tangle my tongue with hers as my hands caress her willing body.

"Damn, Lach. Is she even legal?"

Roger's question pulls my mouth from devouring the blonde's.

Damn, is she? I wonder.

She giggles and nips at my ear.

"I'm eighteen. No need to worry," she pants, breathless from my domineering kiss.

When she whispers she's on the pill, my cock twitches beneath the water.

She giggles.

"Um, Natasha. We need to go to the deck. It's time for lunch."

The sound of Haley's soft voice makes me wince. I release the blonde and move away from her guiltily.

What is it about my youngest cousin that makes me feel like I'm doing something wrong or hurting her in some way?

*Haley*

TO SEE Lachlan kiss Natasha makes me physically ill. I have to do something to stop them from going further. Or I really will hurl all over the sand.

"Um, Natasha. We need to go to the deck. It's time for lunch," I say lamely from a distance, praying he'll let her go.

So unfair.

As though she's a live wire, Lachlan releases Natasha quickly. She tries to cling to him. But he swims away without a backwards glance at either of us.

The butterflies in my stomach sink.

"What, Haley?!" Natasha demands angrily as she storms towards me.

I stare at her with my mouth agape.

"Just because you can't have them doesn't mean *we* don't want a chance to be with them!" Natasha exclaims in a loud whisper as she approaches me. "Did you really think we were hanging out with *you* to be friends?! You're some tech nerd who's boring AF! We knew you have the hottest brothers. And now cousins too? Give us a break for wanting access to them!"

Now my mouth drops to the sand, and my eyes fill with tears behind my glasses.

I should have known it was too good to be true.

Why would the It girls of Brearley want to hang out with me—the geek—all of a sudden?

I've been friendly with girls at school, but not really *friends*. I had hoped to have a real best friend at last. I mean, Lydie is nice to me and all, treats me like her little sister since we're united by the abundance of testosterone around us. But she's so much older and always focused on acing her exams and work at Jackson. We don't spend a lot of time together.

But I guess she's better than this bunch of pseudo-friends…

"Well, you can't cock block us!" Natasha shrills when

she stands before me, and the other girls echo her sentiment.

I take a breath to calm myself before I lose all cool points.

"Well, then go!" I retort. "I don't need *friends* like you, anyway!"

The girls glare at me, then gather their things and leave in a huff.

Natasha's icy blue stare sends chills down my spine. But I glare gray shards of molten platinum at her until she grabs her things and stomps away.

My stomach lurches, and I rush from the beach to my bedroom suite. I've had enough for one day.

Lachlan

"Okay, let's go now before Malcolm and Roger notice and want to tag along. I need a drink and to get laid pronto."

Baz says before we creep out of his bedroom suite to go to a party.

We make it out of his rooms and down the dimly lit hallway past his parent's wing.

CRASH!

"Oh! Ow!!"

Baz and I whirl around to find Haley sprawled out on the floor. A crystal vase shattered beside her.

Unbeknownst to us, Haley—who is forever tagging along

with us since she was a kid—must have heard us when we passed her set of rooms. This time, it appears she tripped on the rug right outside of their parents' bedroom and knocked the vase down when she reached for the table to catch herself.

"Haley? What the hell?!" Baz whisper shouts.

"Are you all right?" I ask, concerned.

When she turns her heart-shaped face up to me, tears shimmer in her platinum gray eyes behind her glasses. Her cute dimples disappear on her flushed cheeks.

As her chin wobbles, I crouch in front of her and cup her face. My hand tingles from the contact.

"Hey, Baby Girl, don't cry," I murmur as I stroke her cheek with my thumb. "It's okay."

Baz nudges me out of the way and reaches for her. His shocked anger replaced by his big brother concern.

"Haley, are you hurt? Did the glass cut you?" He asks as he checks her out.

"What's going on?"

We jolt at the commanding voice of Uncle Morgan and turn to face the Steele Patriarch.

Aunt Shelley hurries past him and shoos Baz and me away.

Haley's cries must have woken them.

As Uncle Morgan reprimands Baz and me, my eyes flick to Haley, who's being led to her rooms by Aunt Shelley. As they walk away, Haley peeks at me over her shoulder.

My heart skips a beat, and I have a sudden urge to care for her, to protect her.

I shake my head, and I glance away, confused by my reaction.

Baz and I decide to forgo the party. Instead, we hang out at the bar and play pool on their mansion's entertainment level.

"Ha! You lost, again, Lach," Baz guffaws as he takes a sip of his Jackson Special Blend Scotch.

Yeah, my head isn't in the game. It's still churning over the emotions Haley brought out in me earlier. I shake it again and sigh as I take a drink from my crystal snifter.

"What the fuck's eating you, cuz?" Baz asks.

I shrug, then plow ahead despite a niggling not to draw attention to my predicament.

"Doesn't it bother you Haley could've cut herself?" I ask in return.

Baz's eyebrows lift, and his eyes narrow on me. They turn a stormy gray. Carefully, he places his snifter on the ledge of the pool table.

"What do you mean, Lachlan?" He asks, still eyeing me.

I give zero fucks he's going all Alpha male on me. I'm one too.

"You did not appear overly concerned for Haley, Sebastian," I reply as I place my snifter down.

"Oh, so you think you can take care of Haley better than me?! She's *my* little sister. *I* know what's best for her, Lachlan, not *you*!" He retorts, as his face flushes in anger.

I don't back down. Something urges me to defend Haley even over her eldest brother who I know truly loves her as he does all of his siblings. Hell, he prides himself on being their third parent.

But again, my mind is in a confused state.

"Yes, I can! She's my—"

She's my what? Not my little sister. And from the way my heart stuttered as her soulful gray eyes stared up at me —touching something deep inside of me—she's not just my cousin anymore, either.

As I think more on it, she's been acting differently towards me all summer, not like her usual self over the holidays and last summer. More shy; averts her eyes when our gazes meet; lingers near me with a faraway look on her face. It makes me wonder.

Haley cannot feel the same. Can she?

But she is Baz's little sister—*my best friend's* little sister. And I cannot have her. No matter what deep part of me she's tapped into all of a sudden. No matter what I sense from her. Besides, she's only a sixteen-year-old girl, and I'm twenty-year-old man.

Fuck. Me.

I lift my face towards the ceiling and blow out a frustrated breath.

"Haley is your *what*, Lachlan?"

Baz's menacing tone draws me from my errant musings.

"My youngest cousin who needs to be more careful, cuz," I answer, schooling my face into a stoic expression.

Baz scans my face for any sign of deceit. None found, he nods and racks the balls.

"Ready to lose again, cuz?" He taunts with a smirk.

I return his smirk with one of my own and take a grateful sip of my Scotch.

Crisis averted.

***

## Click the Link Below or Visit books2read.com/u/4DPzve For Your Copy

*Tempt My Desires Lachlan & Haley Part I*

*I dedicate this novel to my readers! It's been a year since I started writing. This is the final book in the STEELE International, Inc. Series that started my career as an author. I thank you for your support and kind words of encouragement! Here's to many more Sexy Fantasies starring with a crossover series dancing in my head waiting for their stories to unfold!*

*Fulfill Your Desires.*

*xoxo*
*Charmaine Louise*

# WELCOME TO CHARMAINELOUISE — THE SENSUAL LIFESTYLE

GLITZY. GLAMOROUS. STEAMY.

CharmaineLouise New York, Inc. invites you to indulge in *The Sensual Lifestyle* through **CharmaineLouise Books** and **CharmaineLouise Intimates**. CLBrands immerse you in *Sexy Fantasies* with CLBooks contemporary romance novels and give you *Sexy Under Things & Loungewear* with CLIntimates.

**Charmaine Louise Shelton the Founder, CEO & Author of CLNY** loves all things classic, elegant, feminine, and of course with an erotic edge! Favorite outfit of choice is a cashmere cardigan, leather pencil skirt, and seamed silk stockings with stiletto heels. Sexy Fantasy Type: sub with a dash of Voyeur. When not writing and designing, Charmaine Louise travels and spends time with her Maltese buddies, ZIGGY and Jynger.

WELCOME TO CHARMAINELOUISE — THE SENSUAL LIFES...

**CharmaineLouise —** *The Sensual Lifestyle*

~ Visit online at **CharmaineLouise.com**

~ Subscribe to **CharmaineLouise Newsletter**

~ Find us on Facebook **@CharmaineLouiseNewYork**

~ Instagram **@CharLouNY**

**CharmaineLouise Books** *Sexy Fantasies* launched summer 2020. Sizzling, contemporary romance with your soon-to-be favorite Alpha Doms, Powerful Billionaires, and the women they lust after and love for second chances, insta-love, enemies-to-lovers, and more.

Want to chat it up and share your thoughts with other CLBooks Lovers? Read our blog, join our Charmaine-Louise Books Coterie Fan Club and follow us on my author pages and social media to be in the know about the book release dates, exclusive content, giveaways, contests, and more!

~ **Purchase your eBook and paperback novels from my Author Page by clicking here!**

~ Read and subscribe to our blog *The World of Sex*

~ Connect on **Amazon Author Page**

~ **Goodreads Author Profile**

~ <u>**BookBub Author Profile**</u>

**CharmaineLouise Intimates** *Sexy Under Things & Loungewear* debuted in 2003. Inspired by the sensuous sirens and sylph swans of the past and present, the hand crochet cashmere and silk collections are for the sexy: hence, the line names Ginger — Bombshell; Diana — Showstopper; Jackie — Timeless; Lena — Classic. Also known as The Movie-Star from Gilligan's Island; Ms. Ross The Boss; Mrs. Kennedy Onassis; Ms. Horne.

Do you thrive on seduction and being sexy lounging at home? Read our blog and follow us on social media to receive the tips, the latest additions to the collections, private sales, and more!

~ Read and subscribe to our blog *The Art of Seduction*

~ Find us on Facebook **@CharmaineLousieIntimates**

~ Instagram **@CharmaineLouiseIntimates**

**Fulfill Your Desires.**

www.ingramcontent.com/pod-product-compliance
Lightning Source LLC
LaVergne TN
LVHW011800060526
838200LV00053B/3642